THE OCCASIONAL COMMUNITY

Jonathon Manders

The Occasional Community

First published in Australia by Jonathon Manders 2023

A catalogue record for this
book is available from the
National Library of Australia

ISBN: 978-0-6459514-0-0 (pbk)
ISBN: 978-0-6459514-1-7 (ebk)

Book cover image: Nick Browne © 2023

Typesetting and design by Publicious Book Publishing
Published with the assistance of Publicious Book Publishing
www.publicious.com.au

For Cherry, Minna and Sacha

Author's note

This novel is entirely a work of fiction. The places of Paradise and Minamurra depicted in this book are fictitious, they do not exist. Furthermore, the names, characters and incidents portrayed in it are the work of the author's imagination and any resemblance between any of the characters appearing in this book and actual persons, alive or deceased is purely coincidental.

CONTENTS

Chapter One

Welcome to Paradise

*Def. 'A place or state of complete happiness. Abode of
Adam and Eve. Heaven (in some religions).'*

'Welcome to Paradise!' said John Williams to himself as he
strolled along the scrubby sandy track that wound lazily
down to the estuary.

Paradise was the name given to a tract of land along a
narrow peninsular in East Gippsland which separated the
open waters of Bass Strait from an extensive estuarine lake
system. The east and west borders merged into coastal park
and Paradise itself consisted of a number of private freehold
properties separated in the middle by a reedy brackish creek.
The only practical access to the land was by boat traversing the
lake system from a nearby coastal fishing village. Apart from
those who were lucky enough to own the few cottages there, the
only other people to visit were those who could moor for short
periods on a government owned jetty. Many of the properties
held the unique situation of having the lake at one end of the
block and the open beach at the other.

John liked that phrase 'Welcome to Paradise'. He regularly
used it as his standard greeting to friends as they landed by boat
to visit his little sea-side abode.

He'd arrived at his little holiday house a bit earlier in the
afternoon (some called it 'The shack', although John's wife Sal

took offence to the term, saying it inferred some connection with the dubious character of the property's previous owner). It was the start of his four weeks leave from work, and an early burst of warm summer weather heralded the promise of 'salad days' ahead. John and Sal lived five hours away back in the city, so despite feeling a strong connection to this little holiday place, visits were restricted to times when John had four or more days to spare. Adding to the long drive, the final leg of the journey had to be made by boat, as there was no road access from the nearest township of Minamurra, a fishing port the other side of the estuary. John would often refer to Paradise as his 'bolt hole', a place he used to escape to from the stresses of his everyday life. It was a place where he could recharge and clear his head.

Ambling casually along, bare footed, wearing only his favourite faded fishing shorts and old T-shirt imprinted with the words 'Fear no Fish!' John took in a deep breath. The cool damp sand underfoot, and the sweet smell of sun-dried seagrass and leptospermum filled his senses, and he could almost feel the warm salty sea air seeping into every part of his body, revitalising every cell, every nerve ending. Samphire and pigface grew along the edges of the track creating a bright green border before giving way to the sedges and the dry layer of leaf litter beneath the tea trees. The pink flowers of the pigface contrasted sharply from the varying shades of browns and greens.

Along the shoreline small fingerlings darted quickly at John's presence creating a criss-cross of tiny ripples. Further out a pod of Burranan dolphins casually broke the surface as they swam silently by on their way to the ocean entrance. The air was soft and quiet, save the 'hum' of the bush.

'Ah yes, the tranquility' he murmured through a long deep sigh.

Sal wouldn't be coming down for another week, so free to do as he chose, fishing was on the agenda for tomorrow, and to save time in the morning John had decided to collect a bucket load of mussels in the cooler evening from the piles under the government jetty which lay not far from the cottage. Not that he'd need a whole bucket load for bait, but while he was at it, why not collect enough for a meal at the same time, just in case the fish weren't biting? Accompanying a 9 litre plastic bucket he carried with him a device he'd fashioned from some scrap metal which he designed specifically for scraping off mussels from jetty piles. It consisted of a small rectangular steel frame, 'toothed' on the leading edge like the teeth cut into a jack lantern, under which was attached a basket made of galvanised chicken wire. The small contraption was welded to a length of galvanised pipe. The whole thing worked by plunging the device into the water and vigorously scraping the mussel basket up along the piles where they had attached and grown. The toothed 'collar' would scrape the shellfish off which would then be caught by the cage.

'One of my better ideas.' he would boast to people.

'Shit!' John exclaimed, gazing down the shoreline toward the government jetty.

It was evident a large boat had moored at the government jetty sometime between John arriving and during the hour or so he had spent at the cottage unpacking his bags and supplies.

'Boat people!' he seethed,

'They shouldn't be allowed to encroach on my territory.'

'They cramp my style, catch my fish, crap in the sand dunes, and then bugger off leaving soiled tissues and a bloody stain on my piece of paradise'.

But, as they had every right to moor there it would be an 'embuggerance' (as John described it) on his being that he would have to endure.

3

As John Williams approached the jetty, he studied the vessel to try to ascertain who and how many said 'boat people' might be on board.

'Oh shit.' he sighed, on closer inspection.

He could now make out the familiar shape of a 'U-Sail' cruiser. The Butt family had a long established business further up the estuary hiring out these ugly 'boxy' boats, often to inexperienced 'would be' boaties and morons alike looking for a weekend or maybe a week of 'cruising' the estuary, but in reality ramming jetties, sometimes grounding on sandbars and submerged rock piles in the middle of the night and, when the need took them, disembarking to crap in the sand dunes. John's heart sank even lower as he observed a group of men gathered on the upper deck, beers in hand, loud talk and laughter penetrating 'his' peace, like the intrusive sound of the noisy garbage truck back home at 4.30 AM on rubbish day.

'I just love this shit.' John heard a loud voice exclaim, referring to the otherwise pristine environment.

'Why do they bother coming all the way here to get pissed and be noisy when they could save some money and enjoy it just as much at their local pub and leave me alone?' John grated.

The white boat appeared more orange than white in the warm rays of the setting sun. It listed slightly to the starboard side with a greater portion of the weight on-board being unevenly distributed. Rust-stained streaks down the sides of the boat accentuated the orange hues of neglect. The sun's low rays also cast elongated shadows down the port side, accentuating the many dents and scratches that told of a hundred collisions by inexperienced skippers trying to berth at landings or jetties, while the equally inexperienced crews ran around tossing mooring lines haphazardly out at posts or fixtures in an attempt to pull up at a mooring. A section of loose faded blue canvas awning covering the upper deck flapped idly in the evening breeze completing the picture of neglect, and careless seamanship, in John's mind's eye. If the presence of 'boat people' in general at Paradise was repugnant enough, hire-boat people were even worse. But at the bottom of list was a boat load of alcohol-fueled, testosterone charged bellends hell bent on destroying as many brain cells as possible, using a U-Sail cruiser as a vehicle on which to do it. Typically, the relative isolation of Paradise provided these types with a place where debauched drunken behaviour and 'blokey-ness' which anywhere else, would probably see them arrested.

Arriving on the jetty John was greeted by a mouth-watering waft of meat cooking on the portable barbeque on the back deck. The aroma drifting in on the warm breeze tantalised his nostrils, replacing the early beach smells and reminding him that apart from the prospect of some mussels, he hadn't organised anything else for his own dinner tonight.

John did his best to ignore the presence of these intruders and set to work raking the piles with his mussel cage.

A voice from behind asked 'G'day mate! What're yah doing?'

Avoiding eye contact for the moment John replied curtly 'Getting mussels for bait mate.'

'Hey, this guy's collecting mussels!' the intruder called out to his accomplices.

'Is that your tinnie up at the next jetty?' the same voice continued.

'I have a house here.' John replied indignantly, glancing at the inquirer momentarily, but returning to his raking in an attempt to ignore this obvious presence.

Another voice shouted 'Hey guys, look what this bloke's doing!'

John became aware of a second 'boat person' encroaching on his space as he continued to rake and tip the shiny black crustaceans into his bucket.

A third voice, this time from onboard the boat called out 'If we give you a bucket mate, can you get us some mussels to cook? We'll trade you for a few beers.'

John straightened up and turned around to face his enquirers. There were four of them altogether. They seemed friendly enough, older than he had first imagined, maybe mid to late forties he thought. They seemed reasonably warm and hospitable towards him, and genuinely interested in what he was doing. He felt a little embarrassed that he had perhaps pre-judged them.

'Yeh, I guess I can do that. Seems like a fair deal to me.' John replied cautiously, but in a somewhat brighter tone.

So thick were the mussels growing under the government jetty that it took no time at all to fill the bucket the 'boys' had provided him. He almost felt a little guilty at the thought of sponging beer off them for so little effort on his part. As much as John valued his privacy in Paradise, it would be hard to turn away from these people who wanted to engage with him.

'Come aboard and have a beer mate.' hollered the third voice from the upper deck.

John stepped over from the jetty onto the lower deck. A figure appeared beside him from within the cabin, thumb pressed under his lower lip and fingers clenched to resemble a bosun's whistle.

'Weeeee-ooooh-weeeee!' whistled the bloke.

'Welcome aboard me matey!' The same voice said, noticing that John's hands were full, so foisting a cold can of beer in John's baggy front trouser pocket.

'Drop the mussels over near the barbie, grab your beer, and I'll introduce you to the boys.'

John was swept up with all the activity on the boat. Fat lamb chops and pork spare-ribs sizzled busily on the barbeque. A clattering sound could be heard from the galley where someone was rifling through a large ice chest. Another of the crew was on the upper deck singing along to the radio as he cast a fishing line into the dark blue-black water of the incoming tide.

Entering the galley John was greeted with that familiar musty diesel smell that pervaded the old U-Sail hire boats.

'So, what's your name?' the bosun impersonator asked.

'John, John Williams.'

'I'm Darrell, Darrell Rhodes.' the impersonator replied.

'But call me Dusty.'

'John, this is Neville. Neville.... John.'

'Andrew...John, Barry.... John'

John was a little overwhelmed with what seemed an abundance of everything......the rush of names, which he was sure he wouldn't remember, ample quantities of food and beer and good cheer completely filled the boat to its splintery wooden gunnels.

'So where do you guys come from?' inquired John, taking a big slurp of his over frothing beer.

'Dusty, Neville and Andrew are all farmers.' Barry replied.

'Dusty runs sheep up in 'New South', Neville's from the wheat belt and runs a few cattle and Andrew's a pig farmer. I'm a stock agent with East Farmers.' Barry continued.

'We were all mates back at tech school years ago, and around December time on the lead up to Christmas before the big holiday rush starts, we usually try to get away for a couple of weeks reunion. Last year we went Barra fishing up the 'Top End'. This year we thought we'd try hiring a boat down here.'

'How's yer beer going?' interjected Dusty.

Another beer was thrust into John's hand even before he could say, 'I'm fine thanks, I'm still going!'

'Here, you'd better park yer arse.' Neville beckoned.

'Baz says the barbie's nearly ready.'

'Oh, I wasn't going to stay for dinner.' John uttered, backing off a bit.

'Bullshit! Andrew'll be offended if you don't have some of his ribs mate. Won't you Andy Boy?'

After almost sculling the last two cans of beer, John's head started feeling floaty, and surrendering to the situation, he reclined back into the comfort of this warm hospitality. A huge pile of still sizzling meat flew by John's ear and landed haphazardly in the centre of the galley table together with a pile of paper plates. A flurry of broad farmer's fingers descended on the feast like so many seagulls on a discarded picnic.

'Here, get some in yer!' Neville insisted.

Barry grabbed a lamb chop and returned outside to the barbeque. A loud clattering-hissing noise and an accompanying rush of steam through the open galley door heralded the moment Barry emptied the contents of John's contribution to dinner onto the searing hot plate. In no time at all the now steaming mussels flew past John's other ear in a large aluminium pot and landed next to the meat. Barry lent across the table and added a generous slosh of white wine and a dash of chili sauce to the pot, before stirring the mixture loudly with an enormous wooden ladle.

'Not bad for camping eh!' spluttered Neville through his greasy chop.

'Yeh, I wonder what the poor people are doing?' Scoffed Dusty in reply.

Another can of beer was rifled out of the apparently bottomless ice chest and pushed under John's nose. Piece by piece the pile of lamb and ribs was reduced to an untidy mess of bones and shells making the table look more like the aftermath of a bomb site. Around the remnants of dinner, ample bellies stretched grease-stained blue singlets and flannelette shirts alike.

Andrew lent back, eyes bulging like he was about to burst, and let forth a loud and lengthy belch.

'Pig!' called out Neville.

'Oink.' replied the pig farmer.

'Baaaaah!' echoed the sheep farmer.

'Moooo!' heralded the grazier, lifting his big round red face to the heavens.

'You're bloody mad yah buggers!' retorted Barry.

'See what I have to put up with John!' added Barry.

'Ah, pull yer head in Baz yer dirt flogger.' blurted Andrew.

'Sheep shagger.' Barry fired back.

'Sheep farmer, fat bastard.' corrected Andrew.

John was in no fit state to enter the conversation. The last slug of beer had ended up coming out his nose in a convulsive spurt, brought on by the unexpected banter of animal noises around the table. All five men descended into eye watering laughter, rekindled again and again, firstly at the sound of Barry's generous backside breaking wind, then continuing with the sounds of one bodily emission after the next from the various members present. It was as if the hatch holding back a year's worth of energy, built up since the boys last reunion, was thrown open allowing a torrent of merriment to flood out.

Rich tales of life on the farm during the past year echoed across the cabin, and there was plenty of reminiscing over past reunions; 'Remember when Baz blew his eyebrows off trying to start the camp fire with petrol that time up the Murray?'....and; 'How about that time we put Andrew's hand in a bowl of warm water after he passed out and he pissed himself?'

'What about that time Neville followed through playing 'pull my finger'?'

There seemed no end to the stories, which descended further into 'blokey' coarse humour as the evening progressed and the beer took effect. The raucous laughter went on unabated for what seemed hours, punctuated by various name calling and witty retort. The party was underway! John held his aching stomach with both hands for fear it might burst. The back of his throat hurt, partly from the nasal beer enema he'd earlier given himself and partly from the prolonged merriment. He couldn't remember another time he'd laughed so hard. It was an effort just to catch his breath.

Then, as if the seemingly never ending supply of beer wasn't enough, Dusty appeared from the sleeping quarters with a bottle of Chivas Regal.

'Can't let this go to waste, eh!' announced the inebriated sheep farmer, thrusting the prized whisky in the air like some trophy.

Wrenching the cork from the bottle, a loud popping sound punctuated the beer drinking session like a full stop. By this stage it seemed glasses were totally irrelevant as the bottle was passed around the table ceremonially for each in turn to take a swig.

'Come on Johnny boy, get some into ya.' insisted Dusty. 'It'll keep you warm on your way back home.'

It didn't take long for the five imbibers to exhaust the contents of the bottle. All gone so soon? Better open a bottle of port just to keep the festivities rolling! And so on it went, conversation becoming ever so meaningful for true believers, but none the less noisier and delivered through rubbery lips.

Finally, late in the night when John had got a moment to take a deep soothing sigh and collect himself, he became aware that the words in his head no longer resembled the dialogue coming out of his mouth. It was as if someone had anesthetised his lips and tongue and he could no longer 'feel' the words his mouth was trying to make.

'Ahhh, I think it's time for me to go home.' the now incoherent John mumbled.

'Bazz's hit the sack.' replied an inebriated Neville.

John hadn't even noticed Barry was no longer present. Definitely time to get home!

'You need a torch Johno?' enquired Neville.

'No thanks mate.' slurred John in an authoritative voice.

'Me 'ouse' isn't far from here and I know the place like the back of me hand!'

'Drive home safely!' called out one voice.

'Don't fall off the bloody jetty.' blurted out another.

John took one large bold step and disembarked with an ungainly gait from the back of the U-Sail Cruiser onto the jetty. He fumbled around trying to pick up his bucket and mussel cage, but after dropping them awkwardly on the decking several times, decided it was all too hard and to leave them to the morning. The light from the boat and a solar light installed at the end of the jetty illuminated his way shore-ward to the dark scrubby bushes that lined the lake front.

Not long after John entered the scrub and stumbled into several trees, it became plainly apparent he had been enveloped by a dark moonless night. Using the solar jetty light as a 'guiding star' of sorts, he navigated his way back out of the scrub to the water's edge.

'Sure, know the way like the back of your hand smart arse!' he muttered to himself.

'I can't even see the back of my bloody hand it's so bloody dark!'

The evening had cooled somewhat, and the freshened sea air gave John's thinking some degree clarity in his compromised mental state.

'I'll follow along the shoreline till I get to the house track.' he reasoned.

'Can't go wrong with that eh!'

He waded barefoot in the cool water, the soft sea breeze caressed his face, the sand underfoot felt soft too…everything felt soft and friendly. He could hear the swans across the water gently chatting amongst each other, and he imagined the gentle horn-like coos were the pens telling their little cygnets bedtime stories.

Although pitch-black, a cloudless sky sparkled brilliantly overhead, adding to his euphoric sense of well being. He was totally at peace with the world right at that moment.

He stopped for a minute to relieve himself in the estuary and to absorb the splendour of the glowing cosmos above him. Glancing down at the black water he was dazzled by the bioluminescence. Millions of microscopic plankton lit up the water as his stream hit the surface. He kicked his feet in the water, and it was as if brilliant liquid silver light splashed out across the inky black mass.

'Welcome to Paradise!' John mumbled out aloud.

Meanwhile, back on the boat Neville called out to Dusty. 'You be long in the toilet? I'm busting to go.'

'Piss over the side Nev!'

'No, I want to have a crap!…. Don't worry I'll grab a spare roll from the galley and go in the sand dunes. I'd rather do that anyway instead of squeezing into that bloody stuffy shoe box of a loo.'

The next step John took changed his demeanour dramatically. He stumbled on a submerged branch before a searing pain stabbed deep into the heal of his left foot. It felt like an electric prod had shocked its way right up the core of his leg and into his body. Initially he tried to scream out in pain, but opening his mouth, the best John could manage was to draw back his breath in shock. His second attempt to cry out was muffled as he fell face first into the murky water.

John had just waded into a particularly muddy section of the shoreline and stepped with his full weight onto the jagged end of a broken beer bottle. It wasn't the first time, nor would it be the last when past events in Paradise would have consequences for those who sought to stay there now.

Chapter Two

Irish Jimmy's Legacy

*Proverbs- 8:20 "I walk in the way of righteousness,
along the paths of justice"*

Eighty years earlier, a squatter James Tulloch had thrown the bottle into a soak-hole along with all the other bottles and rubbish he had discarded from around his squat. A hundred fierce storms and thirty thousand high tides had since eroded the shoreline at that point until finally the soak-hole and the brackish estuary had become as one.

The ruddy headed Tulloch had arrived at Paradise in the 1930's. He had originally emigrated from Ireland and soon after arriving in Australia sought his fortune in the gold fields near Bendigo. After several years of scouring the mullock heaps that bore evidence of an earlier gold rush, he'd enjoyed reasonable success extracting alluvial gold from the tailings, enough at least to return to his starting point in Melbourne. Back in the relative comfort of the city 'Irish Jimmy's' gambling addiction and fondness of a cleansing ale, or three, set him on a declining financial path to poverty. It would only be a matter of time before his beer-bitten nose, his rubicund cheeks (and the rest of him) were evicted from the bedsit he leased when he failed to keep up with the rent.

For the next twelve months Jimmy wandered the pot-holed highways and dusty byways, swag on his back, his earthly belongings bundled in a yellowed bed sheet tied to a stout pole across his shoulder that swung in time with his swagger. He survived by taking on any itinerant work he could find. Sometimes only lucky enough get enough work for a meal, his roving took him East from the city. He followed the farmlands and logging camps that were dotted intermittently throughout the foothills, flanked by the Great Dividing Range, which stretched all the way from Victoria two thousand miles to Queensland in the North.

He finally came across the remote little fishing village of Minamurra, named after the aboriginal word meaning 'place of plenty of fish'. There he found casual, but regular work as a deckhand on a couta boat. Jimmy made his home in a 'lean-to' he erected near the beach. It was crudely fashioned from old, corrugated iron sheets and bush poles he'd scavenged from around the village. He gradually added 'improvements' and 'comforts' as further scrap materials were found, fashioning benches and seats and the like in the hut. It was far from ideal though. During the chilly south easterly gales that often blew in on the dunes, the spray-laden wind would penetrate the humpy leaving Jimmie's cloths and bedding dank and cold. The local kids would seek him out at night and throw rocks on the rusty tin roof, or bang noisily on the tin walls, then retreat cheekily into the safety of the shadows.

'You little 'sebarstians'.' he'd bellow. 'Piss awf and find someone else to annoy why don't yar!'

But of course, this reaction was part of the entertainment for the youths and only served to encourage their delinquent behaviour, which became more frequent as the months went by. Adding to his torment was a group of nearby '*black fellers*' who discovered his hut and who would pester him for sugar and flour. When he tried to put a stop to their cadging, they resorted to raiding his stores while he was either away in the village or working on the couta boat. Often wet and tired from fishing he would return home to his humpy at dusk to find it ransacked and vandalised.

There was one short reprieve from his torment however, when Jimmy lay in wait in the bushes after nightfall near his camp and managed to ambush his young assailants. All the boys bar one escaped, but the youngest lad tripped over, and Jimmy managed to grab him.

'Leave orf mister!' the small boy wailed.

'Not a chance laddy! Not till I've handed you in to yer dad, or the police.'

'You do that and I'll tell 'em you interfered with me! It'll be my word against yours, and all me mates'll back me up.' the trembling pale faced boy spluttered.

This unexpected threat presented Jimmy with a dilemma for a moment until he thought up a new tact.

'In that case lad I've got no choice but to tie you up and keep you here for a while. At least until those black fellers come calling here again. They wuz asking me if I could catch a young whitey for em.' he explained to the terrified lad.

'They wuz keen on cooking one up. Said they were sick of eating roo and mutton bird.'

In a blind panic, the boy let out an ear-piercing scream sending a dire warning to the others who were still in ear-shot. Tearing loose from Jimmy's iron grip the youth left him with nothing more than his torn shirt in Jimmy's grasp.

'Ah, it'll do for a curtain or a dish-rag I 'spose.' remarked Jimmy, satisfied with the reaction to his verbal threat.

There was no sign of the delinquents for a couple of weeks, but it was only a short reprieve before they would return to their shenanigans with a renewed purpose of revenge for the terror he reigned on poor little Billy.

Despite his setbacks, in the following season Jimmy saved enough spare cash from his modest earnings to purchase his own boat and a large remnant of discarded fishing net. The boat was neither grand nor flash. Clinker built, it was designed as a tender for one of the bigger fishing boats. The lime-based paint on its hull was in an advanced state of flaking off and the exposed substrate was that of the bare grey-bleached timbers. The holes to accommodate the rowlocks were worn and oval but still serviceable, enough for the boat to be rowed. The net was torn and holed, but was not beyond repair again, sufficiently intact at least to make that basically serviceable as well.

His humpy was no longer a place of refuge where he could settle and feel safe. It was too far for Jimmy to consider returning to Melbourne, so now, having the means to get across the water where the estuary breached the sand dunes to the ocean, he set off to explore a more suitable site to re-settle, one that would provide him with a degree of separation from the torment the local boys and the black fellers had brought upon him.

About three miles away on the other side of the inlet to the West, Jimmy found a sheltered hollow in some thick scrub. It was a little way inland from the shore, out of sight of the water, but still handy to it. The locals referred to this area as 'Paradise', the name given to the property by its current inhabitants who were 'selectors' and who were rarely seen in town.

'Yes! Paradise indeed.' he thought. And for the next few weeks he gradually disassembled his hut in the dunes below Minamurra and rowed the bits and pieces across the entrance to his new prospective abode.

'The Selection', as it was termed consisted of five hundred acres of freehold land, the Western portion of which the current inhabitants had cleared and used for farming. This, together with several small scrubby islands that existed close by within the estuary was the home of a reclusive family commune.

For the first few months 'Irish Jimmy' was able to establish his new digs without the knowledge of the land's current owners. It was the odd column of campfire smoke which first caught the selectors attention, although they initially took that to be the presence of some 'Blacks'. However, with increasing scrutiny, the site of a wooden boat dragged up on the foreshore affirmed the presence of a squatter on their land.

By the time the landowners confronted Jimmy, he had put his boat and recommissioned net into service and had begun harvesting fish, both from the waters of the estuary and the open beach at the back of his squat. He'd learned how to 'shoot' his net in the surf by finding one of the many 'run outs' along the beach. Feeding the net into the waves, the underlying rip would drag out the body of the mesh hanging beneath the floats until the full length of the trap was deployed. Securing the standing end on the beach he would pull in on the rope attached to the running end thereby gathering the net in, in a large arc. Initially he would get nothing, but as he became more skilful, most of the time there would be something to reward his efforts on each cast. Some days would produce mullet, others Australian salmon. On the occasions he adventured out at night under a full moon he might bring in an elusive and highly prized jewfish. The days when the surf was too rough, or the tides unsuitable on the beach for fishing, Jimmy would ply his net in the estuary. Using his boat, he would feed the net out into the current and retrieve it in a similar way to that in the surf. The estuary also produced mullet and salmon but offered a much wider variety of fish including bream, luderick, trevally and estuary perch. Garfish were in abundance, but frustratingly the weave of the mesh was too coarse to trap their slender bodies.

Although his catch was at best meagre compared to that which the fishermen enjoyed in Minamurra, the harvest was enough in quantity and variety to barter his offerings in exchange for remaining on the land; After all, Jimmy's squat was in the middle of a shrubby little unproductive patch in the remnant dunes some distance from the habitable part of the property. So, they reasoned as long as this intruder kept out of their way and continued to provide them with fresh fish, they could see some usefulness in allowing him to remain there and something which they could potentially capitalise on in the future.

From little things bigger things grow, as did the Irishman's hut, with Jimmy embellishing the interior and adding more permanency to the structure as materials became available. The final stage of the 'improvements' began after he discovered an aboriginal midden in the bush close by. Hundreds of years of eating shellfish had left a sizable pile of calcified rubble which Jimmy figured out a way to utilise. Sand being also in abundance and with cement powder stolen from the jetty-works in Minamurra, block by block Jimmy began fabricating his own concrete bricks. He made the bricks by using a crude rectangular mould fashioned from driftwood planks that he found washed up on the beach, and he added the bleached shells which served the dual purpose of providing lime and aggregate to the cement and sand mortar. Once a week as part of his shopping list for supplies in Minamurra, Jimmy would steal a little more cement powder from the jetty-works, which he was amazed to observe never seemed to be missed.

Using rocks removed from a sea wall near the ocean entrance for footings, Jimmy gradually clad the flimsy tin walls of his shed with his homemade masonry. Within eight months the drafty iron shanty was transformed into a sturdy one room cottage which still stands today. Glass from a demolished church hall was added for windows, and the pungent odour of creosote used to preserve the timbers permeated the air. All this of course had progressed without the knowledge of the landowners until one day when Jimmy neglected to deliver the promised fish to the commune one morning. A delegation arrived later the same day to remind him of the conditions of his tenancy. They were unpleasantly surprised by the foot-hold Jimmy had established on their land and upset at the amount of rubbish lying around the site. They told him in no uncertain terms to clean the place up that very day, and in the meanwhile, there would be a family meeting to decide whether he could continue to remain on the land.

Life had become reasonably comfortable in Paradise for the Irishman and the thought of possible eviction propelled him into immediate action. Apart from the scattering of unused and discarded building materials around the hut, Jimmy had created his own midden consisting in the main of empty tins and beer bottles. A ready repository for all this rubbish existed in the form of a soak hole located near the water, just out of sight of the track. For the remainder of that afternoon the bush resonated to the sound of crashing iron sheets, clattering tin cans and breaking bottles. By night fall that what could be burnt had been reduced to a small pile of white ash and the intractable waste had disappeared from view as if by magic.

Acknowledging the value of having a resident seafood provider on their doorstep and Jimmy's very limited, if not non-existent rights of residency, the family saw this opportunity to take advantage of the situation. They agreed Jimmy could stay on where he was, provided that in addition to their existing fish quota, Jimmy was to ferry the milk and vegetables the family produced, in excess of their own needs, to the Minamurra market each week. He could hardly disagree.

And so it was that James Tulloch established his place in Paradise unintentionally leaving a painful legacy that would be delivered to John Williams this dark moonless night.

Not much is known about Jimmy's eventual fate but is said the townsfolk of Minamurra tired of his drunkenness and continual pilfering, promised to dance on his grave at the time of his parting. With a typical Irish jape, it is claimed Jimmy responded by requesting in his Will to be buried at sea.

John lifted himself up on all fours and crawled gingerly out of the water. Rising to his feet, the first step he attempted saw him buckle over once more as the gritty sand pushed into the wound, sending another painful shock shooting up his leg like the thrust of a hot lance.

'Oh, dear Jesus!' he exclaimed, hopping up and down on his good leg.

The shock of it all was rapidly setting in, but mercifully he was unable to see the injury in the dark, albeit the pain indicated to him that he had sustained a serious injury. John staggered forward in a sort of hopping-limping fashion, gingerly carrying the weight on his right step via the ball of his big toe.

'Shit – shit – shit - shit.' he panted, scared he might pass out and bleed to death in the dark.

In what seemed a never-ending journey of suffering, he 'hop-stepped' along the shore, then up the dark winding track to the cottage. Several times he managed to step on the odd exposed sharp tree stump near the edge of the grassy verge with his good foot, completing the pathetic scene of misery witnessed only by the stars above. John had to crawl up the four steps that led to the front door, through which he burst like a drug squad detective on a bikie raid. Instinctively he fumbled for a non-existent light switch, forgetting in his acute discomfort for the moment that there was no electricity to the house. Had he planned to be out till after dark, his habit was to light a lamp before venturing out in order to save the frustration of feeling around in the gloom for the matches.

'Oh, for Christ's sake!' he wailed in his anger and pain.

'Please, please.' John begged, as if asking some imaginary being to place the matches before him.

Working his way around the wall to the kitchen like a blind man, he drew his hand along the bench top till he found the stove. With great relief there beside the cooker he felt some matches. The rattle of the redheads within the box gave John his first sense of comfort since that unexpected excruciating moment in the lake. Striking the first match, he shied back briefly as the glare from the flaring brand dazzled his eyes. Luckily, he was able to adjust to the light and locate a kerosene lamp before the taper burnt out, and with a second match he managed to ignite the charred wick, which fizzled precariously at first, but then intensified into a bright steady luminous flame. The warm lamp light bathed the walls of the room in a soft glow, further providing some sense of comfort to John's traumatised state.

Balancing on one bruised, but otherwise intact foot, the injured man holding the lamp aloft, peered into the dark cupboards hoping to locate a basin, some disinfectant and a wound dressing. The best he could manage to find was a square plastic mop-bucket, a half empty bottle of *Pine-O-Clean* and a tea-towel.

He watched impatiently as the cold water from the rainwater tank trickled with teasing slowness from the kitchen tap into the bucket. Barely a few centimeters of water had covered the bottom when John emptied most of the contents of the disinfectant bottle into the tub, turning the clear liquid a ghostly white. The pungent sickly odour of disinfectant permeated the cottage. Collapsing back in a chair, then taking a deep breath through quivering lips, John gingerly lowered the injured foot into the milky mixture. A mild sting layered on top of the throbbing pain like bitter icing on a caustic cake. The taste of trauma welled up in John's throat causing him to gag and subsequently bring up the night's festive takings in a series of violent spasms. The smell of vomit over the sea grass matting combined with the disinfectant to produce a strong evocative odour arousing once forgotten memories of childhood illness when his mother would put him to bed in a dark room with a basin reeking of Pine-O-Clean on a towel beside his pillow.

It was 2 AM and a late moon was finally rising above the tree tops. John reclined back in the cane chair as far as he could, still attired in the same clothes he was wearing when he fell in the water. He stretched his arm out to the bunk-bed beside him and dragged a blanket across himself for warmth and a small measure of comfort. Thinking the gash in his foot was probably impregnated with sand and dirt John reasoned the most painless way to clean out the wound was to let it soak over a good period of time. Exhausted from the ordeal he blew out the lamp at his feet and closed his watery eyes in an attempt to shut out the horrible situation he found himself in. The warm lamp light that had illuminated the room was replaced by cold moonlight which shone through the window behind the chair. The cloudy contents of the mop-bucket slowly turned dark as his blood permeated the mixture.

John's mind drifted back to his childhood when a similar thing happened to him. He recalled with nauseating clarity the time back in his hometown of Warrandyte when he jumped into the river from the steep dusty bank, landing on a broken bottle that lay hidden in the mud. He remembered that on this occasion it was on a stinking hot day and how a kindly wheelchair bound stranger, sitting in the shadow of a willow tree, came forward to tend to his wound and take him in a specially converted car to the doctor. The same kindly soul waited with him at the surgery and later drove him all the way home to the care of his parents.

'We'll have to keep you wrapped in cotton wool in a glass jar, boy.' John's father had declared. 'You're obviously accident prone. Wasn't it just last week you fell off your bike?'

John recalled it was the very first day of the summer school holidays and he had to endure two depressing weeks confined to a chair in the isolation of the stuffy house. Robbed of his riverine recreation, he endured his incarceration with only a black and white television for entertainment.

John's mind re-focused on the present situation and the thought of spending two weeks convalescing in the confines of the cottage with no T.V. further dampened his spirits in keeping with the state of his damp dirty cloths. After about an hour, the hapless figure carefully removed his foot from the bucket, delicately wrapping the thing in the tea-towel. He hobbled over to the bunk from where he'd earlier removed the blanket, lay spread eagle belly down and drifted off into a fitful sleep. Between frequent periods of waking John's dozing mind was filled with a confusion of coloured scenes. Party boats, broken glass and bleeding feet intermingled in a never-ending loop through his troubled dreams. Occasionally he'd mutter some incoherent banter, but there was no-one there to hear or answer the ranting, nor sooth his troubled scowl.

Around 8.30 AM the sound of a kookaburra crashing into the window woke John with a start. Forgetting his wound for an instant, in a state of fright, he jumped out of bed.

'Aaaaahhhh....haaaahh...aaah!' He gasped as the full force of the pain returned like a slap in the face with a cold steel ruler. And the full memory of the night which had been, came flooding back into his consciousness.

With trepidation John surveyed his foot to study for the first-time what damage had been done. The tea towel was badly stained with congealed blood. He returned to the chair where he'd collapsed before to unwrap the dressing. The water in the bucket was opaque and dark pink, and semi-dried vomit cast a macabre backdrop to the object of study. The tea towel had stuck to his foot, and it was a delicate operation to unwrap it without making the throbbing pain worse. Free of the dish-rag, John was able to cock his left leg onto his right knee and study the deep gash that spread laterally across his heal. The wound gaped open, still dirty with a raised flap along one side. John felt nauseated at the sight of it.

'I need to get to a doctor.' he exclaimed to himself.

Without a first aid kit, which he'd promised himself to get, John did his best to improvise some bandaging by first affixing a folded wad of toilet paper over the gash with sticky tape, then wrapping the whole in the cleanest t-shirt he could find, held together again using sticky-tape. The whole affair was then protected from further contamination by a plastic garbage-bag fastened at the knee with a shoelace.

John washed down two paracetamol tablets with half a glass of water, shoved his wallet in his back pocket and ventured out the front door. There he found the kitchen broom which, placed sweeping end up under his armpit, served as a sort of crutch.

In contrast to the previous warm sunny day, the morning greeted him like a frigid handshake. The sun was obscured by grey clouds and the estuary in the distance looked equally grey and uninviting. He could make out little pillows of foam blown up against the shore by an unfriendly wind.

The sight of this man, hobbling along in pain, dirty dishevelled cloths, garbage-bag trouser-legged and having an extremely bad hair day was nothing short of pathetic. But at least he felt some measure of control and purpose, and this helped to exorcize the anxiety and fear that consumed him during the night.

'If I can get down to the government jetty, the boys on the U-Sail cruiser will help me out.' he reassured himself.

'Shit!' John exclaimed, as he'd done the previous day on arriving at the lake.

The boat was gone! The cold southerly wind completed this stage setting of acute emptiness. It felt like cold pellet of lead had been thrust into the pit of his stomach. This solitary figure set against the wintry backdrop could best be described as the epitome of loneliness and isolation.

The boat people had moved on earlier that morning, as boat people do. He was all alone.

Still, John needed to get over to Minamurra to get medical treatment, so the challenge of getting his own 'run-about' off its mooring presented the tired and hungover man with yet another seemingly insurmountable hurdle. His awkward attempt at embarking onto the little tinny from the landing nearly saw him end up in the water. His plastic wrapped shin collided clumsily with the metal gunnel causing John to scream profanities into the empty sky. The trip across proved no less painful as the aluminium boat thumped doggedly into the choppy waves. The jolting planted him up and down on the cold metal seat and caused his foot to bang uncomfortably against the hull. By the time he got to the fishing village he was shivering and soaked all over from the wind driven spray thrown up from the bow wake.

Unfortunately for John the only doctor in town was a semi-retired general practitioner. Doctor Stephens, or 'Doc Howlong' as the local fishing crews called him, had moved to Minamurra twenty years ago in a sea change moment. It had become increasingly difficult for the seventy-year-old to keep abreast of all the continuing advances in the medical sciences, where he once ran a practise in Melbourne. The seaside hamlet offered Stephens a slower and simpler approach to patient care. Many of his patients worked at the fishing co-op and would present with some imaginary complaint when they wanted some time off work.

'And how long do you think you'll need off?' was the standard closing remark offered by the doctor.

The 'Doc' operated his surgery from a weatherboard house situated a little way up the inland road above the village. The front porch had been enclosed and served as a waiting-room. It was furnished with three kitchen chairs, two of which he'd purchased from an opportunity shop down the street. A tatty pile of Practical Science magazines lay on a badly marked coffee-table for his patient's reading pleasure. He'd converted the study into a consulting room. A dark green vinyl-covered examination table sat alongside the window flanked by dusty smelling lace curtains which provided some degree of privacy from any traffic entering the orange gravel driveway. An old leather inlaid desk held a scattering of yellowing prescription pads and journals, and jars with a variety of pens and probes and other obscure apparatus. There was a glass thermometer soaking in a vial of clear blue liquid near the back and a black bakelite telephone and a brass bank-lamp that occupied the remaining space on the cluttered counter. In a partially opened draw a further collection of pencils, pens and other stationary could be observed. Affixed to the wall above the desk were bookshelves crammed untidily with more journals, out of date MIMS dictionaries and anatomy books. An old captain's chair, where the doctor sat and an additional kitchen chair to accommodate the patient, completed the picture.

The doctor's consulting hours were listed as being between 10.00 AM and midday, and 2.00 PM and 5.00 PM on Tuesdays, Wednesdays and Thursdays, however honouring the Hippocratic Oath he'd entered into forty years ago, Harry Stephens would reluctantly but obediently answer any request for urgent medical assistance at any other time. And so it was that the wet and wretched figure of John Williams was granted a consultation on this grey and breezy Sunday morning.

With the final hurdles of berthing the tinnie on the fisherman's wharf, finding the doctor's number in the public phone box across the road, and retrieving his car from the compound out of the way, John drove up the hill 'left footed' both relieved and surprised that the doctor had answered the phone on this day of rest.

John pressed hard on the white button beside the flywire door at the surgery. He could hear the buzzer sound somewhere inside the house. There was an anxious silent pause, then he could hear the sound of footsteps stirring from somewhere within the residence. An internal door banged shut then the dark outline of a portly figure approached from the other side of the screen, and without opening the latch asked 'Mr Williams?'

'Yes. Doctor Stephens?'

'Come in then ...... I don't usually see patients out of hours, especially on Sundays you understand.' continued Stephens, looking quizzically at this dishevelled fellow on his doorstep.

'I'm sorry to encroach on your Sunday doctor, it's just that I'm in a bit of a state with this.'

'Your shoulder you say?'

'No, it's my foot Doc!' as if it wasn't bloody obvious, thought the patient.

John's confidence in the doctor wasn't any further enhanced by the sight of this grey- haired man, grey stubbled face and dressed in an old pair of tracksuit pants (the type with the baggy arse that were stretched out at the knees), matched with an equally unkept looking red checked flannel shirt, opened at the front revealing his singlet.

'I guess it is Sunday.' John reassured himself. 'He probably presents a lot better on weekdays.'

He followed the doctor into the consulting room-come study and hoisted himself onto the vinyl covered examination table.

'Let's get all this off and have a look at it then.' proceeded the physician, lifting his glasses to his eyes from the retaining chain that hung across his chest.

John lay back on the table. Cocking his head up, he peered down anxiously as the doc proceeded to remove the various layers covering his left leg. John studied the doctor, who was squinting intently through glasses, speckled with some sort of matter, remnants of breakfast perhaps, which had fallen from his whiskery mouth and landed on the lenses hanging round his neck below his second chin.

'Mmm...nasty.' observed the doctor. 'And how did we manage this?'

'I stepped on some broken glass last night. Do you think there's any still left in there?'

'Mmmm…. Doesn't look like it, but there's a lot of debris in the wound. You should have brought it to me last night son.'

'I couldn't.' explained John. 'It happened over at Paradise…. I have a cottage over there.'

'I thought that was all National Park land.' replied the doctor.

'No no, there's about a dozen freehold allotments still there in the middle of the National Park.' corrected John.

'Mmm…. I heard they were buying all that back' continued the doctor, studying John's foot.

'News to me.' answered John, discounting the doctor's claim as being mere hearsay.

'It's too late to stitch this, I'll clean it up for you, trim off the flap and dress it. You'll have to keep off it for a week. How long since you've had your last tetanus booster?'

'Oh…no more pain please!' thought John …… 'I…I think the last one I had was about two years ago.' he answered unconvincingly.

'Just as well then, I don't keep any tetanus serum here. Not worth the expense with the rare occasion it's called for.'

Doctor Stephens left the room and John to his thoughts while he went to the kitchen to boil a jug of water and sterilise a soft brush, a pair of tweezers and a scalpel. In the absence of the doctor John gazed up at the ceiling and studied the cobwebs that covered the cornices like some macabre decoration. His attention to his foot was refocused when Doctor Stephens returned with the implements on a stainless-steel dish, together with the remainder of the hot water in an enema bulb, a squeeze bottle of iodine solution, and some dressing materials hermetically sealed in clear plastic bags.

John gazed down at the man attending to his foot as he methodically picked and pulled at the wound, occasionally stopping to flush the site with the stinging hot water which caused John to wince and involuntarily retract his leg.

'You'll have to be still lad, or it'll only hurt more ...... we're nearly there, just a bit more to go.'

Stephens finally and mercifully finished his probing and irrigating. He dried the gash with a plump wad of cotton wool held by the tweezers and patted gently around the margins of the site. He finished the treatment with a liberal dusting of anti-bacterial powder before applying the dressing. First came some butterfly-tapes to hold the wound closer together, then followed some folded cotton gauze, primed with iodine and applied under some clear looking sticking-plaster. John peered down at the discarded dressing wrappers on the worn carpet on the floor and noted the 'use by dates' indicated that the shelf life for these items had expired earlier the year before.

Ignoring John's unspoken, but still noticeable concern for the age of the bandages, the doctor continued, "I've given you a waterproof dressing for now, but you'll need to stay out of the water till I see you next in a week's time.

'Let's say Tuesday morning?' the doctor continued.

'Oh, and keep off your feet as much as possible too. You can settle your account when I see you next. Right now I must get the roast in the oven. Got people coming for lunch.' Stephens concluded.

As the flywire door banged shut behind, John paused briefly to gaze out beyond the village below to the panoramic vista past the estuary to the ocean and sky. The cool southerly had abated somewhat. Silver patches of sunlight glistened on a moderating sea. Out to the east the water on the inlet had shed its herd of 'white horses' and now sparkled invitingly. The problematic foot still throbbed, perhaps even a little more so now with the added pressure of the bandaging applied to it. But despite the continuing discomfort, John's demeanour was noticeably lifting. The emerging sunshine aided in restoring his self-confidence and sense of wellbeing.

The emotional trauma now behind him, John's awareness turned to his thirst and the hollow growling his stomach was making.

'Fish 'n chips, and a can of Coke …… some comfort food. That's what I need!'

Down the inland road the car rolled, the orange-stained gravel beneath the tyres sounding more like rain on a tin roof, than the dry crunching of tiny stones. Wheeling into the main street, he eyed the 'Sharkie's Seafood' sign a little further on. The sight of the takeaway shop triggered a mouth-watering response in John much like the bell ringing in Pavlov's dog's ear.

As well as the fish and chips and the cold drink, John ordered a large take away coffee as a finishing treat. He'd intended to find a park bench by the wharf to consume his meal, but by the attention his still unsavoury appearance was getting from the townsfolk he decided the best option was to return his car to the compound and enjoy his treats during a leisurely crossing back to Paradise. Not that Minamurra was exactly starved of people of unsavoury appearance. Many of the folk who frequented the sleepy port were 'blow-ins' or 'itinerates' looking for a spot of work on the boats, or in the port, as was the case with William Tulloch back in the thirties. There was talk also of shady characters in high powered speedboats that would come in from the ocean in the dead of night and visit, part of a supply train for illicit drugs that would eventually find their way onto the back streets and commission flats in Melbourne.

It was hard to distinguish who might be the druggies from those who were deckhands sometimes, and perhaps some of them were one and the same. Scrawny men with gaunt bearded faces, long hair in ponytails and invariably tattooed. Their standard year-round dress usually consisted of a 'bluey singlet' and faded jeans accessorised with a tatty baseball cap and worn-out thongs. Having dark probing eyes that could detect a sideway glance in an instant, they were people best to avoid or even make eye-contact with. John would often notice them gathered in the 'local' as he passed by the pub to get to the general store for his shopping. Sometimes they'd be there as early as ten in the morning, beers in hand discussing some evil doings no doubt. Occasionally the gathering would include a few of the womenfolk, often with hair dyed some shade of blonde. The women were hardly attractive and equally as tough looking, and as potty mouthed as the men.

The Central, or the 'Blaggards Hotel', as John referred to it, was a place he seldom frequented during his time in the area. The dimly lit smoky saloon smelt of stale beer and the darkened soiled carpet felt sticky underfoot. A rancid whiff of urine would pervade the bar each time a patron opened the door to the toilets, male or female. The word 'luv' was often heard across the bar as in; 'What would you like luv?'

'A pot and a packet of '*Winnie Blues*' thanks luv.'

Regulars to the pub, had their own glass mugs hanging from the rack above the bar with their names etched across the bottom of the vessel. There were certain stools one wouldn't sit at which were reserved by unwritten law for long time patrons, like parking rights for long time employees in an office car park. Stuffed trophy fish which had all turned a similar smoke-stained colour over time adorned the walls between the equally smoke-stained sepia photos of fishing boats and early scenes of horse drawn carriages and wooden buildings in the main street. Occasionally John had stopped in for a counter lunch and a beer, but it was a place where he neither felt entirely comfortable nor welcome.

Returning to his runabout, John manoeuvred the small vessel out from between the beamy fishing trawlers and got underway homeward bound. He was in no particular hurry. Fishing was obviously off the agenda for now, and with the steadily improving weather, eating lunch with the sun on one's back was a pleasure to be savoured.

The little outboard spluttered quietly just above an idle, and the ripples that had earlier that morning been waves lapped gently on the hull. Gliding slowly across the inlet, John's mind drifted off to earlier years when he first came to Paradise.

'Eighteen years! Where's the time gone?' he pondered.

He recalled all those years ago answering an obscure article in a suburban newspaper titled '*Own your piece of Paradise complete with fisherman's cottage*'. The articled featured an equally obscure photograph of the ocean viewed through the branches of some coastal tea-trees. John had been looking for a patch of land near the sea for several years. He wanted to build a modest holiday home, somewhere to get away from his working life. However, with a limited bank balance, everywhere he'd inspected having any sort of view of the water, was well outside his budget.

When he eventually tracked down the real estate agent handling the sale only to discover the land in question was some four hours' drive from where he lived, he was a little taken aback. A further complication was the advice that there was no road access to the block, and the only way to get there was over the estuary by boat. John had never owned a boat. Nevertheless, he made an appointment with the agent and organised some overnight accommodation in Minamurra. The agent organised to have a local boat take them across and drop them off at the government jetty. Paradise Landing as it was known, was built to provide access to the National Coastal Park, but there was a track leading off to the west which was made by the current inhabitant, and which led to this so-called 'fisherman's cottage' in the scrub.

It was only after John arrived at the single roomed estate agent's office to announce himself that the property manager-come-sales-agent explained the full limitations of the property.

'Before we go over, you are aware there are no services over there, aren't you?' She advised.

'What, no rubbish collection you mean.' enquired John.

'No, I mean there's no 'services'…. no water, gas, electricity or phone. There never will be.'

'No roads or fences for that matter either, now that I think about it.' she continued.

'And well, as for the fisherman's cottage……well, it's a bit rustic. In fact, it's not strictly a 'cottage', more of a shed type of affair you might describe it as. But the owner does live there.'

Had John not booked accommodation and driven the three hundred and fifty kilometres to get there, he may well have turned around on the spot and given it up as a waste of time.

'So… when can we get across to it see it then?'

'I'll ring the taxi boat owner now to let him know you're here and he should be waiting for us at the wharf by the time we get there.' she announced brightly.

It was hardly a taxi boat as John had imagined. An open fishing boat, filled with netting and polystyrene floats. There was barely enough room for the high heeled property manager-come-sales-agent and himself to squeeze in beside the skipper and the long wooden tiller that John had to duck under every time the boat changed course.

After tying up at the government jetty the sales agent asked the fisherman if he wouldn't mind waiting for them while they inspected the property. She then proceeded to lead John along a long winding overgrown track for what seemed ages. John recalled watching this well-groomed woman in front of him, neatly attired in high-heels and a pinstriped jacket with matching dress, thinking how incongruous the whole scene seemed.

At one point the woman asked John to wait.

'I'll just go ahead and see if Mr. Wheatcroft is receiving.' she said, disappearing further into the scrubby undergrowth.

A few minutes went by before the woman, clearly flustered, burst forth out of the scrub.

'Ah…Mr Wheatcroft will be ready in a minute Mr Williams, if you'd care to wait. He's just getting changed.' she exclaimed, still shielding her blushing face with a manicured hand.

Randal Wheatcroft, as John remembered him, was a curious man. The cause of the sales agent's embarrassment was the actuality that Randal's 'wardrobe' was rather limited. In fact, Randal rarely ever wore clothes, only during trips into town and on those seasonal occasions when the prevailing weather dictated the need for keeping warm.

In due course Randal, or 'Randy' as the Minamurra youth taunted him, appeared through the bushes to greet the 'scouting party'. Somehow the picture of this aristocratically named gentleman didn't quite fit the picture John was now presented with on this overgrown section of the track.

'Randal!' his introduction went, stretching out a wide-open hand…. 'And you'd be the bloke who's interested in buying my property?'

'Well, I'm having a look at it.' replied John cautiously.

'Perhaps you could lead the way Mr Wheatcroft.' the sales agent interjected, composing herself.

The short broad-faced man with the faint year-round tan and the 'comb-over' hair style bustled energetically through the coastal scrub, his brown, bow-kneed, stick-thin legs striding freely out of the bottom of a pair of loosely fitting khaki shorts which covered his matching broad rear-end.

'Watch out for the 'trippy-grass'.' warned Wheatcroft, referring to the tussocks that over hung the track.

They arrived at the property like actors walking onto a stage set.

'Well, here we are!'

Beyond Randal's outstretched arm spread a picture which at first was a little hard to comprehend. The site resembled something that was somewhere between a camp, a bomb site and a rubbish dump. Drab looking washing hanging languidly from a rope stretched between two trees partially obscured John's view of the scene. The 'fisherman's cottage' was nothing but a small, prefabricated garden shed. An open-sided 'lean-to' hung off the back, its rusty sheets of corrugated iron complimenting the rusty length of guttering attached haphazardly along one side of the structure. Below the gutter a small, galvanised iron tank designed to catch rainwater off the roof sat on the bare sandy ground. With no tank stand Wheatcroft had dug a hole under where the tap was situated to allow him to fill a jug or a bucket when water was needed.

The 'lean-to' which served as a kitchen was littered with a collection of dirty dishes and sooty pots and pans. The improvised shelving along the back wall was filled with an assortment of tinned foods and open packets of powdered milk, sugar and flour. John could make out cans of braised steak and onions, baked beans, and a variety of other unrecognisable tins which had their labels missing. A blackened kettle shared a bench beside a variety of grubby looking condiments. The congealed remains of last night's dinner sat in a dented aluminium saucepan on a greasy looking single burner camp stove. A hole cut in the back wall of the shed served as a doorway between what was the bedroom and the open-air kitchen.

On the other side of an untidy smouldering campfire near the shed, an old khaki canvas tent was draped forlornly beneath a sagging length of rope. Through the open flap John noted a pile of books and some papers, and surprisingly a laptop computer and printer on a makeshift table in front of a small cut-down stool. A petrol-powered generator, obviously intended for providing power to the computer, lay on its side exposed to the elements in the open alongside the tent. All about the ground empty tins, an assortment of bottles and other junk littered the site. A chainsaw and other tools employed by Wheatcroft around the property lay on the ground where the user had last employed them.

The interior of the window-less shed was dark, but John could just make out an unmade bunk along one wall, beside which sat an upturned fruit-box adorned with a kerosene lamp and a traveller's clock. Against the opposite wall was a small rusty potbelly stove. Despite a rough hole cut in the roof directly above the wood heater there was no fluepipe attached to it. A thick black smoke-stain covered the ceiling and extended down the walls to a point level with the top of the doorway to the kitchen where the smoke could escape. The original door at the front of the shed was stopped up and totally obstructed by a collection of indistinguishable personal items.

Doing his best to try and ignore the squalid surroundings that threatened to consume his senses like some terrible scourge John asked, 'And where does the property run to?'

Looking like a weather cock on a windy day, Randal extended both arms out either side of his shoulders and rotated back and forth. 'It sort of stretches out in that direction from down near the lake to up on the dunes near the sea.'

'It's a long narrow block if you follow, from about where that banksia is across to that stump over there.'

John turned his back on the sales agent and this 'dirty little man' and wandered off in the general direction of the estuary to survey the rest of the property by himself. He was hoping he might discover a fencepost or some other marker that would indicate more accurately where the boundary might lie than that of the flailing Wheatcroft. Away from the campsite the bush thickened, the branches of coastal tea-trees gently rattled as they knocked together under the influence of the sea breeze. The muffled roar of distant surf filled in the gapes of silence left by the stirring branches overhead and bird songs punctuated the constant hum of the bush. A little further on native pittosporums and banksias proliferated in a noticeably greener environment. It was as if the block of land possessed its own microclimates. John eventually arrived at a place where the trees gave way to a wide-open area of bull-rushes which lined the muddy banks of a tidal creek. The estuary could be seen from this point at a place which John reckoned to be further west from the landing.

Retracing his footsteps back, John gave the campsite a wide berth and continued up towards the beach. He reached the point where the photo in the paper must have been taken. The expansive blue vista was preceded by a series of hummocks and a seemingly endless stretch of squeaky white sand. Further evidence of Randal's occupation could be seen amongst the sea-grass tussocks. Detritus consisting of remnants of a fishing net, several rusty fishing reels, a crab pot and a broken surf rod littered the dunes. Another surf rod leant against a tree, the empty hook and sinker swaying lazily in the breeze and a feathery length of dry seaweed fluttered from the rod-tip like a ship's ensign. Other than the small pockets of bush where Randal didn't frequent, the remainder of the land had been sullied and stood out as a blot on the landscape. It was far from what John had imagined it to be as described in the newspaper and with an asking price of $100,000 it was out of the question.

Returning to Minamurra, John perused a few other properties on the estate agent's books together with Randal's contact details just in case he had any other questions about the block that Randal could answer for him. There was nothing else listed for sale in the area that attracted John and the next day he drove back to Melbourne dismissing the whole affair as a waste of time.

Six months passed, by which time John had all but forgotten about Paradise, when a letter arrived in the mail from Minamurra addressed to a 'Mr John Williams Esquire.'

It read;

> *Dear Mr Williams,*
>
> *Thank you for your recent interest in my property in Paradise. You may not be aware, but my intention is to buy a cruising vessel so that I might better enjoy the environs of the estuary. The purchase of the boat is predicated on the sale of my property, and so keen to progress with my plans I have instructed the Real Estate Agent that the original purchase price of $100,000 is now negotiable.*
>
> *According, I would like to invite you to make an offer should you still be interested.*
>
> *Yours Sincerely,*
> *Randal Wheatcroft*

The invitation to negotiate a price appealed to John; however, the mention of Wheatcroft's name brought back stark images of the squalor in John's mind. Nevertheless, he contacted the agent to arrange a second visit and this time Randal offered to pick John up from Minamurra on his own.

The estate agent told a different story of Randal's desire to get off the land.

'To be perfectly honest with you, Mr Wheatcroft's health is deteriorating over there, and he really needs to relocate closer to medical facilities.' she said.

'And we've given Mr Wheatcroft instruction to clean up his property if he is serious about getting a sale.'

It sounded like the estate agents were just as keen to get Wheatcroft off their books as was Wheatcroft to get off his land.

So, John once more found himself on the fisherman's wharf boarding a boat to Paradise. On this occasion, having corresponded directly with Randal, he organised to re-visit the land without the company of the sales agent.

Randal's boat was a faded fibreglass sixteen-foot half-cabin. Chalky blue topsides sat above a water-stained white hull. As the untidy looking outboard motor rattled into life John couldn't help but notice the profusion of marine growth covering the hull and the motor leg below the water line.

Randal eased the throttle lever forward and the spluttering smoky engine laboured against the resistance of the barnacle encrusted hull as it pushed through the water. Acrid fumes filling the boat made John's eyes sting and caught the back of his throat causing him to cough and dry retch.

Randal ducked into the half cabin and threw open the front hatch, providing some much-needed ventilation.

'She's been running a bit rich lately John...... May I call you John?'

'Yeah, whatever.' spluttered John, sticking his head out the side to get more fresh air.

Reaching their destination Randal steered the boat into the government jetty. The already damaged bow crunched solidly into a mooring post causing the unfortunate passenger to lurch face-first into the confines of the musty cabin.

'You'll notice I've spruced the place up a bit since last you were down.' said Randal, alighting from the boat.

What John did notice this time was the 'For Sale' sign which had been partially obscured by the bushes on the shore just right of the landing. Its faded lettering indicated the property had probably been on the market for some considerable time.

Randal took John via a different track to that which the sales agent had led him on his first visit. This path took him through several other properties adjacent to Wheatcroft's. John observed several little shacks along the way. A couple were fabricated with corrugated iron. There was one which had been built using discarded car cases and another was clad in asbestos-cement sheeting.

'They're all owned by relatives.' said Randal.

'Most of them come here for their holidays although a few that are retired I see down here more often.'

John could see no evidence though of any new building activity that might have occurred for at least the past twenty years or more.

By the time they arrived at the camp site Randal was in full 'sales swing'. He pulled a crumpled council rates notice out of the back pocket of his equally crumpled khaki shorts and foisted it at John as proof of ownership of the property.

'You can grow some good veggies here y'know. Silver-beet does particularly well in the sandy soil. And the fish have started schoolin' in the lake again, so you'd never go hungry here y'know.'

'Do you have a toilet?' enquired John.

'I just use a bucket.' grinned Randal.

'Offered it to that lady who brought you over last time when you'd wandered off, but she didn't seem keen on the idea...... preferred to hold on she told me!'

'I think I would too.' thought John quietly to himself.

There was noticeably less junk lying about the property. John could see the remains of a huge bonfire just beyond the tent where Wheatcroft had incinerated anything he could find to burn. The fire had left an ugly scar in the middle of the block. Singed foliage on the surrounding bushes and trees attested to the apparent ferocity that the debris must have burnt with. Blackened tins and what looked like the remains of an inner spring mattress protruded out of the ashes and solidified pools of blackened plastic floated on the sand beside the pyre.

Further up toward the sand dunes disturbed patches of ground suggested that what Randal couldn't burn he'd buried.

'It's still like a boil on the arse of nature.' John thought to himself.

But just then as he was about to dismiss the second inspection as another waste of time a sweet-smelling waft of sea-air filtered through the tall tea-trees causing the branches to rattle gently as he remembered they did on his first visit to the site.

'Maybe, just maybe the block could be repatriated.'

'I wonder if the damaged bushland could ever heal itself and be exorcised from this dirty little man?'

'I'll need a bit of time to think about it Randal before I consider making you any sort of offer. There's a hell of a lot of work I'd have to do here to get it as I would like to see it......a hell of a lot of work my friend!'

The journey back to Minamurra was just as unpleasant as had been the trip across. A stiff south-easterly had sprung up and buckets of spray flew across the beam of the boat as Randal powered the struggling old vessel into the choppy waves.

'Duck in the cabin John, or you'll get drowned out here,' yelled Wheatcroft into the wind, his grey comb-over flying wildly off the leeside of his otherwise bald head.

John found himself huddled in what could best be described as a liquid pit of floating garbage. The boat seemed to have regurgitated the contents of its bilge in protest at the rough crossing. Empty beer cans, bottles and rotting organic material sloshed back and forth over the floor of the cabin as the embattled vessel tossed up and down. Mercifully, it only took fifteen minutes before the passenger and crew steered into the sheltered waters of the Minamurra port.

'Oh, and I'll throw the boat in as part of the sale John.' Randal declared as an added 'tempter'.

John returned to Melbourne that night, his mind in two states of reasoning. Thinking with his head, he reasoned that taking on the isolated pigsty (that nobody else obviously wanted) and building a proper cottage would be just too much hard work. Thinking with his heart, he imagined the fishing he could enjoy, the enchanting rattle of the tea-trees and the soothing song of the waves rolling into the beach. Yes, he would need quite a bit of time to think about it.

It was several weeks later, sometime after John had finally put the possibility of buying the land out of his mind that he received a phone call from the woman at the estate agents.

'Mr Wheatcroft informs us you inspected the Paradise property again Mr Williams.'

'Can I tell you he's very keen to sell, and as he's previously mentioned, he'd be willing to come down a bit from the current asking price,' continued the woman in a tempting voice.

'Oh look, you've seen the property yourself and the state it's in,' replied John.

'I'm not sure I'm really interested. He'd have to come down a long way on his price, and I wouldn't want to insult him.'

'I think Mr Wheatcroft would consider any offer at this point Mr Williams.'

John let out a deep sigh. 'Oh look...... I don't know. Tell him fifty thousand,' said John, pretty much as a throwaway line.

'OK....' replied the woman hesitantly. 'We'll inform the owner of your offer.'

A week later, much to John's astonishment he received a letter in the mail directly from Randal himself stating;

'Dear Mr Williams,

I am informed of your offer of $50,000 and consider it to be very reasonable. I therefore can advise you that I have accepted your offer and have left the matter with the estate agent to manage the acquisition and transfer of the property into your name. I am also willing to include my motorboat as part of the sale as previously offered.

Yours sincerely,
Randal Wheatcroft'

Eighteen years on and John still wondered what Randal's reply would have been to an even lesser offer, especially considering he knocked back the inclusion of Randal's rotting 'hulk' as part of the deal. So much hard work and so many adventures and happy memories had amply filled in the time since acquiring the land. And John reflected on how many other Paradise residents had since built or rebuilt their little shacks and shanties into what had now become an established 'occasional community'.

Soon the school holidays would start and the empty houses in Paradise would be coming to life, filled with the presence of property owners, their children and dogs, populating the land that lay between the estuary and the ocean.

As John passed the government jetty on his way to his familiar mooring place, he spotted the mussel cage and the bucket that he'd abandoned the night before. At least if he wasn't up to fishing, he could hobble down the track to get the mussels he'd collected for himself from the jetty piles last night. Remembering he'd topped up the bucket with clean salt-water before he boarded the U-Sail cruiser, he figured they should still be fresh enough to provide for dinner at the end of the day.

The warm sun shone down from a now deep blue sky, complimented by a fair breeze, and it gave John a comforting sense that the state of things was returning to normal. All was well in Paradise once more.

Chapter Three

The Early Settlers

*Proverbs- 29:18 "Where there is no vision,
the people perish."*

The relatives of whom Randal had referred to as owning most of the other properties were descendants of the Scully family. The extended family had a long association with Paradise. In fact, it was the Scully forefathers who first settled there, a generation before those who allowed James Tulloch to squat on the land.

Their story began in 1861 on the other side of the world in Massachusetts, USA. Frederick T. Howland, a Quaker had become convinced that the 'Second Coming of Christ' and the subsequent 'Last Judgement' would come shortly. Obsessed by his belief and with total conviction, Howland started a small commune, with roughly thirty loyal followers initially. The religious sect he created became known as the 'Adonai-Shomo'. Unfortunately for Fredrick, some years later he found himself suddenly 'going' before he could witness the 'Second Coming'.

One fateful day, while riding to town for supplies he came across a hunter in a field. As he passed, a shot rang out, which startled his horse. The panicked mare left the road and bolted into the woods. The horse passed under a low spreading branch at full gallop. The branch subsequently caught the Quaker under the chin, snapping his neck and killing him instantly.

Not long after Howland's untimely demise, a man named Cook arrived at the grieving commune saying that God had sent him to take over and guide the community forward. A charismatic man, the members of the group accepted him initially. However, Cook later began to institute some unusual sexual practices into the commune which led the members to depose him from the leadership and initiate criminal charges against him. With a void left once again to be filled, one of the founding members and true believers, a young Thomas Scully, stepped into the breach and took over the reins.

Prior to Howland's arrival, Tom had engaged in a short but successful business career and under his leadership and sound governance the small group prospered. After several years they were able to purchase 840 acres of land near the hamlet of Petersham, Massachusetts.

Despite the apparent prosperity the group enjoyed in the coming years, in time the older members of the commune began to die off, and several of the younger members, tired of the dogma and all its restrictions, left. With the gradual decline in the original fabric of the commune, eventually a breakaway group of the younger members filed a suit against Scully to gain partial control of the group's property, eventually winning the suit. However as with any drawn out bitter legal battle, those that stood to benefit most financially were the lawyers. The money from the sale of the commune's land was barely sufficient to cover the group's debts and legal fees. Ravaged by all the bad feelings and disharmony within the group, the commune disbanded in 1896.

Fearing the un-sated financial appetites of his pursuers would lead to a second legal bid for the personal wealth Tom had amassed during his time leading the commune, he took flight with his young wife and five children in search of a new beginning.

Travelling west from Petersham, Thomas began to firm in this mind the idea of re-establishing the Adonai-Shomo faith, using his own family as the seed from which to grow a new devoted following. But the ever-present fear that further legal action might still be pending haunted him daily. As the family continued to move west, despite the growing distance from Massachusetts, a sense of the presence of his pursuers seemed to move with them. The thought of losing his personal wealth hovered like a dark spectre in Tom's mind and cast deep shadows over his developing plans. By the time they had gone about as far west as they could go without actually wading into the sea, it was the town of San Francisco that greeted them. It was there that Tom made the decision to leave the United States altogether and migrate with his family to a new land and a new beginning.

They boarded a steamer bound for Melbourne, Australia, a land far away from the 'gold digging parasites' Scully had abandoned back in Petersham.

The long voyage across the vast Pacific Ocean afforded Tom the luxury of time to think. Un-interrupted days and nights free from distraction, Tom studied the Bible together with earlier *Adonai-Shomo* readings and further developed his vision of a new beginning. He wrote a testament titled '*The wondrous vision of the purpose of the Lord*'

'Eye hath not seen, nor ear heard, neither has it been imagined, what God has prepared for his people. We have glimpsed it and are intoxicated by it.'

Tom wrote; 'It was prophesied in Acts 2:13-17 on the day of the Pentecost. After the Apostle Peter had spoken.'

Others mocking said, 'These men are full of new wine.'

'But Peter, standing up with the eleven, lifted up his voice, and said unto them, Ye men of Judea, and all ye that dwell at

Jerusalem, be this known unto you, and hearken my words: For these are not drunken, as ye suppose, seeing as it is but the third hour of the day.'

'But this is that which was spoken by the prophet Joel; And it shall come to pass in the last days, saith God, I will pour out my Spirit upon flesh: and your sons and your daughters shall prophesy, and your young men shall see visions, and your old men shall dream dreams:'

CATCH THE VISION!

By the time the ship had reached Australian waters Scully who, in the privacy of their cramped cabin had preached his new learning to his family daily, was convinced he had found the 'Truth'.

What was about to happen though, would severely test the strength of Scully's commitment to his faith as, steaming into Bass Strait, this voyage of 'spiritual discovery' took a dramatic change of course. After an otherwise uneventful ocean crossing, late in the afternoon, a fierce storm blew up from the southeast. Storm-force winds smashed rolling waves into the stern of the vessel sending great torrents of foaming seawater over the rear decks and down the companionways. Not wanting to risk an almost certain capsize the captain wasn't game to attempt to come about and face the vessel into the tempest. Instead, he did his best to hold his course and try to ease closer towards onshore waters, where it was hoped he might find some shelter, and perhaps the storm would abate in the evening.

As the embattled ship sought shelter nearer the coastline it became grounded on a sandbar just out from the tidal entrance to Minamurra. Some hours passed before the stricken vessel was noticed by the town's people, and by then it was too dark and too dangerous to begin launching a rescue attempt. A small gathering of locals assembled forlornly on the beach to witness the spectacle of this ghostly silhouette that filled the usually empty horizon before them. Each time the rolling sea smashed into the ship, it was as if the barque writhed in agony like a huge, beached whale.

Adding to the dramatic scene, above the roar of the howling gale, the shore folk could just make out the distant eerie groaning from the ship as once tightly secured cargo rasped torturously back and forth across the flooded decks.

As evening faded to nightfall the storm continued to build well into the darkest of nights, and the passengers and crew were forced to endure what seemed to be God's reign of terror with no end. Contrasting alarmingly from the rhythmic rocking of the open ocean they'd become accustomed to, the ship's hull now crashed down sickeningly and intermittently onto the shallow bottom. Attempts by the crew to float the ship off the sandbar only made things worse. Frantic efforts to jettison the deck cargo only resulted in the vessel being blown further onto the bar, the jarring blows of steel against sand intensifying all the while. Every now and then a wave would hit from the side, slewing the boat around and throwing those aboard violently sideways. The cries of Scully's children and the screams of the womenfolk could barely be heard above the roaring, rumbling surf that continued its rage well into the next morning.

That night thought Scully, 'If the *Second Coming* is nigh, then so be it! I am prepared for the Lord's final Judgement.'

But as it turned out, it wasn't the Second Coming, and by midmorning of the new day the wind had subsided just as fast as it had intensified the day before.

By midday the ship was observed sitting forlornly atop the sand bar. Listing to one side, with a build-up of sand on the windward side, its escape route to the open seas was now blocked. The decks were littered with various bits of timber and cargo, items that had previously been packed tightly into wooden crates and stacked neatly atop each other. Lengths of rope that earlier secured the deck cargo dangled loosely over the sides. A rope ladder hung down over the leeward side, and Tom wondered if anyone had deployed it in an attempt to escape the ship during the height of the storm.

With any hope of re-floating the steamer all but gone, a decision was made to abandon ship before any further foul weather beset the vessel, which surely would be unable to sustain any further punishment without breaking up.

As soon as it was calm enough, a small fleet of fishing boats made their way out through the entrance from Minamurra and began ferrying the passengers and crew ashore. Throughout the afternoon a continuous convoy of boats brought first passengers, then crew ashore, together with personal belongings and other items of value. By early evening the steamer was left to fend for itself, a lifeless shadowy silhouette looming out of the sea-mist a few hundred yards offshore.

In the following weeks salvage operations were undertaken to remove as much of the cargo as was possible. A variety of furniture, building materials and domestic chattels were transferred onto the bigger fishing boats and bit by bit taken into port. But with every low tide the stranded vessel sank further into the sand as if being slowly consumed by some mythical monster until, with the next big blow, the dying beast turned on its side and succumbed to the forces of nature.

Some of the salvaged cargo was loaded onto carts and freighted into Melbourne seven days away, but much of it including the building materials was written off and remained in Minamurra to be auctioned or sold at cost price.

Thomas Scully believed that out of calamity comes opportunity, and he had convinced himself that it was no less than God's Will that had delivered them to Minamurra.

'Providence!' he declared.

'A manifestation of God's foresightful care for His creatures.'

Tom heard from the locals that the government of the day, keen to promote settlement and development of outlying communities, was offering those qualified as 'free settlers' the opportunity to take a *'selection'* of land for farming. Surveying the district maps Tom noted a parcel of land across the other side of the estuary that led upstream from the port. The area was still within reach of the tiny fishing community, but sufficiently separated from prying noses. It seemed like the perfect place to settle his family and re-establish the commune.

Within a matter of weeks, using some of the money he'd stashed in his luggage when they fled Petersham, Tom purchased an open boat and rowed it across the entrance to stake his claim on the five hundred acre 'selection'. The land he noted was low and expansive. To the west it was vegetated predominately with mahogany gums and ancient coastal banksias which grew out of a forest floor of tussock grasses and bracken. Occasional sprays of greenhood orchids bowed their heads to the sun. The eastern end (the part closest to Minamurra) was scrubbier and sandier and covered in tea-trees, wattles, and dark green pittosporums. The middle section was punctuated with open patches of grasslands. There were a number of soaks and waterholes nearer the marshy areas that contained fresh water, enough to provide for man and 'stock' alike. The northern edge of the property ended on the low banks of the estuary where layers of black spongy peat lay exposed by erosion from tidal currents and lapping waves. From the south a distant rumbling of crashing waves was carried in on the sea breeze. Adjacent to the selection were a number of small islands in the estuary not far offshore where green grass grew below a lightly treed canopy.

'This is surely proof of the existence of divine Providence.' exclaimed a wide-eyed Scully.

And casting his eyes to the heavens, with hands clasped to his chest Thomas cried out, 'I give thanks to the guardianship and control exercised by you, my Lord in these matters of delivering me to this land!'

'I shall call it Paradise!'

Exercising the same keen business acumen he'd displayed back in Massachusetts, Tom managed to purchase, at bargain rates, most of the building materials and other effects needed to establish a modest home base. Much of the material he purchased had come from the cargo salvaged from the ill-fated steamer. That which was put up for auction he acquired particularly cheaply, as the majority of Minamurra folk eked out a modest living from catching fish and didn't have the means to purchase much else than that required to support a basic existence.

It was a very interesting place that the Scully family had come to settle on. The water and the land teemed with life when they first saw it. The estuary was covered in a multitude of waterfowl. Black swans, beautiful white pelicans and a variety of ducks proliferated in their thousands. Amongst the beach scrub and along the coast many pretty birds could be seen. Wrens, plovers, kingfishers, cranes and honey eaters just to name a few. The morning call of the laughing kookaburras would greet the dawn, while in the evenings the air would ring to the crack of the whipbirds and hoots of the mopokes.

The land was home to all sorts of animals, including a few kangaroos and numerous black, grey and red wallabies. There were bandicoots, like big rats, and many tiny wallabies called paddymelons. Moving around at night was an eerie experience with the 'pat-pat' from the feet of dozens of unseen marsupials retreating from their feeding grounds.

There was evidence of other habitation on the land too. There were mounds of shellfish litter and they found pointed bones that were used to clean out the flesh from cooked periwinkles. Also, on a few of the larger trees near the water's edge there were oval cuts in the bark where canoes had been cut out. Occasionally thin columns of smoke could be seen in the distance, further evidence that the Scullys were not entirely alone in their claim to the land.

Possibly the most interesting thing though, was the discovery of some burial grounds of the natives. The Scullys knew nothing about them until they had been settled for some time. One of the fierce storms that would roar in from time to time eroded the coastal dunes along the beach, exposing the graves that had previously been hidden from view in a burial ground in the sand hills. Albert, Thomas's eldest son came across the first grave during one of his excursions exploring the beach. He brought back a skull, which an alarmed Thomas took be evidence of some foul doings on the land. Tom, concerned for the safety and welfare of his family, reported the matter to the local police in Minamurra. The police upon investigating the site found several other graves and returned to the township with the skull Albert had recovered. They took the skull to a dentist in the district town of Bairnsdale to see if the teeth matched any dental records. The dentist, who had a keen interest in the dental hygiene of the natives was able to confirm the apparently decay free choppers once belonged to an aborigine.

Unfortunately for the reclusive Scullys, the townsfolk got to hear about the investigation into a number of skeletal remains found on their selection, and the rumours soon spread like wildfire about the suspicious goings on over on the land. There was talk about strange ritual practices and sacrifices being carried out by this newly arrived 'secular' family. On the few occasions the Scullys went into town, the men folk would eye them with untrusting stares and the women folk would gather their children into the folds of their dresses like hens protecting their chicks from some predator. All this was certainly going to make it difficult for Tom, who was still developing his 'vision', to win over the confidence of this heathen flock and to educate them in the '*Truth*'; '*The wondrous vision of the purpose of the Lord*'.

Tom would tell his family, 'As you will have noticed during our visits to the village, we are different to them.'

'They are without the knowledge and the 'Truth'.'

'The apostle Peter, in his last epistle, tells us that just as the earth was destroyed by water, with the second coming it is to be destroyed by fire and renewed. Nevertheless we, according to His promise, look for new heavens and a new earth, wherein dwelleth righteousness.'

Fortunately for the Scullys, as the relationship between those in Paradise and those in Minamurra deteriorated through mistrust and scuttlebutt, the Scullys became more self-sufficient and relied less on the need to interact with the townsfolk. With the help of Albert, who was sixteen years old and younger brother William, who was fifteen, Tom had managed to clear a reasonable portion of the more arable sections of land where he grew a variety of grain crops and vegetables. To avoid having to fence off other areas to raise stock, Tom occupied a couple of the closer islands where he kept a few dairy cattle and goats. Apart from the produce harvested from farming the land, the abundant wildlife provided them with a bountiful source of protein. Tom and the boys all became great rifle shots. Although easier to hunt, the swans were not often shot as their black flesh was not very good eating and as such was not relished very much. The ducks however, were a different story, they were considered very good to eat, and although they were far more timid than the trusting swans, they were worth the extra effort to bring to the kitchen table.

The wallabies were also hunted by the Scully boys. Apart from the meat, which was harvested, the pelts were put to good use. Tom had discovered the bark of the coastal wattles contained a high level of tannin and boiled up in a large drum over the campfire, was ideal for tanning the skins of the animals. All the family had warm wallaby-skin rugs as extra coverings on their beds, each child's rug arranged according to chosen colour. The dining room also had a beautiful opossum-skin rug that Katherine, Thomas's wife, had stitched together.

Despite the isolation and lack of contact with the local community, the family flourished on the land. Without the distractions of the civilised world, and with no inhibitions, Tom studied his Bible with increasing fervour and intensity, searching for further evidence of the 'Truth'. On his 'voyage of discovery' into the meaning of life, he began sifting through the various theories, and scouring the scriptures very carefully and fully, and he slowly but surely changed his thinking from orthodox views.

Daily, Tom would gather his family and indoctrinate them into the way of his thinking.

'Gradually I understand the purpose of God in His dealings with mankind, and I am becoming very enthusiastic and exhilarated with the concept of the future as revealed in the Bible!' he explained.

Quoting from the Psalms, Tom ranted, *'How sweet are thy words unto my taste! Yea, sweeter than honey to my mouth!'*

'Through thy precepts I get understanding; Therefore, I hate every false way. Thy word is a lamp unto my feet, and a light unto my path.'

Apart from the bounty provided by the land, the Scully members were somewhat starved in the context of culture and conversation afforded by contact with the wider community and so, with no other source of knowledge, what Thomas preached to them became their reality.

So convinced in the truth of his own beliefs was Thomas, that he felt compelled to share his great discoveries with those outside his immediate family. He was keen to find ways to expand his commune. He would establish a camp on a remote section of his property from which he could share his teaching and inspire his followers. But before that he would need to begin to spread the good word, which meant engaging the townsfolk and gaining their trust.

A lone missionary in a mass of souls in desperate need of enlightenment was how Tom saw himself. Unfortunately, that was not how the local 'masses' saw poor Tom. The general view of Scully was that of a man who was a reclusive eccentric, one who was ruthless when dealing in business......and of course there was that business about the bodies in the sand-hills.

Not surprisingly then, Tom's first attempt to preach to the flock was a disaster. Positioning himself on a box on the wharf, Tom directed his sermon to a group of fishermen who were busily unloading and sorting their catch after a long night's fishing.

He began with a prophecy about the second coming. *'Eye hath not seen, nor ear heard, neither have entered into the heart of man, the things which God hath prepared for them that love him.'*

'And I saw a new heaven and a new earth; For the first heaven and the first earth were passed away; and there was no more sea.'

'No more sea you say!' answered an amused voice.

'That would stuff up our fishing wouldn't it boys!'

The gathering of men paused from their work to focus on this impromptu source of entertainment. Having caught their attention, Tom held out his hand by way of question and addressed them directly.

'Now, how many of you have scalded your hand in boiling water on the stove? It burns does it not, like the fires of hell!'

'And you reach into the ice-chest to sooth your agony do you not?.......But let me tell you, there're no ice-chests in hell, only more boiling water!'

'Hey Tassie!' interjected one of the fishermen to his mate.

'This bloke thinks he's Jesus Christ......I wonder if he can walk on water?'

Before Tom could get midway through his next sentence, two of the burley unshaven men picked him up bodily, then carrying him to the edge of the wharf, threw him unceremoniously into the port. Tom disappeared beneath a huge splash. Raucous laughter on the jetty drowned out the popping of rising bubbles beneath. Then there was a brief silence as one and then another peering face stared down curiously over the edge of the wharf onto the empty expanse of the water. Moments later the temporary stillness was broken by a thrashing, spluttering Thomas as he exploded above the surface. Sporting a garland of sea grass, a loud gasp was rent from the flailing man's mouth, his eyes bulging like one who had just seen the devil himself. The raucous laughter on the pier erupted once more ringing in Tom's ears like a salvo fired from a flotilla of enemy ships.

Tom beat a hasty retreat to his boat and, hauling himself in like a half-drowned rat in a soup-tin he pulled back on the sculls with all the strength his enraged and embarrassed body could muster. As a final act of belittlement, in his haste he managed to slice one of the oars across the surface of the water sending him sprawling flat on his back into the bottom of the boat. Thomas's tormentors were doubled over in laughter at the sight in front of them and it was all he could do not to cry out in his anger and his pain.

The trip back to Paradise was arduous and difficult. Rowing into a brisk headwind and against the outgoing tide, Tom was exhausted by the time he reached home. Still soaking wet, and refrigerated by the chilly breeze, his face had changed colour from the previously enraged red to a curiously ghostly blue. Several remnant strands of sea-grass fluttered in the wind along with his wispy hair. His clothes hung heavily off aching limbs and his white knuckles contrasted starkly with his dark wet jacket. It was a pitiful vision that approached the little homestead.

It was the twelve-year-old Florence, Thomas's youngest who noticed him first.

'Mummy, mummy! There's a strange looking man in a boat down at the lake!'

'Oh my Lord,' exclaimed Katherine, spotting the bedraggled figure pulling into the bank.

'That's no strange man Florence......well not a stranger at least; It's your father for heaven's sake!'

'Albert! William! Come quickly and help your poor father and see what's wrong with him.'

Katherine was clearly shocked at the sight of Thomas in his state of disarray. The man she had come to know as one who was always composed and who always had a 'presence'. This pathetic figure resembled more of a village idiot than an enlightened preacher. Disembarking clumsily from the boat, he tripped over into the water before sloshing his way up the track toward the bewildered gathering before him. Albert and William found it strangely amusing but dared not show their mirth. Tom's youngest boy, young Thomas however grinned broadly and blurted, 'So did you fall in Daddy?'

'Not exactly 'fell'', replied Tom through chattering teeth.

'Anyway, it's no business of yours to be worried about.'

Tom was clearly becoming agitated by the disport his demeanour was providing for the children.

'So how did it go in town then Tom?' asked Katherine, trying to diffuse the imminent hostilities.

'Well ......' said Tom, pausing to gain some composure.

'I would have expected it to have gone a little better than it did.'

Clearly, Tom was not prepared to share his humiliating experience with the children, and so they were left to imagine what extraordinary event could have occurred to deliver their father home in such an unfortunate state.

Part of the tenet of Thomas's teachings was the complete abstinence from tobacco, liquor or any stimulants such as tea or coffee, so without the aid of any of the material substances for comfort, he was left to console himself with little more than his faith and a warm glass of water.

'Katherine, there are none so blind as those who will not see,' remarked Tom, rolling out that old acorn.

He would have to think up a different strategy if he was to have any influence on the hearts and minds of those in Minamurra. Fortunately for Thomas (who was no longer willing to risk ridicule in town again), his children were able to provide a conduit with the outside world as he gradually relinquished his steely grip on them and allowed them to visit town once in every while to pick up stores. The children had the advantage of being able to present a much more normal profile than the self-proclaimed preacher, and keen to learn about the outside world, were much more interested in learning from, rather than preaching to, the locals.

When in town the boys, particularly the older two who were quite good looking, and having a naturally occurring interest in the fairer sex, as young 'men' are want to do, found it relatively easy to engage in conversation with some of the village girls. They were more guarded though when it came to Sarah, William's twin sister, engaging with the local boys. Nevertheless, all the Scully children, including little Florence were able to develop friendships in time, heralding the first real evidence that the family had integrated with the community.

Thomas on the other hand remained reclusive and became even more convicted to his faith, if that be possible. Sadly Katherine, who was twelve years younger than Thomas, being loyal to her husband would sacrifice her opportunity to seek friendship outside the family to be with him and support him through his self-imposed exile.

This didn't diminish the children's appetite for spending time in Minamurra however, and even through the colder winter months, the season for storms and rain, they would seek every opportunity to row across the estuary to the village.

The boys would boast that no matter how bad the weather might get while they were engaged in the township, they were never forced to spend a night in town. Though driven back by great gales and heavy seas, they always managed to force their way to Paradise finally, sometimes with almost-swamped boats. With the great rushing run out tides that would occur during winter when the westerly winds blew hardest, occasionally they were nearly swept out to sea through the entrance despite desperately frantic rowing, catching the rocks in the entrance and hanging on until they could tow the boat to safety, or the tide slackened.

The Scullys lived constantly in the sound of the sea. You could even tell which way the wind was blowing by the direction from which the sound could be heard. It rumbled most of the time, and Katherine would often worry about the boys out on the water during rough weather. At one time when she fell very ill with a fever, the ocean's moaning sounded to her like the growling of a lion which, in her delirium she imagined was devouring her children. But these desperate battles against the elements were a factor in developing the tenacity of purpose and determination which helped the family survive in their imposed isolation. In the following years, when Minamurra would host the annual rowing regatta the Scully boys, then in their mid to late teens, would enter in the 'open class' and nearly always bring home the rowing trophy. It was another factor which helped restore some respect for the family and helped integrate the children with the village community.

By the time Albert and younger siblings William and Sarah were nineteen and eighteen years old respectively, they had each discovered love and had established steady relationships. Thomas could hardly deny them the opportunity of marriage, especially in the case of the boys as it was not the tradition that his permission was the one that needed to be sought. He was however in a position to place the importance of family values above the sanctity of matrimony, and he insisted that any prospective daughter or son in law be part of their family and reside with them in Paradise. This of course was the answer to Tom's dilemma about how to expand his family commune.

In order to make such a requirement attractive, or at least palatable to the prospective spouses and their families, he divided up his land into five one-hundred-acre blocks, one each for the would-be new couples and one set aside for young Thomas when the time came. Florence though, he reasoned, could inherit the remaining land on which the family homestead stood in the years to come. Although she would ultimately have to share that portion of land with Thomas and Katherine while they still lived, it was undoubtedly the pick of Paradise having the best pasture and having been predominantly cleared.

And so, in time the family grew. Under the teachings of Thomas, they proved to be a very stable, if not orthodox type of strong people. Never having doubt in the stability of Thomas's simple social system they lived in the bosom of what they had been taught to be real Christianity. They each built their own houses, lived on their own land; They were all good rifle shots and really feared no one ...... or their opinions for that matter. Nobody interfered with them. The women folk, (as Thomas referred to them) he described as co-labourers in the effort to develop the land. In one of his many written affirmations, he described them as those noble, non-smoking, non-drinking, natural thrifty wives who have been a great help to us in our struggles. And years later, when they inevitably began to produce offspring; 'They have rejoiced in presenting to us such healthy, robust, breast-fed children who will surely grow into such splendid triumphant youth.'

'I think this be further evidence of the *Truth*; We have glimpsed the glorious vision of the purpose of the Lord!' he expounded.

By now the family had cleared enough land to produce grain, fruit and vegetables, well in excess of their own needs, and they were able to start taking the produce to Minamurra to sell. While the green groceries were seasonal, the Scullys were also in a position to supply the township with milk and eggs on an almost daily basis, despite Thomas's reluctance to encourage the family to visit the village too often. Thomas appointed himself as secretary and treasurer of the business and managed the accounts which also included having the final decision on how the income would be spent. The first major purchase was a bigger boat, one with a sail. Young Thomas would later recall how it was one of his pleasures to lie on the smooth white deck under the jib in front of the mast on a warm sunny day. From there he would watch the masses of birds swimming away from the gliding vessel. If the boat got too close, the big swans would take fright and start to run across the surface of water until they could fly; Young Tom would listen to their feet patting on the water and observe their broad black and white wings climbing into the breeze. Elsewhere flocks of birds would fly overhead above the tall sails in a 'V' formation. When they were out sailing in the evening and early mornings the swans would pass over them, trumpeting with a constant and steady beat of wings.

With the larger boat and a source of income to supplement Thomas's dwindling nest egg, the Scullys were gradually able to purchase an array of farming equipment and household items to make their self-sufficient lifestyle better established and more comfortable.

Now that his 'following' was finally starting to grow (be they still only family as such), Thomas revived the idea of creating a communal camp, or retreat as he'd call it, near the far western boarder of the property where he could preach to his flock. He chose a leafy spot amongst the mahogany gums which overlooked the upper reaches of the estuary.

With the help of the boys, he cleared half an acre of scrub and built a church-like structure which was constructed primarily of bush poles and clad in corrugated iron. Atop a steeply pitched roof sat a tall symbolic spire clad in bark. The windows consisted of wooden shutters, hinged from the top, allowing the screens to be propped open with sticks to let in light and air. A simple dais stood at the back of the chapel on a raised platform. Half a dozen uncomfortable looking wooden benches lined each side of the tiny hall. Despite having lined the ceiling with old newspapers covered in hessian, on a warm day the heat of the sun could be felt radiating down through the hot iron roof. In contrast, even on the hottest days cool air would rise up from between the gaps in the bare wooden floorboards. A separate open structure was built in front of the chapel providing an 'outside kitchen' and eating area, beyond which a campfire setting with surrounding log benches was cobbled together. Finally, behind the chapel a couple of lean-to sheds were put up and furnished with crude bunks so that people could stay overnight if required.

Building the bush camp proved quite an undertaking. The upper reaches of the estuary being so shallow, it was impossible to navigate either of their boats closer than a kilometre or more from the site. All the building materials had to be carted in from further down the lake by horse and dray and by the time the project was finished they had created a well-worn track to the camp.

A place to learn and rejoice in the '*Truth*', Thomas named the place 'All Smiles'. He hoped that in time he could offer the camp as a summer school, where the youth of Minamurra and surrounding areas could come on holidays to enjoy the rustic setting and experience the wondrous '*Vision*' as taught by 'The word of the Gospel according to Thomas Scully'. A nice idea maybe, but the reality was, apart from hauling his obedient family up there each Sunday for a service and a picnic, that 'All Smiles' never got to accommodate anybody from outside the immediate family who might be seeking enlightenment.

Even the Scullys (other than Thomas) tired of the weekly journey to 'All Smiles', particularly in winter when it was cold or wet and the puddles along the track would quickly turn to mud under the passing traffic. On those unseasonal days it was much easier to congregate in the family homestead for their weekly service and enjoy a traditional Sunday roast in the warmth and comfort of indoors.

With time came the look of neglect to Thomas's communal camp, and worse still in the absence of 'white fellas', the aborigines started using the place as their occasional campsite, lighting fires in the chapel to keep warm on colder nights and stealing sheets of iron from the outbuildings to shore up their own humpies further west of the Scully land. Then came the young truants from Minamurra, who would sneak up there under the cover of darkness to binge on stolen booze and metre out their dislike for the Scullys by way of vandalising the buildings and desecrating the site with litter and broken beer bottles. Some even used the chapel as a toilet. Within five years the place bore deep scars of abandonment and there was little to smile about with the demise of 'All Smiles'.

In 1923, just on twenty-five years after settling in Paradise, Thomas John Scully formally from Massachusetts, passed away. He was eighty years old. He left behind him a legacy of unorthodox beliefs and modes of life, which he'd developed following his flight from Petersham back in 1896, and which his descendants still hold. By the time of his death the third generation of Scullys to live in Paradise were growing up and thriving on the land.

Without Tom, Katherine who was still a relatively young sixty-two-year-old, took her leave to start a new life in Minamurra. Here she would discover the pleasures of other female company and simple joys such as 'window shopping' and morning teas, something she never experienced on the selection. Florence, who had up until now devoted her life to supporting her mother and father suddenly found herself alone in the homestead and having no longer any reason to continue leading the life of a spinster left the district altogether to start a new life in Melbourne.

With Florence showing no further interest in remaining in Paradise, Katherine divided the 100-acre block left to her by Tom's passing into a number of smaller allotments. In her final Will and Testament, each of the many grandchildren was left a parcel of land. Not all the blocks in the subdivision were the same size. They were allocated according to how favoured by Katherine each grandchild was. Some of the blocks covered ten or more acres and had water frontage, while others by contrast were tucked away in the scrub and were barely half an acre in size. Still keen though to preserve the Scully status in Paradise, she put a caveat on the properties which decreed that no land should be sold to any person outside the family.

As they got older, the majority of the grandchildren were educated on what they called 'the mainland'. Some attended school in the nearby district township; others went to boarding school in Melbourne. This third generation shared the same tenacity of purpose and determination as did their parents, and nearly all went on to study at university to excel in disciplines such as Engineering, Medicine and Law.

By the mid 1940's the late Thomas and Katherine's surviving children began to move off the land. Albert had tragically drowned in the estuary one night attempting to secure his boat during a sudden storm, apparently after suffering heart failure soon after entering the cold water. Albert's wife, haunted by the sight of his lifeless body floating face down on the bank of their property departed soon after, vowing never to return. William and Sarah resettled with their children in Melbourne. Young Thomas, with his love of boats had joined the Royal Australian Navy during the height of the Second World War. After serving in the Atlantic and the Middle East he married a young American military nurse he met on-board a hospital ship and lived out the rest of his life in his father's home state of Massachusetts.

Somewhere during the gradual exodus from Paradise James Tulloch disappeared too. One day he simply failed to turn up for his regular fish-delivery and produce run. A search of his abandoned cement brick hut some days later left little clue as to where or what may have happened to him.

Inevitably, there reached a point in time when there were no permanent residents living in Paradise. The last one to go was Albert's eldest son Maxwell, who returned from studying theology to follow his grandfather's studies, which he did as a lonely isolate caretaker of the vacant properties. Most of the remaining stock which was of any value was sold at auction and so went the cattle and horses. The goats which were considered to be of little value were left behind and continued to breed on several of the islands. A few pigs and a number of hog deer which the Scullys had introduced at one time escaped and turned feral.

Maxwell in one of his late writings said; 'It is rather morbid; The dream has vanished and 'searching feet of change' have altered everything. Mother and Father are now dead. Not the first time that death has occurred amongst my family, but none the less here I am left. Death is so permanent, and I realise we can never meet as a united group on this land again in this life.'

The final exorcising of the land from the first Scully generations occurred in the 1950's when a campfire to the west of Paradise escaped and was driven through the property by a roaring hot mid-summer north westerly. Many of the original houses were burnt down, although some structures like 'All Smiles' and Irish Jimmy's were strangely spared. As a result of the fire, the government of the day keen to better manage the wilderness to the east and west of Paradise declared the land either side to be National Parkland.

Paradise itself was preserved by the fact that Katherine had had the foresight to make it her Will that the property be retained in the fold. In the absence of permanent occupation, the bush slowly regenerated and over grew the pastures and paddocks which once waved at the sun in acres of corn and grain. Old relics of carts and other farm machinery rusted quietly, hidden by the scrub. It was almost as if the land, once awoken by Thomas John Scully was drifting back into a long ancient sleep.

But in the next 15 years things began to change. The Scully members and their descendants began to gather again in Paradise on their holidays, far exceeding in number the original seventeen or so. And keen observers amongst them started to note and point out the remarkable change that had come over the group. From the lowly beginnings as selectors and free settlers on the land, the family had in a few generations blossomed out in many lines, with medical, legal, educational, nursing, religious and missionary practitioners within their ranks.

Little shacks and cottages soon dotted the allotments, and a network of sandy tracks, like giant cobwebs, criss-crossed the land.

Some of the buildings were very basic and were fashioned from materials scavenged from the land. The ones constructed from old car cases were the inadvertent beneficiaries of an offshore oil drilling project during the 'Sixties'. As it was the custom to discard unwanted packing and rubbish into the sea, much of this flotsam had eventually washed ashore along the coast in front of Paradise. Some of the grander erections were given evocative names, such as 'Whispering Waves', and 'Birdsong'. Invariably, to deter would-be vandals in the absence of any caretaker, most of the huts were heavily shuttered and heavy padlocks hung from rusty pad bolts on the doors.

Chapter Four

The Occasional Community

The Second Commandment;
'Thou shalt love thy neighbour as thyself.'

After a more comfortable night than the one previously, John arose early to a brilliant crisp January morning. The delicate scent of early summer hung lightly in the air. A calm sea caressing the sandy beach murmured in the background, and the silent trees stood still while the first rays of a rising sun bathed their upper branches in warm golden light.

As his morning habit would have him do, John made his way down the track to survey the estuary. Hobbling with a tender limp he was able to manage without the 'broomstick-come-crutch' he'd depended on the day before. Still in shadow, the sandy path was damp with heavy dew and the sand stuck to the sole of his one sandal and the ball of his injured foot. He peered across the water to the government jetty. The water sparkled brightly and played dancing reflections over his squinting face. Shielding his eyes from the glare John noted the absence of boats on the pier, then scanning out to the north he took in the sight of dozens of black swans feeding in the distant shallows off the shore of Bandicoot Island. Turning to the west, a huge flock of pied cormorants fluttered noisily on the water like a low dark cloud that had settled out of the sky to hide from the rising sun.

Looking further west nearer the horizon he spotted the familiar sight of a dark red sail which surely, he reckoned, must be old Joe Tucker arriving in his restored couta boat '*Emma*'. Joe was a long-term occasional resident, one of those retirees that Randal had once referred to. He'd married a Scully girl while he was still studying for his engineering degree, and after he'd graduated, together they established a small but successful engineering works on the outskirts of Melbourne. Joe and his wife Jane would bring their two young children down to camp on the property during school holidays. Then after he retired, with more time to spend in Paradise, they built a rustic cottage right on the water's edge with its own little jetty to moor his beloved Emma.

Despite not having direct family roots to bind him to Paradise, Joe was fiercely committed to preserving its amenity and passionate about crusading against any suggestion of change in the area. In keeping with the heritage of the land, he constructed their cottage from a collection of driftwood and old weatherboards that he salvaged from a demolition site in Minamurra. Even the old weatherboards he considered to be too contemporary, and when fixing them to the walls turned them around inside facing out so the 'offensive' painted surface would not be seen. Oddly, there were two curious additions to the building that resulted from a visit by the local building inspector one day.

Council people tried to avoid Paradise as much as possible, because they knew most of the buildings there had been built without a permit and to try to deal with the ire of the feared Scully tribe was just too painful to be contemplated. Joe's house was an exception though. The other little shacks and cottages were all hidden from view in the bush and if one didn't know they were there, one would take the land to be completely devoid of human habitation. Joe's cottage conversely was highly visible, and the council had at one time received a complaint from a passing motorboat. Joe was told the structure was illegal and would have to be pulled down. Further, he would never be permitted to build so close to the water in full view of the estuary again, much of which was now declared Coastal Park. With the help of his in-laws, those who were of a legal persuasion, Joe identified a loophole in the council by-laws. Amongst other temporary structures permitted on his land was a caravan! Drawing on his engineering skills and anti-establishmentarianism Joe, in a moment of creative brilliance, designed and built a huge axle and a pair of concrete wheels which he attached to his otherwise immobile home. In a letter to Joe the council outlined their intent to proceed with legal action should he not demolish this recalcitrant guise, but realising the futility of taking the Scullys to court left the advice as an idle threat. The ever-present wraith of council action never dampened Joe Tucker's enthusiasm for spending time at the cottage.

He once said to John, 'You know, Jane and I get so excited, just at the thought of coming down here. We're just like a couple of kids about to go away on school camp!'

While in Melbourne, Joe kept Emma upstream of the estuary in the Edwards River west of Minamurra. A slow trip could involve up to a half day's sailing to get to Paradise in a light breeze. But Joe was in no hurry, he hated rushing and the trip down the river allowed him to wind down so he could enjoy his stay in Paradise right from the beginning.

Gradually, ever so gradually, the distant red dot grew larger and took form as Joe guided Emma toward the land, till finally Joe's craggy grey bearded face could be seen scowling below the boom.

'Oh dear, I wonder if the cranky old bugger's still in a foul mood?' John whispered to himself.

'Last year he did nothing but bitch about his neighbour, Susan Weeks.'

Unfortunately for Joe, he managed to build his cottage right on the border to the neighbouring block, and when this 'new' person erected a comparatively large house, which stood on stilts and which overshadowed Joe's rustic erection, he was mortified. He took an immediate dislike to Susan as well as her house and never missed an opportunity to vent his spleen in other's company.

If John was waiting in anticipation to hear Joe bang on again about Ms Weeks, he was not going to be left disappointed. Meeting Joe on his jetty the one-man greeting party beckoned for Joe to throw out a line so he could assist hauling Emma alongside. No sooner had John grasped the line than Joe rasped; 'G'day Williams. That lesbian isn't around at the moment, is she?'

'Who?' Taunted John.

'You bloody well know who.'

Joe was aware John was quite fond of Susan and was more than happy to press the point that he wasn't.

'That Weeks woman; God, have you seen the size of her arse?'

'She'd be doing us all a favour if she took it elsewhere and spoiled someone else's view.'

'Actually Joe, no I haven't seen anybody else around. You're the first.' replied John politely.

Tying the mooring lines off with his broad knobbly hands Joe continued his rant as if ignoring John's reply; 'Did I tell you last year that woman was knocking on my window with a sugar bowl in her hand?'

"Could I borrow a cup of sugar? She said through the window."

'Bullshit! I knew what she was up to! It was just an excuse to try and strike up a conversation.'

'I'd rather talk to a pelican!'

'So did you give her some sugar?' John asked timidly.

'I wouldn't give her the wind from a sneeze to cool her porridge!' bellowed the now animated face of Joe Tucker.

John, fearing he might have inadvertently triggered the fuse to a ticking time bomb cut in with a quick change of conversation. 'Emma's looking good Joe. Did you have her out of the water this winter?'

But the ticking fuse continued to tick, ignoring John's question; 'Y'know the stupid bitch asked me last year if I liked that monstrosity of a house of hers. I told her I'd like to buy it, and she took it as a compliment......until I explained that the first thing I'd do by way of improvements would be to tear the bloody thing down. She hasn't spoken to me since, so that's a blessing!'

'There is one thing that I wanted to ask you.' said John, in a more assertive tone. 'I was at the doctor's yesterday, cut my foot. Anyway, when he asked where I was staying, he mentioned something that I disregarded at the time. Something about the government acquiring the Paradise land to turn into coastal park. You hear anything about that?'

'Ha! They'd have a bloody good fight on their hands if they ever tried that one on.' rasped Joe, glaring at John.

'The bloody council would love that though. They've wanted to get us off the land for years you know. But no, to answer your question; I haven't.'

Joe's firm reply gave John a degree of comfort, as if anybody would have known anything Joe would be the first to hear. So, it probably was just 'scuttlebutt' after all, thought John, discounting the remark once more.

'OK, I'll catch you later Joe. Is Jane coming down?'

'I'm picking her up tomorrow from Minamurra, if you need anything in town.'

'Thanks, I'll let you know. I'll catch you later.'

John limped back to his cottage to fix his breakfast leaving Joe Tucker on the jetty to unload his boat and continue to mumble into his beard......about Susan Weeks no doubt.

Over a bowl of cereal John recalled his first encounter with the 'grumpy Joe'. When John decided it was time to build his cottage, he hired a large barge from Butt's boat yard. Three truckloads of building materials (including the kitchen sink) were loaded on in Minamurra and the whole shebang towed across to Paradise early one morning. To save money in transporting, he'd decided to barge the entire building-lot over in one passage. John had hired a small work team from Butt's to help load and unload the materials. Scanning down the materials list in the timber yard, it didn't look to be an overly onerous task until a visual appreciation of the fully loaded vessel asserted the daunting size of the job at hand. At the Minamurra wharf everything was loaded on by derrick crane, but at Paradise it was a different story. For a start the barge, grossly overloaded could only be towed into chest deep water off the shore before becoming grounded. Then all the neatly fastened packs of timber, cladding and roofing iron etc. had to be pulled apart and waded ashore piece by piece. It wasn't long before the hired hands, chilled by the cold water and tired of the whole unloading process, completely lost interest in what they were hired to do. By day's end instead of having neat bundles of building materials securely stacked on the property next to the building site, there was an unorganised pile of everything spread out along the shore. As evening approached, the 'rent a crowd' dissipated...... all of them called it a day and retreated home to the warmth of a good hot dinner and a dry bed. So, John was left to his own devices, exhausted and cold with a mountain of stock next to the lapping water as the tide began to run in and the last light of the day also retreated.

'We might be able to come back tomorrow to give you a hand,' The last hired hand said as he pushed off in a tinny.

'But you'll need to ask the boss first to see if he'll let us go for the day.'

John surveyed the mountain of timber products and iron on the shore, and to his horror observed the rising water. For the next five hours he hauled as much of the stuff back away from the advancing flood as he could on his own, until finally around 11 PM, totally exhausted with a full moon now high in the sky, he shuffled back to his campsite and collapsed into his swag.

The next morning, still nauseated from the stresses and strains of the previous day John made his way to the foreshore to inspect how much of his delivery had survived the night without floating away. Thinking he was alone in Paradise, he was caught by surprise at the sight of a grey bearded man, waddling bow leggily towards him.

'So, you're the new invader, are you?' the old man growled without any introduction.

'I'm the bloke who's bought Randle Wheatcroft's property......John Williams.' John answered.

'Yes, we all know about Randal. How long's this mess going to stay here I'd like to know.' continued the man.

'I was hoping to have had it all up on the block yesterday actually, but I underestimated the size of the job it would seem. And I was hoping the Butts boys might have shown up today to help, but it appears they're a no-show.'

'Yes, well the 'Mayor of Paradise' will have something to say about this no doubt.'

'Mayor of Paradise?' queried John.

'Simon Scully' the man answered. 'He hasn't run into you yet?'

'Well, no……I didn't know there was a mayor.'

'There isn't, but he thinks he is. He'll seek you out soon enough.'

'Sorry.' said John. 'Your name was….?'

'Joe …Joe Tucker's who I am……I hope you're not planning to build some monstrosity.' the man finished, turning his back on John and waddling back along the foreshore.

'And thank *you* for all your help and the warm welcome.' muttered John to himself.

'What'd you just say?' enquired Joe sharply, reeling round to eyeball John.

'I was just saying nice to meet you, and I should have all the stuff up at the block by the end of the week!'

'Grumpy old bugger!' whispered John ever so quietly, taken aback by the apparent keenness of Tucker's whiskery hearing.

Clearly, Joe was averse to any form of change, or anything on the land that might challenge his values and ideals. And for John, was the stark realisation that he was an outsider entering into an otherwise closed community. Despite this rocky first meeting, Joe softened somewhat in time and in comparison, to the likes of Susan Weeks, John considered himself to be better accepted into the enclave.

The next morning John discovered a rusty old handcart and a length of rope which had been left next to his pile. Obviously, it was Joe's gesture toward assisting to see the offensive materials removed from sight as early as possible. The cart as it appeared, was a relic from the early farming days. It had been refurbished at some stage with a few packing case boards crudely affixed to its rusty iron frame to form a tray and the addition of a couple of very agricultural looking wheels fitted with balding pneumatic tyres, which were half flat, and which squealed dryly when the cart was rolled forward. Two splintery wooden shafts were lashed to the sides to form handles by which to haul the thing along.

Day in and day out John, like a human draft horse, hauled mind numbing cart loads of stock inland. It was a job that seemed to take forever. The semi-inflated and perished rubber tires pushed heavily into the soft powdery sand, and every now and then the whole cart would tip over sending the load into the scrub. The rope which came with the cart was equally difficult to deal with. It was an old length of trawling cordage and was stiff and resisted any attempt to be formed into a knot. Still, with gritted determination and blistered hands he managed to move the last of the materials by the end of the week.

Joe had a reputation for being perversely irritable. Word had it that he was thrown out from a cricket match one time for setting fire to the hat of the spectator sitting in front of him. He'd told the young bloke to remove a large straw sombrero because it was blocking his view. The offender responded to Joe's directive by saying, 'Chill out gramps, it's a free country you know.' Joe's blood, which was nearly always on the simmer at the best of times, came to an immediate boil. Not wishing to engage in any further discourse with the offender, Joe simply pulled out a cigarette lighter and ignited the back of the hat, which with the help of a stiff breeze quickly became fully involved in fire. The effect was as immediate as it was dramatic, Joe was frog-marched out of the stadium by the attending police, banned from attending future matches and sued by the howling youth for injury and mental anguish brought about by being set on fire. Joe was also someone to avoid in a parking lot. Should a car park too close to his, and obstruct his access, Joe would walk the length of the car, coin in hand pressed against the duco.

'They're either ignorant, or arrogant, and there's no excuse for either!' he'd bellow.

As the morning progressed in Paradise other people started to arrive for their holidays, and the hum of activity could be heard about the bush-blocks. From across the creek John could hear the booming voice of Dieter Urquhart.

'Daniel, I tawt I told you to help your brudder Markus mit der gas cylinders. Did you tink they'd find their own way up to der house?'

This was followed a short time later by the bell like crashing of gas cylinders falling out of a wheelbarrow, then further booming; 'You know Daniel, you're not an ideas man!'

Coming from the east the buzzing sound of a chainsaw intruded into the quiet of the bush.

'Sounds like Alan Bagshaw's arrived.' thought John.

'I don't know what it is with his preoccupation for chain-sawing, or whipper-snipping the minute he gets here...... obsessive little man!'

A rifle shot rang out from further across the creek beyond Urquhart's place heralding the arrival of Simon Scully's family. They were always shooting at something or other. It was one property to avoid straying onto.

'So, the 'Mayor of Paradise' has graced us with his presence too.' thought John.

John's first meeting with Simon occurred not long after he'd started building the cottage, as Joe Tucker had forewarned. Walking over to the stack of framing timber beside the track, John spotted a tall thin figure striding purposely toward him.

Following a few paces behind this man was the much smaller, demure figure of a woman. It was Simon Scully and his wife Peta. Like all the direct Scully descendants, Simon's thin frame, bottle-bottom glasses and protruding teeth gave him a strange almost bird-like appearance. His pink 'terry-towelling' hat matched with a green checked cotton shirt and beige cargo pants made an unfortunate fashion statement. One would never have known he was a retired barrister. Equally at odds was Peta's almost subservient demeanour, who had worked with Simon as a legal secretary.

'So, what have we here?' said Simon, surveying the building works and initially ignoring John's presence.

'So, you're John Williams, they tell me, and I'm Simon Scully.'

'So, are you going to be staying long?' he continued without introducing his wife.

'Well, I…I …'

'We're all Scullys here you know. Some of us are direct descendants; the others have married in……'

'Um, I plan to use this as a holiday house.' replied John to the earlier question.

'Most of us are professionals …… you know, medicine and law, that sort of thing. What do you do John?'

'Well, I, I….

'Were you aware there was a caveat on this property? Not that it would be legally enforceable anymore.'

It was obvious that the 'Mayor of Paradise' wasn't at all interested in John's answers. He was there to state his presence and make it clear to John what was the lay of the land.

Scully continued to inspect the building site while he delivered his introductory interrogation to a dumb-founded John Williams. He paced out the building footprint and scribbled down notes on a tiny pad he'd produced from one of his many pockets. He appeared to act as if he possessed some divine authority. Peta, on the other hand stood silently in the background like some dog that was waiting patiently for her master to come out of a shopping centre and take her home.

'Well, I'm glad we've had the chance to have this little talk.' concluded Scully.

'By the way, this is my wife Peta.' he added, almost as an afterthought.

Peta stepped forward and waved a pale hand which offered the same warmth and welcoming as a wet fish.

No sooner had Simon and Peta appeared unannounced than, having conducted his business with John they left, exiting through John's property on a tour of the next property no doubt.

Whenever John met a new member of the little community, after the initial introductions they'd always enquire if Simon Scully had been to see him yet. John found that not all the community were as abrasive or cool towards him when he first arrived. Many of them were more than happy to see the back of Randal Wheatcroft and all his junk. In fact, John came to learn that a number of property owners on hearing Randal had a potential buyer, came down from Melbourne and other places to help Randal clean up his block so that it might have a better chance of selling.

It wasn't until the first big storm blew in that John discovered what had been done with some of the heavier items of rubbish that had littered the property. Walking over the sand hills one day to the beach, he nearly broke his big toe on what turned out to be Randal's old pot belly stove which had partially been exhumed from its shallow grave during the blow. During the next few years other objects came to the surface too as the dunes moved under the influence of the prevailing winter winds. There was an old kerosene fridge, the leg of an outboard motor and after one particularly savage gale, the remains of Randal's tent hung, splayed out way up in a tree like a gigantic, crucified fruit bat. Dieter Urquhart, John discovered, had scoured the block prior to his arrival after purchasing the place and cleaned out anything remaining of potential value such as Randal's petrol generator and his chainsaw, both of which had been left in the weather where Randal had last used them. A lot of what remained of Randal's stuff after the pre-sale clean-up John himself ended up burying; Only John made sure the holes were dug sufficiently deep in stable ground. The only thing he left was Randal's shed and the lean-to which he would joking refer to as 'Wheatcroft Mansions', and which he used to store his tools and other chattels that were not wanted in the house.

With a late breakfast done and a second cup of plunger-coffee downed, John focused his attention on cleaning and tidying the cottage. His wife Sal was coming down in a few days to join him. Sal had been opposed to John purchasing the property all those years ago. She'd seen photos John had taken of the block while Randal still lived there and was aware that the area had a reputation for sand flies, march flies and snakes. Sal realised she would have no control over John's decision to purchase the property but had exercised her right to distance herself completely from the process. For Sal, who considered anything less than five-star accommodation to be little better that camping, coming to terms with the comparative isolation and basic living that Paradise offered was a huge challenge. Not surprisingly then, John was always keen to present the place in the best light for her.

John had organised to pick Sal up from Minamurra to coincide with his follow up appointment with Doctor Stephens.

It would not only save him an additional trip over to town but provide him with a few extra days to deal with the self-inflicted aftermath of that fateful night on-board the U-Sail cruiser. Even though he'd cut out the vomit impregnated squares of seagrass matting and burnt them in the laundry copper, the smell of vomit and Pine-O-Clean seemed to persist within the cottage. There was also a blood-stained trail across the decking outside, which had impregnated the porous treated pine and set like a dark colour-fast dye.

With copious amounts of bleach and elbow grease John eventually managed to erase most of the damning evidence. Sal was particularly averse to anything to do with the spilling of body fluids and John was particularly keen to play down the whole sordid drama associated with the lacerated foot. He could just hear her saying, 'That's it John, you won't be going away again by yourself. I leave you alone for a couple of days and you just go stupid. How would I be able to cope without you if you killed yourself?'

Even though the cleaning of the cottage preoccupied John's attention he was aware of the background sounds coming up from the estuary that indicated the arrival of more of the community. He'd been around long enough to become familiar with the sounds of the boat motors and to recognise what engine noise belonged to whom. Apart from the Urquharts, the Scullys, the Bagshaws and Joe Tucker, who had arrived earlier, he was aware that Rick and Gloria Head had made the trip over, as well as Susan Weeks.

There would be time to catch up with them all in the coming days as it seemed that no matter how well set up people were in their shacks and cottages, there was always more to bring over when they first arrived. A new mattress, some extra chairs, a wardrobe for the spare bedroom.... there was always something. Then of course there was the food supplies, bags of ice, gas bottles to run stoves and gas fridges, clean bedding and boxes of beer and wine (with the exception of the direct Scully descendants who totally abstained from alcohol, coffee and tea). So, on the first day of arriving, most people already weary from the long drive from home were intent on settling in and getting set up for their break. The catching up and socialising would come later as the community re-established itself in Paradise. There would be drinks by the lake, dinner invitations and conversations starting up from where they left off many months ago. The government jetty which had been devoid of boats, save the farmers on the U-Sail vessel, would soon be packed bow to stern with boat people. Yachties, cruisers and hire boats would all be vying for position on the jetty. Those that couldn't find a spot would push up bow first against the shoreline and tie off to a tree or cast an anchor out on the sand where an unsuspecting pedestrian on an evening stroll could trip over, bark their shin or stub a toe or two. The holiday periods marked a time when the usual quiet isolation of Paradise and the adjoining coastal park precincts would be transformed into a hub of human activity, and when the best and worst of human behaviour could be observed.

There was a clear demarcation between the various sub communities in Paradise. Those on the land referred to the floating population simply as 'boatpeople'. Within the boating community the yachties referred the motorised vessels collectively (be they large or small) as 'stink-boats'. At the bottom of the pile were the 'day-trippers' and those on hire boats, particularly the raucous types who would stay overnight and who were prone to engaging in raging parties till the wee hours of the morning, or those who would light campfires on the shore, occasionally setting fire to the scrub.

Late in the afternoon, John having done as much tidying up and sanitising as he could, limped down the estuary to see how many boats had come in. He noticed Susan Weeks' familiar silhouette in the distance on the jetty, which was adjacent to Joe Tuckers' house. John was quite fond of Susan; He admired her independence and sense of adventure and beyond that found her level of intellect stimulating. As an active conservationist, she had a particular interest in marine biology and had spent many months on her own in Paradise studying such things as the annual prawn migratory habits and the effects of farmland run-off on the aquatic grasses of the estuary and its tributaries. As she regularly arrived on her own, he wandered up to see if there was anything she needed a hand with, as she would never ask for help, but often needed help with hauling something up to the house or attending to something broken on her boat. John was intercepted by a scowling Tucker near the front of the jetty.

'Oh my Lord, will you look at that!' Joe exclaimed as he directed John's attention to the back view of Susan who was walking toward the end of the jetty. She's got a swagger like a cowboy wandering onto a film set!'

Joe's ambush caught John quite by surprise and presented him with an unexpected dilemma. If he rebuffed Joe's remark, he risked jeopardising the level of friendship and trust that had taken so many years to establish. On the other hand, agreement would provide Joe with the opportunity to openly taunt Susan in John's company, with an equally undesirable impact on John's relationship with her.

'You mentioned you were going over to town tomorrow if I wanted anything Joe.' John cut in diplomatically.

'Got the kettle on?'

'What! Are you going to give me a huge list?' barked Joe through his beard.

'No, not at all, I was out of milk. Wondered if you wouldn't mind picking me up a litre.' lied John.

'And I thought you might have a cuppa going. Haven't had one in two days…. can't drink it without milk!'

'Come in then, it'll save me from having to look at that woman any longer, and anyway I wanted to talk to you about Jane.'

John, while trying in vain not to appear too keen to hide from Susan's view, nearly pushed past Joe to get in the front door.

'Jeez, you must be thirsty for a cuppa you thirsty bastard.' exclaimed Joe.

The front door opened straight into the kitchen. Over on the opposite corner in an inglenook a slow-combustion-stove burned quietly, a large cast iron kettle sat atop on an all-day simmer. Wisps of steam drifted lazily from its darkened smoke-stained spout. A heavy white enamel washbasin occupied the middle section of a long bleached wooden bench where the sun reflected through a cottage window and illuminated the richly stained red pine ceiling boards. A brass garden tap fed the basin with rainwater from a rusting galvanised iron tank that stood outside the kitchen between Joe's house and that of Susan Weeks'. Timber shelves made from driftwood planks, filled with condiments and spices lined the opposite wall. At the far end of the kitchen a cavernous larder housed more wooden shelves stocked with bountiful amounts of flour, tinned foods and other kitchen consumables. A 'Tilly Lamp' hung from the ceiling not far from bunches of dried herbs and lavender that infused a fragrant aroma complimenting the scent of the seasoned pine lining boards.

Joe beckoned John to sit at the kitchen table in a cosy corner by the casement windows. Light cotton curtains provided privacy from passing eyes, while still allowing a soft glow of sunlight to radiate into the room. Like most of the furnishings in the house, Joe had fashioned the table from second-hand timber and tea-tree branches. The nail holes and scars on the tabletop that told a thousand stories of its past had been soften by the addition of bees wax and turpentine, giving the piece a soft buttery feel and appearance.

John sat down and shuffled along the bench-seat that stretched along the wall beneath the window. His sandy thongs made a shuffling rasping sound against the worn linoleum.

'Oh crap! Sorry Joe, I should have taken my thongs off at the door. I've brought sand in.'

'Don't worry about it John. What would Paradise be without sand?' said Joe, running a broom under the table and adding it to a neat pile by the entrance way.

Adjacent to the kitchen shelves a doorway led into the dark sitting-room-come-main bedroom. Through a gap in the red door-length drapes John could just make out the fireplace built from old bricks which had survived the bushfire responsible for burning down the original Scully homestead. A pair of candelabras adorned a heavy Cyprus pine mantelpiece. The foot of a double bed fashioned from tea-tree branches protruded into view from the opposite side. It was covered in a colourful patchwork quilt, and it was easy to imagine Joe and Jane tucked up in bed on a cold stormy night, the roar of the surf in the background, watching the fire-light flickering warm patterns across the exposed beam ceiling above them.

The rustic charm of the interior of the cottage seemed to fit well with the craggy faced host who was busy pouring out two generous mugs of steaming tea.

'I don't know if I ever told you, but Jane had a hip replacement a couple of years ago.'

'No, I wasn't aware Joe, although I'm aware she hasn't been down too often in the last year or so.' John answered.

'Well, the operation went as well as we could have wanted, and it's made a huge difference to Jane's mobility. It even cured her of being pigeon toed, strangely enough. The thing is......' Joe continued between sips of tea, 'The thing is, she's become a bit vague since the 'op'...... gets a bit bushed sometimes; Y'know...forgets where she is at times. Anyway, her sister thought it would be good for her to spend a few weeks down here, get her away from the rat race and give her a break and some peace and quiet. The sister's putting her on a bus from Melbourne tomorrow morning...I'm meeting the bus in Minamurra tomorrow afternoon, as of course you know. I'm only mentioning this to you John, because she hasn't been down for a bit, and I know she likes to explore the tracks and look for orchids at this time of year.....If you do happen to see her wandering about looking a bit lost, if you wouldn't mind, could you please point her in the right direction home?'

John sensed a different tone in Joe's voice, there was a fragility there which John had never known to exist in this man, and who all of a sudden seemed to diminish in size as his wizened body arched over the table and took John into his confidence.

John felt an awkward uncomfortableness in Joe's manner......even a bit claustrophobic. But he needn't have, as this rare 'soft' moment proved to be short lived with John's next remark.

'I'll certainly keep an eye out for her, but shouldn't you be letting Simon's family know?'

'Like hell I should be!' burst out Joe. 'And you won't be either!'

'Them and their weird beliefs.... all that Adonai-Shomo rot that their family brought them up on. They'd have her taken away from me and locked up in some bloody God bothering loony bin, nothing surer!' bellowed the old man.

John peeked nervously out from behind the curtains to check whether Susan had heard Joe's outburst, but fortunately it appeared she had already got what she needed and returned to her house next door.

'Well, I'm sorry to hear about Jane.' said John, returning his attention to Joe. 'I'll make sure I keep an eye out for her, and I'll make sure nothing is mentioned to the Scullys.'

It had taken eighteen years for John to get this close to Joe Tucker, and with this brief insight into Jane's welfare John felt a new bond with his fellow neighbour, and something to be shared with the exclusion of the other Scullys.

'OK Joe I'd better be getting back home for now...... a few things to do.... By the way Sal's coming down on Tuesday. She'll keep an eye out for Jane too.'

'Leave the cups where they are, I'll put them in the sink.' said Joe as a parting gesture.

As John stepped out onto the veranda, he glanced back, just in time to see a brief smile break out across Joe's craggy face. It was the first time he could recall ever seeing any warmth in Tucker's face, other than of course those times when it was flushed with rage.

John was tempted to slip next-door and call in on Susan for a catch up while he was so close by, but decided not to chance it. He was sure he could feel Joe's piercing eyes following him off the property and along the foreshore, and any show of friendship with Ms Weeks at this point in time would surely undermine the bond he had worked so hard to establish with Joe. John hated what he considered to be a weakness in his own personality. When was he ever going to be his own man with the strength of character to be able to openly declare his opinions and loyalties with others? While he considered Joe to be often bigoted and prejudiced, he non-the-less admired the strength of this man's conviction, and the simple black and whiteness of Joe's outlook on life and others. What would it be like to enjoy such freedom afforded by uncompromising views and opinions John wondered? He thought of the Scullys too and their uncompromising beliefs and views, and how they openly celebrated the differences between their own kind and the rest of the world. And he recalled Simon Scully telling him once there was no right or wrong way to do things, only *the* way.

When John got back to the cottage he was surprised to see Simon on the veranda waiting for him to return. Simon appeared hawk-like to John, hovering in anticipation to swoop at the precise moment on an unsuspecting prey.

'Simon! I was just thinking about you then.' said John quickly in an effort to avert Simon's first strike.

Simon had a manner of talking which was more akin to talking at you, rather than to you. His conversations tended to consist of tightly spaced statements which he'd deliver with the rapid fire of a 'gatling-gun'.

'Thinking about me were you then John. Were you indeed! Well, as you know, I'm not one to confabulate so I'll get straight to the point.' Simon continued. 'I need your assistance with a delicate matter.'

'Well, you'd better come in then.' John invited, trying to give himself some head space to think where Simon might be going with all this.

'My goodness!' exclaimed Simon. 'What's that terrible smell in here?'

'Oh that? I thought I'd got rid of that. You can still smell it in here, can you?'

'I had an accident the other night. Stepped on a broken bottle in the water near the government jetty. I was a bit heavy handed with the disinfectant.'

'It smells like someone's been sick to me.' replied Simon.

'Oh, that too.' replied John without trying to explain further.

'Damn, I must have missed a bit.' John thought to himself.

'If it was just this side of the government jetty,' said Simon. 'You probably stumbled into old Irish Jimmy's rubbish dump. He used to squat on this land you know. He built that concrete hut near the government jetty. We used to fossick in the mud for old bottles down there when we were kids, still got some at home together with a couple of aboriginal skulls and old spears which have been handed down......I hope you went straight away and got a tetanus shot. There used to be a lot of rusty old iron in there as well. Anyway, I digress when I said I wouldn't.' continued Simon getting back to the point. It concerns our cousin Jane Tucker. You know Jane....... yes of course you do! Well Jane has dementia. You know what dementia is......yes of course you would. We've been keeping an eye on our Jane. Joe doesn't know it, so we'd appreciate you not telling him. One of our other cousins Jill informs us she's putting Jane on a bus tomorrow and sending her down here unsupervised.'

'I'd imagine Joe would be over in Minamurra to meet the bus. Wouldn't he?' John cut in, pretending to not know about Jane.

'That's not our concern John. It's Joe's whole irresponsible attitude to her condition.' Scully continued. 'You know, this is something that happens to people who use aluminium saucepans and who drink alcohol John. Did you know that? If she'd stayed with the family all these years and not been led astray by that Joe Tucker, she'd still be in good health now I have no doubt.'

It now occurred to John where Simon was heading with the conversation. Simon and Joe had not been on speaking terms for as long as John could remember. Indeed, the only single thing John could think of that the two shared in common was the fact that Dieter Urquhart's dog, which held a primal dislike for both, had on separate occasions bitten both of them in apparently unprovoked attacks. Helping to maintain the rage, the Scully boys would use every opportunity to remind Joe he was only a 'prick relation' and they would refer to Joe's beloved cottage as Jane's place.

'Anything could happen to her down here John.' added Simon 'She could go wandering off in the night, wander into the lake or the ocean. Who knows? 'I even have reliable information the feral pigs are breeding up again near 'All Smiles'. They're known to eat people you know. Imagine if she wandered up there and that happened......awful, awful!'

'So how does all this require my help?' ventured John cautiously.

John could sense he was being painted into a corner here. He wasn't allowed to tell Simon he already knew about Jane, and he wasn't allowed to tell Joe that Simon already knew. Either way between Simon and Joe, whoever found out that the other one knew what the other knew, John would be sure to be caught in the middle by association. Knowing Scullys' reputation, if things got out of hand and push came to shove between the Scullys and the Tuckers, there'd sure be legal ramifications and John would find himself as a lead witness in court.

'I see you talking to Joe. Goodness knows why, but he's never listened to me, so.........'

'Simon, I come down here to get away from family matters and other stresses.' John cut in. 'I don't want to be caught up in something that could end in a family fight, or worse in a legal battle.'

'Oh, but you are John, you are, simply by the fact that I'm engaging you to assist us.'

John felt like someone had just poured a cold vial of acid into his stomach. The biting sensation in his gut clouded his thought process and left his head spinning. He was overwhelmed with a feeling of fear and loathing for Simon who had just now trapped him, without John even being tempted by a bait.

'Look, let's just see how Jane is when she gets here tomorrow.' replied John, stalling for time.

Simon Scully knew John would normally be calling in to see the Tuckers when they were both in Paradise, so John was aware that there was an expectation on Simon's behalf that he would be calling in at Joes when Jane arrived in the afternoon. Not paying them a visit would clearly be in defiance of Simon's wishes for John to talk to Joe about allowing the Scullys to intervene in Jane's care. And Joe would be expecting him to call in and collect his litre of milk anyway.

'I'll leave it with you then John.' Simon finished. And then Simon was off down the track with his usual forward leaning purposeful strides.

John spent the next half-hour looking in vain for any signs of the missed 'sick smell' Simon had said he could detect, before giving up and turning his attention to fuelling the kerosene lamps and cleaning their chimneys before night fall consumed the little cottage once more. He retired to bed soon after eating a light evening meal of baked beans on toast. The golden flames of the kerosene lamps filled the cottage with a warm aroma that complimented the glowing yellow light that illuminated the walls. It should have been a relaxing evening there in Paradise for John. Instead, he spent a long and restless night tossing and turning on his bed, trying to figure out how he would manage the events of tomorrow.

Now, if he were to be his own man, (as he would like to be) and not be compromised by what he saw as a basic weakness in his own character, he would front Joe Tucker first thing in the morning, tell him Scully had been to see him and was aware of Jane's condition and intended to take her away from Joe. But it would be like pulling the pin on the first grenade to start an all-out family war and John was fearful of all the collateral damage Paradise would suffer and for the consequences he himself might incur in the fall out. Perhaps Jane wouldn't turn up after all. Perhaps Scully might talk to Jane's sister overnight and talk her out of putting her on the bus from Melbourne.

'Why can't these bloody people sort out their own problems,' John muttered in the empty hours of the night.

The uneasy night, made more restless by a fresh south-easterly that sprang up in the early hours, led John to rise late from bed. He forwent his usual early morning habit of walking down the lake to survey the water and settled instead on staying indoors and breakfasting on his customary two coffees over toast with strawberry jam. He would have stayed indoors for most of the day if it wasn't for the sound of raised voices booming up from the estuary just before lunch time. Venturing out onto the decking John trained his ear towards the water. The voices grew louder and were punctuated by the sound of barking dogs. From a little way down the track, he could make out that the voices he could hear belonged to no other than Simon Scully and Joe Tucker. John, who was still limited to some extent by his injured foot quickened his pace to a sort of half skip-half hop, so intrigued he was to find out what this latest development was all about.

He stopped just short of the foreshore and peered through the bushes, keen to maintain his obscurity. At first John struggled to comprehend the curious sight there out on the water. Joe Tucker was at the tiller in Emma under full sail for Minamurra. A short distance off his stern in a small aluminium run-about was Simon Scully, desperately bailing and being dragged backwards behind Emma. The short chop brought up by the sou-easter was spilling over the transom and swamping Simon's boat as fast as he could bucket out the water. A large gathering of boat people and day trippers lined the government jetty to watch the unfolding spectacle. One man in a camper chair with beer in hand was clapping and cheering them on. A number of barking dogs off the boats were out on the jetty too, adding to the chaotic picture.

'You heathen son of the Devil.' screamed a crimson faced Scully, between bail loads.

'Go to hell you arrogant prayer mumbling bastard.' barked back Joe, tightening his grip on the tiller. And stop following me!'

John snuck along the top of the embankment down to the government jetty to get a better look. He stood at the back of the gathering group of onlookers and peered over their shoulders. The puzzling thing was that Simon's outboard didn't appear to be running, but he was keeping pace with Tucker…backwards at that….to the point where he was in danger of being totally swamped and in danger of sinking.

'No wonder Jane's welfare can't be guaranteed with behaviour like yours, you blaspheming reincarnation of Satan!' yelled Simon.

Oh dear, so the subject of Jane's care has been broached thought John.

'Piss off Simon, you lunatic! And leave me and Jane alone, you cult-crazed zealot! You're bloody mad you buggers.... the bloody lot of you!' snarled Joe.

At this point as the two-man floating circus approached the jetty. John could finally see the problem that had propelled the two men into this public display of bile-spilling and animosity. The leg of Simon's outboard motor was entangled in a mooring-line attached to a cleat on Emma's stern. Without power, Simon was being towed along under the force of Emma's massive gaff-rigged sails. Apparently, according to a couple of the eyewitnesses on the jetty, Simon was returning from shopping in Minamurra, and just as he was coming about to moor on the lea of the private jetty Joe, who was attempting to sail off his mooring and travel to Minamurra to pick up Jane, was caught unprepared by a sudden gust of wind. Emma had heeled over and shot out straight in front of Simon who, taking evasive action to avoid a collision veered sharply behind the couta boat. The trailing stern line which Joe had not yet hauled in, fouled Simon's propeller and stalled his engine. Joe in turn, keen to avoid any contact with Simon had sailed on, raising the mainsail as well as the jib to put some distance between them, and the quicker the better!

The two men were like fighting dogs, goaded by being shackled together by a lead. Unable to escape each other's wrath, the heated exchange went from trading insults on each other's seamanship, to more personal matters such as insults regarding Simon's parentage to religious motives (or lack of in Joe's case) and finally the issue of who to best look after Jane's interests.

As the two boats passed the end of the jetty, Simon now fearing for his life, leaped from his stricken vessel and made a desperate lunge for the ladder at the end of the landing. Without Simon's stabilising weight, the tinnie skewed sideways and slammed stern first into one of the sturdy mussel encrusted piles. The mooring line connecting the two boats stretched taught momentarily before snapping off one of Emma's cleats, and firing back like a giant elastic band, thus breaking the umbilical cord of hatred that had moments before connected the two in bitter argument.

Simon (the Mayor of Paradise) clambered up the ladder like a half-drowned cat. His dripping pink terry-towelling hat was plastered over his head like a large slice of compressor meat. It draped down over his wing like ears and was saved from covering his eyes by his fogged-up bottle-bottom glasses. His wallet and other 'personals' could be seen protruding through his soaking wet grey tracksuit pants. And as he stood there to catch his breath before firing a last verbal volley at the disappearing Tucker, a large puddle formed around him on the decking. The barking dogs all retreated to their respective boats, tails between their legs.

'Quick, where's my camera Diana?' John heard someone chuckle.

And; 'Stay close to mummy now. I don't want you to go near the man.' from another to a small child.

Seemingly oblivious to the audience behind him, and the trail of various items of shopping floating away on the outgoing tide, not to mention his half sunken boat caught under the jetty, Simon delivered his final threat.

'We'll sue you for this Joe Tucker…yes we will. We'll take back your land as well as our Jane…You know that don't you Joe…. you know that, don't you!'

'Bite yar bum Simon.' Joe retorted from a distance. 'And you owe me a mooring line and a cleat by the way you bloody Jesus freak!'

John was in awe of the raw aggression these so-called mature men could deliver on each other, and he quickly slipped away into the scrub before Simon, (who was now working out how to salvage what was left of his boat) had noticed his presence.

This unexpected tirade between Simon and Joe brought great relief to John, and he felt joyously unburdened now that he had escaped from Simon's trap. From upheaval comes opportunity thought John, and with Joe Tucker in Minamurra for at least the next few hours it was the perfect opportunity to call in on Susan undetected. John was aware Susan had travelled extensively since he last saw her, and he was interested to learn of all her recent adventures. Equally keen, he was almost salivating at the opportunity to deliver the juicy gossip surrounding the stellar performance he had just been witness to.

John found Susan standing on her balcony overlooking the estuary. She was scanning the water with a pair of large field-binoculars. He figured she must have been observing the performance between Simon and Joe as surely, like everybody else she would have been drawn out by the explosive exchange of insults between the pair.

'Can you see them? They're a sub-species of bottle nose dolphins.' Susan said, without lowering her glasses. 'Burrunan dolphins or Tursiops Australis to be precise. They're unique to this area.'

John climbed the steps to the balcony and peered out beside her. He could see a small pod of four, maybe five shiny black dolphins breaking the surface as they cruised smoothly past.

'And there's a calf! ....Now that's a good sign.'

John stood there in awkward silence, conceding to the fact that the mammals had Susan's full attention for the time being.

'I suppose you witnessed that fall-out between Simon and Joe a little earlier.' John eventually said.

'I couldn't be less interested.' Susan answered, finally lowering the binoculars and acknowledging John's presence. 'Anyway, how have you been John? She said, moving the conversation on. It must be at least a year since I saw you last. I think the last time, you and Sal were here for dinner.'

'Yes, I think it was.' replied John. 'Sal will be down in a couple of days, so it must be our turn to have you over for dinner then.'

'That would be lovely, I've so much news to tell you.... if you're interested of course.'

'Oh, of course.' replied John.

'Have you noticed the decline in the size of the sea grass beds since last year?' Continued Susan, raising her binoculars toward the water again. 'They say it's because of the presence of large numbers of the black shore crabs which have been introduced into the lake system.'

'The only thing I've noticed recently, which was introduced into the lake system, was your two fighting neighbours this morning.' answered John, wanting to get back to the gossip.

'John, I really have no interest in the machinations surrounding those two men. Joe can be so difficult at times and I'm sure it's bad for his health, and as for Simon; What kind of behaviour would you expect to observe with an Asperger? Life is too short to indulge yourself with bad wine John.'

John thought about Susan's last statement for a moment, and he realised to what extent he'd been drawn down into the dark negativity of Simon and Joe's conflict, when after all, here he was supposed to be in 'Paradise'!

'You're absolutely right Susan, life is too short to be worried about that sort of thing.'

'Care for a cuppa?' said Susan, moving the conversation on again. I'll put the kettle on.' She continued, without waiting for John's reply.

John followed Susan into the large airy kitchen- come-living room that opened through wide bi-fold doors onto a balcony. A fresh breeze flowed easily through the room and the sun reflecting off the water cast dancing patterns across the lime-washed lining boards on the ceiling. While Susan busied herself with the tea making, John gazed around the walls and shelves taking in the collection on exotic artefacts and maritime memorabilia Susan had acquired during her many travels. Amongst the many curios decorating the room, an old wooden racing-scull hung suspended from the high ceiling and there was an accompanying wooden surfboard leaning up against the far corner. In the adjacent corner on the floor sat a large, rusted iron anchor beside a brass diver's helmet.

'God only knows how she got that up here.' thought John.

He always found the place stimulating. Each time he visited there'd be something new and interesting to see and to talk about. He found it hard to understand why Joe had such a set on her as it would seem the two had potentially much in common to celebrate.

Meanwhile, back next door to John's place, the fastidious Alan Bagshaw, having cut up a month's worth of firewood and having nothing more to chainsaw, set about with his '*whipper snipper*' to trim back the grasses and the samphire along the verges of the track.

'We have to keep this clear in case of snakes!' Alan would exclaim to John on every visit.

Susan had once shown John how to use the samphire in a salad, and it seemed to him to be such a waste on Alan's behalf to constantly mow the stuff down. While Susan and John chatted over tea, the buzzing drone of the 'whipper snipper' dominated the background sounds around Paradise, save the occasional bellowing voice from the Urquhart's place, the distant carol of children's voices or the crack of the odd angry shot from the Scully property out the back.

Down on the government jetty the boat people and day trippers, who'd arrived in their numbers overnight and during the morning, were busy going about their business, eating lunch or enjoying an early beer or wine. Thin columns of blue smoke rose momentarily from portable barbeques before being caught by the wind spreading their enticing aroma along the lakefront. Children, who from a distance looked like tiny dots of moving colour were either noisily playing on the foreshore or swimming by the jetty. Boat traffic passing by Paradise left a criss-cross pattern of bow wakes sending a constant pulse of mini-wavelets lapping along the shore, stirring up the silt and creating a band of coffee coloured water along the shallows. Paradise had come alive with the 'occasional community'.

Susan loaded up the tea-tray with the teapot, cups, a sugar bowl, a small jug of milk and a bowl filled with Japanese rice crackers, then carried the tray to an outside setting on the deck.

'Please help yourself.' She beckoned to John, as he stepped out behind her and took his seat.

Over his cup of tea and a handful of crackers John gazed out over the easterly aspect in the direction of Minamurra and down towards the government jetty. The colour and movement of all the activity in his view seemed to be coordinated in some strange but aesthetically pleasing continuum of chaos. He could feel the positive vibes from Susan's environment and her presence washing over the angst that he'd experienced through the night before and earlier that morning.

John picked up the binoculars from the table to get a closer look at the activity along the shore-front.

'Oh, I can see Rick and Gloria Head coming in.'

Rick was another one of the so called 'retired' community members. Formerly a financial advisor, he'd amassed his fortune by investing heavily in the early IT industry. He'd bought up Apple shares exclusively which had provided him with an extremely comfortable lifestyle ever since. Twice married, his second wife Gloria was some twenty years his junior. John always thought of them as a strange match and often wondered how much Rick's advancing age and his wealth had to do with the viability of the partnership. Whether it was the way they dressed or their mannerisms, in a funny way they reminded him of the two characters from Gilligan's Island.... Thurston Howell the Third and his wife 'Luvie'. Christened 'Richard', he'd shortened his name to Rick for obvious reasons.

The design of John's cottage had inspired the Head's, although Rick had the means to hire builders to construct his which, while displaying similar design characteristics, was substantially larger than John's place and was set up with the latest solar hot water and electricity. Unlike most of the other Paradise folk, Rick would engage people from Minamurra to come over and take care of the maintenance, the cutting of firewood and anything else that needed to be done around the place. Frankie Banister of 'Banister's Bait Boat and Auto' was one who relied on Rick's need for services to supplement his income during the off-season. Frankie, a bit of a larrikin would refer to Rick as Dick and would say to people on the occasion when he went over to do some work there as working at 'Dick Head's' place. Much to Rick's annoyance the local youth had caught onto this and took delight in calling him Dick Head whenever he was in earshot of them.

Rick always welcomed a visit from John. It gave him a break from the intensity of Gloria's company and a chance to discuss the matters of the world which Gloria seldom showed any interested in.

'Could I interest you in a 'G & T', or a whiskey John?' he'd offer on John's arrival at the front door. I have a lovely single malt that needs to be drunk.'

'He's on a diet John. He's only allowed one drink.' Gloria would interrupt, referring to Rick in the third person.

'Goodness knows where you'd be without me to look after your health Rick.'

'Probably in a much happier place.' Rick would retort, his tanned face winking widely at John.

'Oh John, he's lucky I don't leave him......Really!'

'You may leave anytime you like my dear.' Was the usual reply to that statement.

It was a play act between the Heads that anybody visiting would be entertained with. Many of the Paradise couples would dine out on the constant duelling between Rick and his younger wife.

'If you can excuse me Susan, I might wander down and give the Heads a hand up with some of their stuff. There's always something they have difficulty in hauling up to the house.' said John. Even though they'd never ask, I know they're always grateful for a hand. Rick's not getting any younger you know.'

John left Susan's place just in time to see the familiar red sail of Joe Tucker's boat approaching the private jetty. He decided to wait for Joe to come in so he could greet Jane. The Heads would be occupied for a bit anyway tying their boat up and unlocking the house before unloading their things. As Emma drew into the jetty John peered down under the low boom to see Jane. Instead of the willowy composed figure with the long raven locks John was expecting to see, there sat a small woman with short grey hair and a confused almost haunted looking face.

Joe threw John a line and with a slow pull Emma came along side. Jane peered at John, but she may as well have been looking at a cormorant. Although their eyes met, there was no sense of connection in Jane's expression.

'Jane, this is John. You remember, John Williams...... the one who invaded your family's land eighteen years ago.'

Jane smiled, and looking back at Joe answered, 'Yes, John! I remember.... John, of course!'

John could sense some connection had finally been made.

'How are you going Jane? Long-time no see!'

'Yes, it has been a long time, I think. How long has it been Joe?' she asked.

'You haven't been down here for a while Jane, maybe more than a year at least.' said Joe, before shifting his attention to John.

'Laughing Boy hasn't been sniffing around since I left this morning has he?'

'Laughing Boy?' enquired John.

'You know, bloody Scully. Who else would I mean! ......I had a run in with him this morning.'

'Oh yes, I heard the noise. Was that what it was about?' answered John, not wanting to disclose he witnessed the whole performance.

'Anyway, I'll expect you to call in. It's good for Jane. She responds well to company.... gets those brain cells moving again.'

'I'll be sure to do that Joe.' replied John, as he helped Jane out of the boat and onto the jetty.

John left Joe and Jane to their own devices and made his way towards the government jetty to where the Heads, having beached their boat had begun the job of unloading their supplies. Gloria had already been up to the house and brought down an old wheelbarrow which they used to carry stuff up from the estuary to the house. John observed Gloria in her thin, low cut sheer dress, made up with bright red lipstick and contrasting metallic blue eye liner, and thought how incongruous she looked trudging into the shallows beside the boat with the rusty old barrow. Rick had remained in the boat with their three dogs, sorting things out and placing various items of shopping and homewares to the side of the boat where Gloria could reach in and load them into the barrow.

'Hi there Rick. Hi there Gloria! Welcome to Paradise!' John sang out over the din of the dogs barking and snarling at him from behind the gunnels of the boat.

'Let me give you a hand, only I can't go in the water with my foot.'

'Oh, thanks John, but we'll be fine once Rick gets his act together.' answered Gloria. 'What on earth did you do to your foot?'

'I cut it on some glass in the water not far from here a few nights ago. It was a bit of a drama at the time, but it's all good now......just have to keep it dry for a few more days.'

John waited for Gloria to push the heavily laden barrow out of the water.

'Here, let me help you it's easy for me.' he said, moving in and relieving her of the handles.

'Well thankyou John, you're very kind.'

'Not at all ......not at all.' John groaned as he struggled to push the thing through the soft sand.

'I told her she'd overloaded it John. She never takes my advice.' The voice from the boat called out.

Gloria returned to the boat to grab a few bags of shopping then followed John up to their house. He made one more trip with her, the second time carrying up a nine-kilogram gas cylinder, which he figured either of the Heads would have had trouble carrying.

'Thank you so much John, it's saved me a lot of effort.... especially if I was relying on Rick to help me out. He's such an old dodderer these days.... Honestly!'

Gloria stepped forward and gave John a big fat kiss on the cheek, partly as a show of gratitude and partly as a reward for his effort. He could feel the wetness on the side of his face and a lingering smell of her heavy perfume. He knew she would have left a big red smudge mark on him, but politely waited till he was facing away from her before he used the palm of his hand to wipe it off.

'Tell Rick I'll call in to see you in a day or so when you are settled in.' John called out over his shoulder as he headed back to his cottage.

John spent what was left of the day preparing for the evening, re-cleaning and re-fuelling the lamps, splitting some wood to heat the old copper so he had some hot water to clean up and wash in. There was always something to do, and one of the pleasures of Paradise was the daily routine of doing the simple things to maintain comfort that anywhere else would be taken for granted as part of the daily grind of modern-day life.

After sundown, under lamp light, John planned his Tuesday in Minamurra, writing out his timetable using pencil on paper like a synopsis for a play. He had his follow-up appointment with the doctor in the morning, who was expecting him during surgery hours between 10.00 AM and midday. Sally's bus was due in at around 2.00 PM, provided it was running on time, and assuming she hadn't missed the connection between the train and

the bus in Bairnsdale. Then there was the shopping to do ……
he could fit that in between the doctor's and Sal's arrival. If the
doctor didn't have any other patients and saw him promptly, he
would have enough time to indulge in fish and chips for lunch
again before heading for the grocers. Then of course he wanted
to catch up with Frankie Banister to get some fuel for the boat
and get the low down on the fishing. John was also keen to see
when Frankie might want to catch up over at Paradise for a fish
and a beer or two one evening after work. In a normal day back
in Melbourne it wouldn't seem too much to fit in, but John's
experience in Paradise had taught him that even the simplest of
errands to Minamurra could take all day, and without careful
planning the day's activities could easily fall short of expectations.
And so, John's written plan needed to contain not only the basic
objectives of the trip, but also a number of contingencies should
the initial plan go awry.

Tuesday morning arrived and before he did anything else,
John tuned the transistor radio to the local weather report. It
was always prudent to allow for the weather in one's plans, as
the crossing over to Minamurra could be challenging in rough
conditions. He wanted to time his trip to arrive on Doctor
Stephens' doorstep no later than 10.00 AM. The doctor never
gave out appointment times, only the day on which he wished
to see you, so depending on the particular day, one may be
seen straight away if it was quiet, or if busy, wait in turn to
take a seat on one of the kitchen chairs out front on the porch.
If you were unfortunate enough to still be waiting around
midday, the doctor was want to disappear out back for an hour
for his lunch.

John did his usual pre-departure rounds, as most others also
did, to see if anybody else in Paradise wanted anything while
he was over in town. Most people had just arrived during the

last couple of days, so there was little he needed to add to his shopping list, save Rick, who wanted a bag of ice for his drinks and Alan who asked if he could pick up the local newspaper.

After casting off from the private jetty John slipped quietly by the cabin cruisers nudged up to the shore overnight, and quietly by the government jetty where more cruisers were moored. A passing boat pushed up a wash which slapped noisily against the aluminium hull over the purr of the idling outboard. The boat people were sitting in small groups out on the landing that rose above him. Large fat-gutted men and women in T-shirts and shorts chatted while they warmed their bodies in the sun, like waking lizards. As John slipped past them, he picked up various snippets of conversation. One group were commenting on the noisy boat on the end of the jetty which had played loud music till after two in the morning. Another group were making plans to get together for dinner that night and deciding who would be bringing what to the table. Yet another lot were comparing notes on where they'd camped in previous nights. Some people remained on their boats, cooking late breakfast, or out on the stern-decks reading or fishing off the back of their vessels. The 'noisy boat' on the end of the jetty sat silently, its occupants apparently still asleep and seemingly oblivious to all the activity along the rest of the landing.

Further on past the government jetty a 'squadron' of yachts were rafted up together along the shore.

'Yachties never do like mixing with the stink-boatpeople.' John thought to himself.

There was a distinctive difference between the yachties and the motorised boat people that John observed. For a start the yachties didn't lounge around reptilian-style in deck chairs. Obesity in these people was the exception, rather than the norm. The men could often be seen sporting beards, and gaily striped T-shirts rather than the three-day growths and silly little faux skipper's caps covering the cruiser lizards …. And the sailing population appeared to be generally older in years and maintained a more active transience, not staying for more than a couple of nights on the shores near Paradise before sailing on to explore the next destination.

Steering past the yachts John could hear the steel cables, (or 'sheets' in yachty terms) clinking rhythmically like engine valves against the aluminium masts in the stiff easterly breeze, and there was the constant whir from the wind generators. The little wind vanes on the top of the masts danced excitedly to the tune of the wind, and small triangular flags fluttered off the main stays. John wondered how they could sleep at night with the constant whirring and 'clink, clink, clink' resounding down the masts into the cramped cabins. For that matter, he wondered what attracted people to camp in such close quarters, as one of the main attractions for him coming to Paradise had been the comparative solitude and peace that the place used to offer, and in fact still did for most of the year.

Once clear of all the boats John opened the throttle and the outboard engine roared into life propelling the run-about up onto the plane and sending it skipping across the water. The government jetty shrunk away to a distant dot on the horizon as the port of Minamurra came into view through his watery eyes. It wasn't long before he was tying up outside Frankie Banister's place and retrieving his car from the compound. John tried to enter the backyard quietly so he could get his car out without engaging in a conversation with Frankie, which he feared might cause him to be late for his appointment with the doctor, but the scraping of the wire gate across the gravel alerted two dogs that barrelled out of the workshop snarling and barking. Frankie was not far behind them.

'Well, look what the cat dragged in.' declared Frankie on seeing John.

'For Christ's sake call your dogs off Frankie, they scared the crap out of me!'

'It's all right I've fed them breakfast. They won't eat you ......can't guarantee they won't bite though! Anyway, that'll teach you for trying to sneak into my yard un-announced like you did last week.' Frankie continued.

'Sorry about that.' said John 'I was in a hurry last week.... had a gash in my foot and had to get to the doctors, which is where I should be now.' replied John.

'Old 'Howlong'! I wouldn't send my dogs to him. Best of luck then!'

Frankie Banister was a small irritated looking man. A shock of red hair flew back from his florid forehead as if he'd just struck a finger in a light socket, and his rosacea blighted face glowed angrily in the sun. Of Welsh descent, he never held back with what was on his mind and his high pitched nasally voice had a slightly annoying twang, especially when he was having a whinge about something. His business was divided into three parts; A shop front where he sold a variety of stock which included boat parts, bait and fishing tackle, a workshop and a storage yard. The orange gravelled yard was filled with boats and trailers that sat above patches of overgrown grass and weeds. It was also where many of the Paradise residents parked their cars during their stay across the water. Out the front on the cracked concrete apron two weathered looking fuel bowsers stood across from a propane tank for filling gas bottles and an ice-chest filled with bags of crushed ice. The workshop separated the yard from the shopfront in which Frankie spent a good deal of his time servicing and repairing outboard motors. An electric buzzer on the wall would alert Frankie when someone entered the store from the road, to which the standard answer was, 'Be with you in a minute!'

The walls of the fibro and tin workshop were darkened by years of soot from an oil heater that Frankie had made from a large metal drum and bits of copper tubing. Thin laser like beams of light cut through the haze from nail holes in the second-hand tin which covered the roof. The heater was fed with discarded engine oil through a rubber hose from a collection tank outside. A domestic hair-drier clamped to a metal stand blew air through a short length of silver ducting into the heater and across a series of steel plates in the base of the drum where the ignited oil dripped down from a needle valve. It was surprisingly efficient, and except for the first ten minutes when thick acrid smoke would belch from the stainless-steel chimney, the rest of the time it burnt relatively cleanly. In the depths of winter at full tilt Frankie could get the whole unit to glow a deep cherry red, although twice that John knew of, when Frankie had the thing really roaring, flames shot out unexpectedly from the air intake and nearly burnt the hair off his head.

Fluorescent lamps which hung low from chains below the roof cast a pale light over the cluttered room. Various workshop machines, steel work benches and tool racks crowded the gritty concrete floor. The workshop was never free of noise. Even when Frankie was not calling something a bastard, hammering or grinding, or carrying out some other tasks, a battery of white plastic bait-tanks bubbled quietly across one side of the room and there was the constant hiss of air escaping from a loose compressed air fitting. A large air-compressor near the wooden garage doors would cut in on regular intervals to top up the pressure when it dropped below a pre-determined limit. Sharing a shelf stacked with grimy workshop manuals an old bakelite AM radio played out a constant stream of country and western tunes.

'There's a gas bottle in the boat that needs filling, but I'll call in to pick it up a bit later Frankie if that's alright.' said John.

'Yeah, whatever John. I'll still be here, unless of course I'm not.' joked Frankie.

John wandered over to his car, trying hard to ignore the dogs that were sniffing at his heels and growling. With each growl he could feel the hair on the back of his neck standing on end, and the worst bit was that he knew the dogs could sense that too.

John made it to the doctor's just after ten. To his disappointment a rusty old ute in the driveway meant he wasn't going to be the first to be seen. He walked onto the porch come-waiting-room without pressing the bell and took his seat opposite a swarthy looking character presenting with an open wound above his left eye accompanied by a rather swollen bluish cheek. There was a distinct aroma of fish and beer emitting from the man and it was obvious from his general appearance he'd come from one of the trawlers down on the wharf. The fisherman sat there forlornly over a can of warm beer, an occasional drop of blood fell from his brow and landed on the top of the can from which he took infrequent sips. By John's reckoning he must have come off the boat that morning and gone straight to the 'blaggard's' pub for an early session, and there, managed to get in a fight, something which wasn't particularly hard to do with the company that frequented the hotel.

John did his best not to make eye contact with the other patient, but it was difficult seeing there wasn't much else to look at in the tiny room. Finally, Doctor Stephens appeared at the waiting room door. John peered at the doctor in disbelief ......he looked like he was still dressed in the same baggy arsed tracksuit pants and red checked flannel shirt he wore during John's last visit! At least John found some re-assurance in the doc's professional etiquette with the observation that he appeared to have had a shave and combed his hair since last time.

'Oh dear, it looks like the fish have been fighting a bit harder lately.' said the doctor addressing the man sitting opposite John.

'Doc, tell me; Have you ever had a broken nose?' retorted the fisherman, lifting his bleary eyes from the messy beer can.

'Well, no I can't say I have Bill.'

'Well, if you'd like one, I'd be more than happy to give you one......smart arse!' the fisherman answered.

'See what I have to put up with here.' said the doctor to John, totally ignoring Bill. 'Most likely he'll be back again next week, with the other side of his face rearranged. Let's have a look at you then.' Stephens said with a sigh.

John sat nervously in the porch listening to the drama unfold in the surgery. He could hear 'Bill the fisherman's' threats and objections to the treatment expounded in loud profanities as Doctor Stephens had his way with him. The abandoned blood-stained beer can on the chair next to John in the waiting room only served to exacerbate John's anxiety. Finally, after what seemed an endless session of torture, the somewhat subdued fisherman stumbled back into the waiting room to reclaim the remains of his beer. John noticed the sutures which Stephens had closed the now iodine-stained wound looked more like a fishing-line snarl. They'd been drawn together so tightly that Bill's left eyebrow was now fixed in a constant raised expression of pain.

As the fisherman stumbled out the door Stephens called out, 'I'll see you again in ten days' time, and remember you still owe me for the last two consultations you've had!'

'Next!' called the doctor, and John found himself looking around the waiting room just to make sure there wasn't anyone else who might have been waiting whom he hadn't noticed.

If John's anxiety wasn't already high enough, the sound of the ute roaring off outside, spraying gravel against the side of his car from the spinning wheels, took it to a new level.

The doctor, sensing John's nervousness beckoned him into the surgery with a reassuring smile.

'Come in, let's have you then.' he grinned. 'Now let's see, Mr Williams......ah yes.' mumbled Stephens while referring to his notes. So, how's the shoulder feeling then?'

'Shoulder?' queried John. 'No, no, it's my foot. The gash on my foot!

'Ah yes, here we are!' continued Stephens consulting his notes further. 'Let's get you up on the table and have a look at it then.'

John slipped his shoe and sock off, and then lay back on the examination table with his leg dangling over the end. His still tender foot felt bare and exposed in the open air. Stephens wheeled his chair around to where he could examine the foot at close range and took a seat. Leaning forward he trained an office lamp that stood near the table toward John, and John could feel the radiant heat from the lamp on his sole. Layer by layer the doctor carefully pulled off the dressings and placed them in a dish on the floor. When the last piece of dressing was removed Stephens polished his glasses on his shirt, then placed them on the end of his nose. Leaning forward for a closer look, John could feel the doctor's breath against his foot.

'Do you get many patients like Bill?' enquired John, trying to start up some small talk and distract himself from the thought of further painful treatment at the hands of the old man.

'I get a few animals like Bill......enough to think at times I would have been better off having studied veterinary science instead of medicine.' the doctor sighed.

'Now, this is looking quite good.' Stephens announced to John's relief.

The doctor left the room for a short time then returned with the means to clean the foot up. He re-bandaged it with a light dressing which he trimmed to size with scissors, then removing his glasses, he turned the lamp off.

'You'll probably be able to do without this dressing in a few days, but you'll need to keep an eye on it and stay out of the water for a bit longer.' the doctor advised.

Stephens left the room once more while John put his sock and shoe back on. John peered up at the now familiar cobwebs around the cornices then checked his watch. After what seemed like ages Doctor Stephens shuffled back into the surgery with John's account.

'I only accept cash or cheque.' he said. 'I can send you an invoice if you haven't got it on you now.'

John took the account from him and fidgeted in his pockets for his wallet and any spare cash. It turned out he had just enough. The doctor took the notes and coins and placed them on his desk amongst the pads and journals and other stuff. He picked up one of the pads and wrote out a script for some vitamin E cream, then another in the form of a receipt.

'Once you've finished with the dressing, it will help to use the cream twice a day till the scar completely heals. Now, is there anything else I can help you with today?'

'Actually.' said John. 'There was something you said during my last visit that bothered me......I wasn't quite at my best, but I remember you saying something about you thought the land at Paradise was being bought back, to link up the coastal parks either side I presume.'

'There's been some talk around town recently that those blasted Scullys and the others over there were finally going to be moved off the land.' said the doctor. 'Not sure who I actually heard it from, but about time.'

'Well, that can't be good!' replied John. 'I own one of the smaller properties over there.' he continued in a protesting tone.

'Well, fool be you.' replied the doctor in a clipped voice. 'They'll give you nothing for it if it's true.'

The doctor's apparent lack of detail or concern caught John off balance. It was like having a bomb dropped at his feet without being provided with the advice on how to deal with it. John's head was spinning as he stumbled out of the surgery. His vision narrowed to the point that he didn't even see the old lady waiting in the porch as he hurried out and caught his shin on the woman's sturdy walking frame. John tripped forward and face-planted the flywire door causing a tear to open up above the cross-brace. The door banged noisily against the outside wall then recoiled with the help of the retaining spring, slamming shut with an equally loud bang. The thought of losing his beloved cottage caused him to feel sick in the stomach. Who could possibly be considering a compulsory acquisition of the land? The Coastal Parks people? The State Government? The National Parks mob? It was well known the Scullys had been unpopular with the Minamurra folk for nearly one hundred years, so no-one in town would be likely to care what happened one way or the other, in fact they'd probably support such a thing. Even the doctor didn't seem to care. Still, maybe it was just hearsay John reasoned in an effort to reassure himself.

John took several deep breaths when he reached the car. He'd surprised himself with his reaction to the doctor's simple and unsubstantiated statement. He felt embarrassed about the accident he'd just had with the doctor's door and ashamed not to go back and apologise for any damage he might have incurred. Still, the doctor had managed to hit such a raw nerve and had done so in such a dispassionate way. He hadn't even made the effort to feign empathy, 'fool be you indeed!' .... It left John with a bad taste in his mouth, and he was tempted to feel disappointment by the fact that young 'Bill' hadn't carried out his offer to flatten the doctor's nose.

John rolled down the gravel road into Minamurra. He parked his car in the only available spot nearest the supermarket which stood a little way past the 'blaggard's' pub. On his way past the hotel John noticed Bill the fisherman back with his mates out under the porch, swilling beers and well on his way to getting into another fight. John got caught out when the half-tanked fisherman's bloodshot stare suddenly made eye contact with him.

'Whadar you look'n at arsehole?' rasped Bill

John quickly looked the other way and quickened his step pretending not to hear the taunt.

'Hey, you!' the voice called after him… 'Deaf as well as stupid are ya?'

John kept walking, not looking back. It seemed the fisherman hadn't recognised him from the doctor's surgery and John figured his anonymity was something best maintained.

The supermarket was more of a mini market than anything else, but what it lacked in size it made up for in stock. The proprietor, Geoff Evans was a portly man with a generous belly that completely filled out his creaseless blue apron and tightly stretched dark green rolled up at the sleeves. He had an overall dapper appearance accentuated by a neat little bow tie that peeked out from his equally generous second chin, and his glistening curly blonde hair that crowned his shiny plump head. There was a large lolly-stand near the check-out at the entrance to the store with bags of fresh liquorice and candies which welcomed shoppers with a sweet signature aroma. Geoff, who never seemed to come out from behind the till nearly always had a lolly in his mouth which he would masterfully roll around and suck whist at the same time maintain conversation with the customers. The shelves in the shop were packed as amply as Geoff was. There was something for everyone…Apart from the usual greengroceries, tinned goods, dairy and other refrigerated items, Geoff stocked newspapers and magazines, fishing-tackle and hardware items. Right up the back he kept a small selection of wine, beer and spirits. You could tell which products turned over less often than others by the amount of dust on them. In all the years John had shopped there nothing ever seemed to change. There was always the same familiar odour of the liquorice, the same little trolleys that rattled over the same worn checker tiled floor and the same buzzing sounds emitting from the fluorescent tubes in the ceiling.

John slowly traversed the three narrow aisles, one hand guiding the trolley that seemed to have a mind of its own, while the other held the shopping list at eye-level so he could take in what was on the list while at the same time peruse the contents of the shelves. A shopping list for Paradise was a little different to one he might make out for Melbourne. High on the list were items such as matches, kerosene, candles, tinned and dried foods as well as long life milk and other non-perishables that could last for a bit should he not be able to get back over for a while due to bad weather. He also stocked up on an adequate supply of beer and wine, something he'd normally buy from the hotel at a cheaper price, but for the desire to avoid that blaggard Bill, who seemed to have a set on him. John slipped his debit card into the ATM to get out some cash out before fronting the checkout counter.

'And how are we today?' greeted Geoff, swallowing on his lolly.

'Yeah, fine thanks.' answered John as he began to empty the trolley.

The shopkeeper flew into action clearing the items and sliding them down the opposite end of the shiny counter as fast as John could unload them. All the time while the shopkeeper's eyes scanned the goods for prices, the fat fingers of his right hand danced independently across the keys on the cash register like he was playing an instrument. John noticed the wobble of Evans' double chin and a trickle of perspiration down his temple as if the shopkeeper was conducting the checkout activity as an exercise routine.

'Is that all?' said Geoff marking up the last couple of items.

'Yes, thanks Geoff.' said John.

'No chocolates? Two for one on special!'

'Ah, no thanks.'

'No crisps?...... A dollar off the large packets!'

'No thanks!' repeated John, recalling that the last packet he bought from Geoff was stale.

'OK then, that'll be eighty-four dollars and seventy cents.... Make that eighty even then.' said Geoff through his lolly in a gesture of generosity.

John handed him two fifties he'd just withdrawn, aware that Geoff's impromptu discounting was a ploy the man often used as a safeguard against customers' desire to return items that turned out to be not quite right when they were opened at home.

Despite the weight of the eight fully loaded plastic bags on his straining arms, John went to the trouble of crossing to the far side of the road in order to put as much distance between himself and Bill the fisherman as he passed by the hotel. Whether Bill was still there or not, John didn't know, but mercifully he was able to pass without drawing any further unwanted attention from the pub. John placed one lot of bags on the pavement while he fumbled through his pockets for his car keys. Only after he finally located the keys did he realise he'd left the car unlocked; Such was the distraction of what the doctor had said, which still played on his mind.

It was one o'clock, enough time to indulge in fish and chips for lunch before Sal's bus was due outside the post office. Even before he got to the fish and chip shop John could smell the aroma of chips wafting in the breeze. Like freshly ground coffee, John thought, how much better fried chips smelled than tasted. John was aware of the noisy hunger pangs his stomach was making as he placed his order. He wondered if the woman on the other side of the counter could also hear them. The fish and chips in Minamurra were the best he'd ever tasted, much better than what you could get in the city. For a start the chips were hand-cut and par-boiled before being deep fried in lard. When they came out of the boiling vat, they would be crispy-golden on the outside, and wonderfully fluffy and soft inside. Equally crisp and golden were the generous fillets of succulent beer-battered fish, fresh off the boats. After a light dusting of salt and a sprinkle of vinegar, John's eagerly anticipated lunch was wrapped in butcher's paper and handed across the counter to him together with a complimentary soft drink.

John found a picnic bench a little further up the road overlooking the wharf opposite the Post Office. His mouth watered as he un-wrapped the steaming parcel, the tang of vinegar rising up into his nostrils like smelling salts. He sampled a single scaulding chip, then ripped back the pull tag on his soft drink and took a large swig of bubbling lemon squash. The effervescent squash tickled the back of his nose and made his eyes water. He released a long satisfying burp, the best part of it being that Sal wasn't there to chastise him for doing it.

While waiting for the bus to arrive, John filled in the rest of the time sitting in the sun, sharing his chips with the 'rent a flock' of noisy seagulls (which seemed to have appeared out of nowhere soon after he'd opened his lunch parcel) and reading Alan Bagshore's newspaper. He didn't have to wait long before the V-Line coach pulled in enveloping John in a cloud of dust and heady diesel fumes. Sal stepped off the bus with a small overnight bag. There was a loud hiss as the bus driver released the pneumatic handbrake and the bus pulled out on the road with a roar from the hot smelling diesel engine.

John stepped forward to give Sal a welcome kiss, but before he could say anything Sal cut in; 'You've just had fish and chips for lunch, haven't you, and don't say you haven't because I can smell them on your breath!'

'OK so I did. So what!'

'Well, you won't be having them again this holiday. Look at that stomach of yours!' replied Sal, pointing at it with her eyes.

'So, what have you been doing with yourself today, apart from eating 'fat food'?' she asked.

'I had a doctor's appointment this morning, and then I did some shopping......'

'Doctor's appointment? What's wrong with you? Are you sick?' ......

'No, no! I had a bit of an accident last week. Sliced my foot on a broken bottle and......'

'Oh please...don't tell me about it; just the thought of it is making me feel sick!'

'Well, it's all good now.' reassured John. 'I doesn't hurt anymore and there's just a light dressing on it which I can take off in a few days the doctor tells me. Anyway, hop in the car, we'll get the groceries into the boat, then I need to pick up a gas bottle and some ice from Frankies.'

'I hope you've got the cottage all clean and tidy, I'll be cross if it's in a mess. You know how I like to have it nice and tidy.' warned Sal. 'Have you put any flowers inside for me? I won't be happy if there're no flowers.'

John pretended not to hear Sal's last remarks, instead filling her in on who else was down for the holidays, and of course all the drama between Simon and Joe which had occurred the day before. They drove the short distance to where the boat was moored opposite Frankie Banister's, unloaded the shopping, then John left Sal with the boat while he parked the car in the yard and picked up his gas and ice. He could hear Frankie working on a motor in the workshop.

'You BASTARD!' Frankie shouted, before throwing down a ring spanner with such force that it rebounded off the concrete floor and nearly took off his nose.

John cautiously cleared his throat to announce his presence, not sure whether the next missile would be launched in his direction.

'Having a spot of trouble with that?' He said awkwardly, feeling that he'd come in at an inopportune time.

Frankie was working on a portable generator that looked like it had seen better days.

'It's rooted!' exclaimed Frankie. 'That bloody Dick Head wants me to fix it for him. Who does he think I am, bloody Houdini the magician? With all the money he's got you'd think he'd just go out and buy another bugger.'

'I think Houdini was an escapologist.' corrected John.

'Yeh, whatever!' snarled Frankie.

'I'll be calling in on Rick on my way back. Would you like me to tell him it's unserviceable?' offered John.

'Don't bother, I've got to go over tomorrow myself.... something wrong with his bloody fridge as well.'

'Um, while I think of it Frankie; Have you heard any stories going around about Paradise being compulsorily acquired for coastal parklands? It's just something the doctor mentioned this morning.'

'I wouldn't listen to anything he says, wouldn't know a shoulder from a foot, that bloke!' replied Frankie.

'So, you haven't heard anything then?' enquired John.

'No, but I did take a bloke over about a month or so ago…. he wasn't any of you locals. Some bloke dressed up in a suit. Said he wanted to look at the properties over there…didn't say why, but he looked a right 'burke' all dressed up like some city wanker trudging around in the scrub with his shiny shoes and all.'

'Did he say where he was from?' asked John with sudden interest.

'Nah…I didn't ask ……slipped me a hundred bucks for the pleasure of my company there and back, that's all I was interested in.'

'Well, if you see him again can you find out more and let me know. There's something fishy going on.' said John, frustrated by Frankie's lack of information.

'Speaking of fishy.' replied Frankie. 'When I've finished with Dick Head tomorrow, I was planning on dropping a line in over at your place if you're interested in joining me for a fish and a beer or two.'

'Sounds like a plan.' said John

'Your gas bottle's out the front, and you can grab your ice on the way out too. I've already put it on your account…… probably see you tomorrow then. I'll bring over everything we need.' concluded Frankie, returning his attention to the so called 'bastard' of a generator.

John grabbed the ice and gas and lugged them over the road to his boat. Sal was waiting impatiently; keen to get across the water and rest up after her arduous day's travel.

Chapter Five

Of Wives and Neighbours

*John 8:44 "Ye are of your father the devil,
and the lusts of your father ye will do......"*

John and Sal had an easy crossing to Paradise. Helped by and incoming tide and a gentle tail wind, they pushed across with the warm sun on their faces.

'Oh, would you look at the colour of that beautiful blue water!' exclaimed Sal.

The flood tide was midway through flushing the inlet with clean ocean water, and Sal could see every detail on the bottom of the lake, even when passing over the deeper channels. She observed the patterns on the sandy bottom, the sea grass beds and the occasional fleeting fish. As the government jetty gradually came into view, she remarked on the appearance of so many boats moored on the landing and along the shorefront. John slowed the runabout down as they approached the five-knot zone where the holiday flotilla had formed. A jet ski flew past them at high-speed throwing up a huge rooster-tale, the motor growing angrily at the rider's command.

'They should have an open season on those bloody things.' shouted John.

'Now come on John. I haven't come all this way just to hear you whinge about every little thing. Just go with the flow. You're on holidays you know.'

Motoring quietly past the yachts and the cabin cruisers, John took in all the passing snippets of conversation as he had done in the morning. The yachties were busy polishing their decks or adjusting rigging and the lizard-like boaties were still reclining in little groups on the government jetty, soaking up the sun. The odd puff of blue smoke rose out of the bush in places, indicating a campfire was going, perhaps to heat someone's water, or cook someone's meal. As John steered the boat in near the shore, Sal drew a deep breath and took in all the smells that were familiar with Paradise......the sweet sea air, the Bergen, the aromatic wood smoke and the dry tussock grasses. With each successive breath she could feel her journey-fatigued state gradually eroding away by the rush of energy-filled air as it passed into her lungs and dissipated throughout her body. This was part of the magic of Paradise that everyone who arrived there would feel.

As they nudged up to the private jetty Sal remarked again on the number of boats moored about the Paradise shoreline.

'Apart from the 'boaties' Sal, I think most of the property owners are here too by now.' answered John. 'They all seem to have arrived much at the same time.' he continued.

'So, have you spoken to anybody yet?' enquired Sal.

'Yes a few of them, and I've asked Susan over for dinner some time.... I'll fill you in on all the gossip while we walk to the cottage.'

'Before I listen to anything I'll be in need of a rest first, once I've unpacked of course. You can tell me everything after that.' interjected Sal before John could go further.

John grabbed Sal's overnight bag in one hand and balanced himself with a shopping bag in the other. He figured it might be easier to carry up the rest of the stuff at his own speed while Sal had her nap.

Halfway up the track they came across Alan Bagshaw. Busy as a badger and dressed in a neat pale blue windcheater, black compression-pants and pristine white Nike runners. Alan looked more like he had just come out of a 'yuppies' gym rather than his rustic bush block. He'd chain sawed and whipper snipped his way through much of the day and now his attention was apparently focused on 'tidying up' the track. Rake in hand Alan was engrossed in fastidiously smoothing out the ruts and scuff marks left in the sand from the numerous passages of barrows and foot traffic.

Glancing up briefly from his 'important' task Alan offered the Williams a greeting in the form of; 'Welcome Sal, I see you've got John working.'

Sal, wanting to show some tolerance smiled thinly replying: 'Lovely to be here Alan…. Always hard at it, I see.'

'Your paper will be at the cottage if you care to collect it later.' added John.

Sal harboured an ardent dislike for Alan's compulsive tidiness. His incessant desire to continually cut and trim, usually employing noisy machinery, she felt it all stood for the very suburbanite attitude that ought to be totally absent from this natural seaside setting. Alan was also a fitness fanatic, and no doubt, when there was nothing left for him to tidy, snip or rake he would be taking off for a run along the ocean beach…. hence the footwear and the compression attire (which made him look more like a monkey that had grown frog's legs than a contemporary Homo sapiens).

'Why would he bother John? I mean really! Hasn't he got anything better to do with his time down here? And really, men his age shouldn't wear those ridiculous pants. You could see his 'goolie bits' poking through for God's sake!'

'He's a 'MAMIL'.' replied John

'What?' snapped Sally.

'A Middle-Aged Man in Lycra.' smirked John.

'Oh, don't be so stupid.' Sal fired back, adding…. 'And I haven't come all this way to listen to your ridiculous 'dad jokes'. More importantly, have you brought up the things that need to be put on ice?'

'Why don't you have a little lie down first and unpack later.' suggested John, sensing a growing level of irritation in Sal's demeanour. Then, having sorted the shopping bag and placing Sal's bag by the bed in an effort to placate her, he turned his back (as politely as one can) before smartly closing the door behind him and retreating from the cottage.

John returned to the boat to collect the rest of the shopping and drop off Rick's bag of ice, which was surely now beginning to melt. It was a beautiful afternoon, sunny and warm with the promise of a balmy gentle evening to come, but despite that he also felt a growing level of irritation within himself. While he'd looked forward to Sal's company, he was frustrated by her peremptory attitude since her arrival. There was all that news he'd wanted to share with her, and conversely news she might have that he would want to be informed of, but apparently such information would only be exchanged according to her priorities and not his. Added to this, with all the walking around during the day, his foot was now ached once more. A deep throbbing within his heel goaded John like a cattle prod. But then it came to him…. the base source of his irritation; What was at the bottom of all this vague talk about re-claiming the Paradise land holdings? There was something going on, but no one seemed to have any detail or hard evidence of exactly what! It seemed there was just 'hearsay', which of course didn't help abate John's discomfort from the uncertainty.

'Maybe someone else here knows more?' John thought. 'But with all the machinations abounding in Paradise, who could one implicitly trust for reliable information.' he reasoned.

John was aware the Scully's had a generational reputation for their financial acumen and underhanded dealings. Was there some financial opportunity festering below these rumours John wondered? There was nothing in his thinking that eased his angst.

Meanwhile, down at the private jetty, the Urquhart berth was a hive of activity. Dieter and his two boys were busy loading their run-about with an array fishing-lines, bait of various descriptions and smells, and cans of cold beer. Dieter was dressed in his trademark faded khaki bib & brace overalls and gumboots. Digesting the vision before him, John often wondered how this big man would fare if he ever fell overboard. The Dutchman seldom wore a lifejacket, and it wasn't like you could ever lift his 140 kg. body back in the boat easily if he ever fell in. As John approached, Dieter with the intent to stymie any idle conversation, cut into his verbal directions to the boys to address John.

'Can't talk now John, der boys and I are going to try and skveeze in an hour or two's fishing outside der entrance before dark.'

John had always been too nervous to venture through the entrance in his own boat. He knew just how treacherous it could get, especially during an ebb tide when the strong outrush of lake water pushed against the incoming ocean swell. In his eighteen years' experience in Paradise, he'd witnessed so many boats come to grief trying to navigate the entrance and the bar during unfavourable conditions. He remembered Frankie once telling him, 'My advice to people coming in to buy bait and asking about 'going out'; Sure, you'll probably get out OK, but I won't guarantee you'll get back in.'

'So, where's my invite?' enquired John provocatively.

'You've got your own boat, so no excuses for you not taking yourself out any time. You're such a 'big girl's blouse' when it comes to fishing in the ocean John. You'll need to grow some balls if you want to get der decent fish.'

Reflecting, John was surprised how this big burly Dutchman hadn't become yet another statistic over the preceding years. He'd lost count of the nights Dieter had somehow found his way back along the inlet from the 'Blaggard's pub, so drunk on his arrival at Paradise he couldn't get out of his boat and climb onto the jetty. But fortunately, there always seemed to be someone with him that could help. And then there was the night Dieter had drunkenly moored his vessel stern first into a stiff westerly. John remembered waking early one morning to a bellowing Dutch voice crying out 'Some bugger's schtollen der fucking boat!' John recalled how Dieter's big rosy 'pie face' had gazed out across the water for any sign of his missing craft, unaware that during the night the boat had slowly filled with water, lapped over the stern by the wind, cupful by cupful, and which now rested peacefully on the weedy lake bottom just three meters below where he stood. On reflection the incident seemed quite comical, but at the time it was a very sobering event. Anyway, John reasoned against being stood-up by Dieter, that Frankie Banister would be over tomorrow and the pair of them would spend some very pleasant time fishing off the surf beach. Even if the fish weren't to be 'as decent' as Dieter might catch, it promised to be just as enjoyable, and considerably safer at that.

In no time it seemed, the Urquhart's shoved off and John retrieved the now dripping ice bag from the floor of his boat. He headed up the track that led to the Head's cottage, the dripping ice bag held at arm's length like the severed head of some strange watery creature he'd killed.

Within sight of his destination, the Head's forward greeting party/come early warning system activated and launched themselves at him, barking, snapping menacingly and relentlessly despite John's best efforts to pacify them with some soothing 'good boys' type verbal reassurance. Once alerted, Gloria who was sunbaking topless out the front in only her knickers, sat up abruptly from her place on the outdoor lounge and, drawing a scanty shawl around herself, retreated through the front door.

'Sorry John! I'll be with you in a minute.' she called, disappearing indoors.

Momentarily, John was left to his own devices with the three marauding poodles, teeth bared, ramping up their attack. John instinctively swung round to take a boot to the dog closest to his heals, but as fast as he could turn, the three attackers turned with him maintaining their assault from the rear. It was just as well John was deprived from taking a swinging kick at the dogs, for only a second later Rick's beaming face shone out the door to greet him.

'Oh, don't mind the dogs. They don't eat very much.' joked Rick. 'And don't worry about Gloria, she won't bite either…. just come in.' he continued.

Responding to Rick's advice John advanced towards the cottage once more, and without making it look too obvious, swung the ice bag about menacingly to create a sort of force-field between himself and his canine attackers. He was met at the door by the now slightly more dressed Gloria who had pushed in front of her aging husband. In a single movement she swept down and collected all three snapping poodles in her arms, then continuing with the movement, thrusted forward planting a big red lipstick kiss squarely on John's startled face. However, the sound of a snarling set of dog's teeth so close to his throat sent John stepping back involuntarily and caused him to jar his already throbbing wound on the ground.

'Arrrr…damn it!' John screamed.

'Sorry John!' apologised Gloria, for the second time. 'Please do come in.'

The interior of the Head's cottage was all about boats and sailing. A string of gaily coloured ensign flags hung from part of the exposed beam ceiling. A pair of crossed rowing sculls above a life buoy attached to the back wall was complimented by an old wooden ship's wheel on the opposing wall. Access to a mezzanine floor, where two ship's bunks afforded a sleeping area, could be made via a ladder which had been salvaged from a ship's passageway. An old wooden single scull hung from the beams beyond the flags. Seashells and old photographs of sailing boats adorned the remaining spaces.

Rick gestured John to drop the bag of ice in an 'Eski' beside the door. 'That should get us out of trouble for now thanks John, I've got that Bannister bloke coming tomorrow to look at the fridge. These gas fridges are a bit temperamental aren't they, eh? Tell me what I owe you.'

'Nothing Rick, don't worry about it.' replied John, noting that the three poodles hiding behind the day bed were still baring their teeth at him.

'Well then, will you let me get you a drink? Seeing we now have ice.' asked Rick. 'A whisky, a G & T?'

'Don't let him talk you into anything you don't want John.' cut in Gloria. 'It's a bit early for most people.' She continued, addressing Rick. 'They're not all alcoholics like you my dear.'

'What have I told you before Gloria? It's always five o'clock somewhere. So, which was it you were having John?'

'OK, well, perhaps a whisky on ice then.' replied John

John was quite keen on the idea of having a shot of whisky, not only might it help take the sting out of his foot, but might also help settle his nerves, put on edge by those bloody dogs.

'Well, seeing you two are having drinks, you may as well fix me a G & T while you're at it Rick.' said Gloria in resignation while she put some biscuits and cheese together.

Rick prepared the drinks ensuring John received a generous serve. It didn't go un-noticed by Gloria.

'I'm sorry John, here I go apologising to you again. You must tell Rick if he's given you too much. He's so heavy handed at times.'

'No, it's fine Gloria, just how I like it thanks.' John replied.

'I'm sure John's big enough to speak for himself Gloria.' stated Rick in a patronising tone. 'And I'll fix you another when you've finished that one John.'

John pulled up a couple of directors chairs to the small trestle- table in the middle of the room where Gloria had set out some plates and the biscuits and cheese. The three of them sat down, John in a position where he could keep one eye on the dogs, who had become suspiciously quiet.

'You know John.' Gloria started. 'We'll be eating at the soup kitchen before long with the way Rick's giving away our money. That Bannister man who's coming over tomorrow to look at the fridge.... costs us a fortune to have him do anything. Rick thinks he's marvellous. Gets him over here all the time to fix things and do odd jobs, and Frankie charges us like a wounded bull. He's outrageous. Rick may as well just leave him with an open cheque book.'

'So, I suppose you're going to do all the repairs and odd jobs then dear.' exclaimed Rick. 'And by the way may I remind you, it's not 'our' money, it's 'my money' you're talking about.'

'Anyway, it's all the same in the end.' retorted Gloria.

'She thinks Bannister should work for nothing John. That's what she thinks.' whispered Rick out the side of his hand.

'Well, your little house looks a treat. It's a credit to you both.' John gestured, attempting to defuse the developing 'domestic'.

'That's very kind of you to say that John, we do our best. Get John another whiskey dear, and I'll have a top-up too while you're at it. But I don't want you having any more Rick. You become so augmentative after a couple of drinks, and I don't like it.'

With a stiff whiskey under his belt John could feel himself relaxing and becoming more comfortable. And it seemed to be having a positive effect on the dogs. They too seemed to have become more settled. Gloria on the other hand appeared to be becoming more animated and outspoken by the time her second drink was in front of her. John was well aware she had a reputation around Paradise for becoming a bit of a flirt after a couple of 'G&T's, so it should not have come as a surprise when Gloria took a photo album from the adjacent bookshelf, and placing it in front of him, lent over exposing her sun dried breasts from between the folds of her flimsy shawl on the pretence of showing him some images of the recent work they'd done around the house. And John knew that there'd be a seductive kiss yet to come when it was time for him to leave. Rick was obviously well aware of Gloria's tendencies, and rarely said a word. Apparently, it was all part of the game.

Not wanting to appear engaged in Gloria's dalliance, John returned his attention quickly back to Rick.

'Rick, there's been some vague rumours about suggesting there might be some interest in compulsorily acquiring some, if not all the freehold properties in Paradise to extend the existing coastal park. Have you heard anything about that?' John enquired.

'I've heard nothing, but I can tell you one thing. I doubt they could ever afford it. I mean how many places in Australia, or anywhere else for that matter, enjoy the luxury of having both ocean frontage at one end of their properties and lake frontage at the other? These properties are now priceless.' replied Rick.

'But doesn't compulsory acquisition suggest you might just get what you're given?'

'Well, as I say I've heard nothing, and anyway they, whoever 'they' might be would have a fight on their hands...especially with the Scullys! They'd have to burn us out!' exclaimed Rick in a dismissive tone.

John felt somewhat comforted by Rick's remarks and took solace with the thought that what they (whoever they were) might want and what they might get to be two completely different potential outcomes. He also felt comforted in the realisation that others in Paradise would be prepared to put up a decent fight should the rumours prove to have any substance. He admired Rick's defiance and again it caused him to reflect on what he perceived to be a weakness in his own character.... that being the ability to be his 'own man'.

The sound of kookaburras carolling outside to announce the evening alerted John to the fact that Sal would have already expected him to be back at home, probably at least an hour ago.

'Heavens! Is that time?' muttered John in clichéd terms. 'Sal will be wondering where the hell I am.'

'Thanks again for the ice John, you're so kind. I'll see you down to the track.' Gloria offered.

'No no, it's fine Gloria. Really! And I know my way out; You're probably keen to get on with thinking about dinner.' responded John.

John rose to his feet, and pushed back his deck chair, scraping it noisily across the timber floor, inadvertently activating the Head's 'early warning system' once more. The three poodles instinctively positioned themselves to protect the doorway, which now just happened to be John's only means of egress. Resisting the intimidation facing him, John made a direct advance on his escape route, which if he was still in full control of his faculties may have paid off. Instead, sedated sufficiently by two fat shots of spirits, mistimed his footing and step on one of the dog's paws.

The reaction was both instantaneous and profound. The black poodle, whose paw had been squashed under John's foot, let out an unearthly scream, which in turn set the white poodle off into a howling fit and the beige poodle scurrying under Rick's chair. All this sent Gloria into a dramatic and animated response. Both the black and white dogs beat a hasty retreat and joined the third dog snarling and cowering under Rick's chair.

'Oh, my poor little darlings! What ever happened to you?' exclaimed a maternal sounding Gloria.

Rick, who obviously had little empathy with the hounds, broke into a short splutter of laughter, perhaps it was more of a snigger, followed by a longer burst of involuntary coughing, as if attempting to atone for his indiscretion. John, who thought he was going to be 'for it', was relieved to see that Rick's overt display of amusement rapidly turned Gloria's object of ire away from himself.

'Oh, so you think this is funny Rick? Poor little Zsa-Zsa! And look at little Pippi, she's so upset too!'

Meanwhile Gloria's 'little darlings' were shivering in fear but continued snarling defiantly from under the comparative safety of Rick's chair. With the heated interchange building between the dogs, Rick and Gloria, John saw his opportunity to beat a hasty retreat.

'Sorry about that, no harm done, I hope! Let me know if there are any problems, won't you?' added John, as he beat his retreat from Rick's cottage down the shadowy evening track.

Walking homeward along the shoreline, a low setting sun reflected strongly on John's face from the sparkling estuary waters. He noted the familiar outline of Dieter Urquhart's boat, reduced to a black shape against the brilliant orange sunset, gliding silently toward the sanctuary of the private jetty.

John raised his hand to shade his eyes, and called out to the boat; 'So how did you go?'

'Who vonts to know' a broad Dutch voice replied.

John knew Dieter well enough to know there was a direct correlation between how much alcohol Dieter had consumed and how broad his accent became. It was obvious the Dutchman was well primed....and the boys seemed pretty happy as well.

As John drew closer, a rosy pie-face that seemed to glow almost as brightly as the sunset barked out; 'Oh, it's you! Look boys it's der big girl's blouse come to inspect our catch!'

'So how did you go?' repeated John, ignoring Dieter's demeaning remark.

'We've done better.' blurted the Dutchman. 'But we done OK.'

As the boat bumped awkwardly alongside the mooring, Mark the older boy heaved a fish box onto the jetty. John strode out to study the catch which was partially obscured under a mess of empty beer cans. He could see a number of good-sized flatheads surrounding a much bigger fish which he recognised as a gummy shark.

'You've done well!' exclaimed the impressed 'Big Girls blouse.'

'We nearly didn't.' piped up the excited younger boy. 'Dad nearly broached the boat coming in over the bar.... we bottomed out on the edge of the channel.'

'Don't bullshit Daniel.' snapped a dismissive Dieter. "Vee ver fine, just a shmall hiccup.' he continued.

John's attention was drawn to Mark who appeared to be rolling his eyes as if in support of Daniel's claims. It was Daniel, John recalled who once told him; 'Some people should never be allowed to own a boat.'

John watched on as the Urquharts packed up their runabout. He was keen to get a better look at the catch. Mark disembarked and hauled the fish-box over to a cleaning-board by the water's edge. As if having received some secret signal, a squadron of honking pelicans descended on water in front of the bench. They were followed by the squawking seagulls, and then by the timider cormorants. Dieter joined Mark at the cleaning board while Daniel went on up to the house with the rest of the gear. With filleting blades flashing against the setting sun the men immersed themselves in the cleaning process. Within minutes fish frames and scales were flying in all directions. John looked on entranced as glossy white fillets separated from darker pieces of detritus as if by magic. The sound of flapping feathers and snapping beaks added to the frenetic spectacle. The water boiled from the feeding fury of the competing birds. Every now and then, a gull or a pelican would break off and fly out over the water with a fish remnant that was too big to be immediately swallowed. Closely tailed they'd be harried by a flight of compatriots, keen to relieve the bolter of its bounty.

Then as quickly as it had all commenced, the last fillet was cut away and the process was finished. Mark washed down the board as Dieter fed the pile of fish pieces into a wad of plastic bags he'd produced from his pocket. Feeding time over, the birds disappeared with the same speed they'd arrived at a little earlier.

'They look great.' remarked John, referring to the fish fillets.

'Vell, you know vere to go if you vant to get dem.' answered Dieter, without looking up while rinsing off his fat pink fingers.

John took this to mean that nothing would be forthcoming as an offering for dinner. And without suggesting that just a fillet or two would make for a welcome surprise for Sal, John turned his back on the boys and retreated toward his own place. Halfway home he glanced back at the jetty. In contrast to all the action just a short time ago, it was still and empty, save a lonely dark figure at the end gazing forlornly out. Jane Tucker, John deduced.

A thin wisp of barbeque smoke, the sounds of a banging door, wood chopping, beer cans popping, and merriment drifted across the backwater creek which separated the Urquhart's place from John's. The Urquharts were already preparing their ocean feast. Dieter and boys were batching for the time being. Jan, Dieter's wife (Simon Scully's niece) wouldn't be down for another week. She rarely stayed in Paradise long while all the 'boys' were there together. Jan and Dieter had never socialised much with the Paradise community, and in keeping to themselves for the most, there was not much of interest to share with her boys when they were all together, the boys and Dieter as they were, being pre-occupied mainly with drinking and fishing. Her connection with Simon through her father (another Adonai-Shomo descendant) didn't help either. Simon disapproved of Dieter and had, on several occasions tried to have him cast out of Paradise on the premise that the land on which Dieter built his house belonged in fact to Jan's mother, and as such was not a suitable place to harbour one who partook of alcohol and who did not speak the 'Truth'. To make matters worse, when Dieter built on the tiny allotment, he neglected to have the land properly surveyed, and much to his chagrin, suffered the full force of Simon's wrath when it was discovered he had erected the kitchen and bathroom over a section of Simon's land. Simon had insisted the house be demolished and was hell bent on taking the matter to court, which may well have happened save some eleventh-hour intervention from Jan and her father. Jan's father suggested the land title could be signed over to Simon as a form of compensation and leased back to the Urquharts on a peppercorn lease. Dieter had attempted to blind-side the idea by secretly putting the house up for auction. Unfortunately for Dieter, word had got out about the misalignment problem with the building, and only one person fronted up on auction day, and he was just a 'tyre kicker'. The issue went unresolved for many years until one day, for reasons only known to Simon, he made Dieter an offer. Simon's freehold spread over several separate titles. While he was not permitted to subdivide, he was able to re-align one of his boundaries, that which contained the parcel of land adjacent to the Urquhart's block. Simon re-surveyed his land and moved his eastern boundary just enough to separate the part that Dieter had built over from the rest of his land. He then offered the tiny allotment to Dieter for ten thousand dollars. How could Dieter refuse! While the purchase of Simon's land resolved the alignment issue, it did nothing to resolve Simon's dislike for Dieter, and Dieter's dislike for Simon. At least the Dutchman could remain in Paradise without further contest.

The sound of footsteps on the wooden decking heralded John's arrival home. Sal had already lit the lamps in anticipation of the encroaching evening.

'Where the hell have you been?' snapped an obviously irate Sal. 'And what's that strange sickly smell in the house?' she added, before John could answer the first question.

'I finished my nap ages ago and I've been wondering where you'd got to.' she continued

'I got held up at the Head's.' answered John in a somewhat dismissive tone. 'Then I watched the Urquharts cleaning their fish. Anyway, what's all the stress? I wasn't far away.'

'Susan called in earlier. Invited us over for some pre-dinner drinks, but it's probably too late for that now, and Alan Bagshaw came knocking, looking for his newspaper.'

Returning to Sal's first question, John replied; 'Oh is there still a smell? I was sick the other night, probably ate a bad mussel.'

'Is that so.' answered Sal in a very 'knowing' tone. 'Are you sure it had nothing to do with how much you drank? And yes, the place stinks.' Sally fired back. 'You'll have to do something about it tonight before we go to bed. I'm not sleeping with this smell, and that's final.'

'Anyway....' continued John getting to Sally's second point; 'there's plenty of time to catch up with Susan. I'd actually suggested to her the other day she could join us here for a meal one night.'

'So did Bagshaw get his paper?' John finished, cutting in before Sally could make further comment.

After their initial sparring, John and Sal's conversation settled down to where they were able to discuss each other's news the past week while they'd been apart. John was particularly keen to share with Sal his account of the incident involving Joe and Simon out on the lake, and how the 'Mayor of Paradise' had made a such a fool of himself in front of all the boat people. Then, continuing on the subject of Joe, John reflected on the dramatic change in Jane Tullock's demeanour.

Sal had always admired Jane. She'd often remark on Jane's graceful presence, her dignified manner and her beautiful long locks of dark shiny hair.

'I didn't even recognise her in the boat.' said John.

'Joe said she'd become a bit vague since her hip operation, but Simon came over to see me and seemed to think it was far more serious. He didn't think she should be here at Paradise at all. Said she was suffering some form of mental decline......
some referred to it as 'Sundowners Disease'. But Simon described it as Alzheimer's.'

'Oh my goodness.' exclaimed Sally. 'I think I might have seen her on our track a little before you came home. There was a small frail woman, she looked like she was lost. I asked her if I could help, and she said she was OK, then wandered back toward the estuary. I thought she must have been from one of the U-Sail cruisers moored at the government jetty.'

'But now that you mention her...oh my goodness!'

'That would have been her.' confirmed John.

'I noticed she was standing at the end of the private jetty as I returned home this evening. I hope she's back home safely with Joe by now.' he continued.

'So why did Simon want to share this with you?' inquired Sal.

Sal knew Simon well enough to know he never shared information, particularly that of a personal nature, unless there was some purpose in doing that.

'I think Simon is looking to mount a case for taking Jane away from Joe. He doesn't believe Joe is fit to look after Jane in her current state. He asked me not to discuss it with Joe and said he intended implicating me as a witness, should the matter go to court.'

'Well of course you won't be John. Will you! You did make that quite clear I hope.' insisted Sal.

'I don't think I'll need to now, since he and Joe had their blow up on the lake.' remarked John. 'But best to be aware both of them will be looking for any support to strengthen their arguments.'

'Oh dear, I feel so sorry for Jane, and Joe.' lamented Sal.

Moving the conversation on, John asked; 'Oh, and while I think of it. Did I mention Frankie's calling in tomorrow afternoon to do a spot of fishing off the surf beach with me?'

'Well, if that's what you've organised, it's no use suggesting we catch up with Susan tomorrow night then. Is it?' replied Sal in resignation. 'And, what am I going to be doing then?'

'Frankie's coming over to do a job for Rick. We'll be going fishing after that. Maybe he'll bring Faye with him too?'

Sal was quite fond of Faye (my poor suffering 'other half', as Frankie would put it), and this seemed to soften Sal's attitude to John's piscal plans for the following day.

As the evening drifted into night, and John and Sal talked of better things, while the brilliant warm colours of the sunset Paradise had bathed in, mellowed into softer pastel shades after the sun had disappeared. The sea breeze abated as if to provide the water birds with a mirror smooth bed for the night. The sounds of the daytime activities diminished as the sounds of the night crept quietly in. An evening star flickered weakly overhead in the clear darkening summer sky. The transition into night at Paradise was typically a peaceful affair, as if the whole world was preparing to slumber. Just on dark, the evening bird song sounded a chorus in a final declaration of days end.

The Williams retired early to bed (as one is oft to do in Paradise) and lying there by the adjacent window, they gazed up at the cosmos with its ever-brightening stars while the sound of breaking waves on the ocean beach gently penetrated the quiet landscape, helping to lull them off to sleep.

It was a generally peaceful night, save the occasional crack of gunfire from the Scully direction, then the panicked squawk and clatter of birds fleeing from their cover in response.

They rose early the following morning. Sal prepared a breakfast-tray to have down on the lake front while John loaded a small foldout table and a couple of plastic chairs into a trolley. The crisp dawn air brought with it the promise of a warm sunny day to follow. Sal and John made their way down the still damp sandy track with their breakfast fare. The air was sweet smelling and everything seemed renewed and refreshed from the previous day. Bush birds tweeted sweetly in the tea-trees while the water birds bathed and preened busily along the water's edge. In contrast to the soft evening light, the early sun burned brightly on the land etching every detail in crystal-sharp focus.

Finding a good sunny spot by the lake, close by where the track finished, John set up the table and chairs. Sal placed the tray on the table and removed the large saucepan lid covering the still steaming offerings of toast, poached eggs and bacon, and of course a large pot of hot tea. The warm sunshine was tempered somewhat by an early morning breeze, as a body of cool air from the distant mountains drained down across the coastal plains over the estuary and out to sea. An overtly energetic Alan Bagshaw dashed past dressed in a swimming cap and Speedo branded 'budgie smugglers'. He ran briskly down toward the government jetty before taking to the water to swim the return leg against the outgoing tidal current.

'Really, why would you?' uttered Sal, as she poured a second cup of tea, and pulled the collar up on her tracksuit top to ward off the chill on her neck.

Over at the private jetty they observed Joe Tucker's solitary figure strolling out quietly to survey the scene. A huge black cloud of cormorants took off in front of him as he approached the end of the landing. Several bright blue puffs of smoke emanated from Joe's whiskery face and drifted away on the morning breeze. John remarked on how unusual it was to see a man smoking a pipe these days. There was no sign of Jane. John raised an arm and waved to Joe in a gesture of silent salutation. Joe didn't reply, and John wondered whether it was simply because he didn't see John's distant greeting, or whether he'd chosen to ignore him.

By the time the Williams had finished their 'alfresco' meal, including John making a quick trip back to the cottage to fix a coffee for himself, the sun had risen high enough to begin stirring the boat people on the government jetty. One by one, pyjama clad figures, and others in lesser attire appeared from within the musty confines of their vessels. Some wandered landward in search of the composting toilets provided by the Parks people. Others busied themselves, wiping over dew-covered windows and airing out cabins while one couple could be seen collecting dishes from the previous night's supper eaten on the jetty. A single fishing rod glinted briefly in the sun as a line was cast out from the back of a boat. Then the comparative silence was interrupted by the distant drone of an outboard motor somewhere. The spluttering roar of an old tractor bursting into life could be heard over on the Scully land. Paradise was waking to greet the new day.

John rose from his chair and headed over to where Joe stood.

'I just want to catch up with Joe, Sal, before he disappears inside. Leave the tray and things, I'll bring them up on my way back.'

John quickened his step as he noticed Joe starting to wander back to his house. He wanted to see that Jane was alright and to tell Joe about Sal's sighting of Jane last evening on the track, and of seeing her hovering over the end of the landing.

'Joe!' he shouted. 'I just wanted a chat with you before you go in. Beautiful morning, isn't it?' John added, trying to put a positive tone to it all.

'Oh, hello Williams, I suppose it is. Was that Sal and you sitting by the lake before?'

'Yeah. I waved to you.' answered John. 'You obviously didn't see me.'

'Obviously.' growled Joe in a voice suggesting he'd chosen not to notice John's friendly gesture.

'Joe, I was a bit worried about Jane last night, and I didn't want to discuss it in front of her.'

'Well, you might as well follow me in then. Jane's asleep. She won't hear anything. She seems to sleep a lot these days does Jane.'

John followed Joe into the kitchen. The woodfire stove was going and sunrays penetrating the thin haze of wood smoke through the small kitchen window illuminated silvery wisps of steam that drifted up from a blackened kettle. Joe gestured to John to take a seat at the kitchen table.

'So, what's this about Jane?' asked Joe, placing his smouldering pipe down in front of him.

'I was just concerned that Jane got home alright yesterday evening. She was wandering about along our track, and later I think I saw her out on the jetty. Sal saw her too and thought she looked a bit lost. Anyway, you did ask me to keep an eye out for her, but obviously everything's OK.'

'Well, sort of.' hesitated Joe. 'She went missing. Must have been about the time you last saw her. After looking everywhere, I feared the Scully's had taken her away, so I went over and confronted Simon. It wasn't very pleasant. I probably shouldn't have called him a 'God bothering bastard'.' admitted Joe.

'The silly bugger got so excited he started to hop up and down on one leg. I thought the fool had stood on a nail or something. Then a couple of his nephews appeared, you know the so-called surgeon and the financial adviser, and that's when things really went bad. Scully reckoned the fact that I didn't know where Jane was just proved I was incapable of looking after her. I still thought that religious zealot must have Jane hidden in the house somewhere, so I tried to get past him and go inside. That's when that Aiden picked up a gun which was lying on the front porch and threatened to shoot me. Those bastards are barking mad I tell you.' continued Joe in an amplified voice. They ran me off the property at gun point. Threatened to shoot a hole in Emma too! It's no use going to the police. You know how the Scullys close ranks. It would be my story against all of theirs, and the locals here, be they coppers, council people or civilian folk have always been reluctant to take them on. They're bullies you know, always have been. Anyway, by the time I got back here I found Jane had come home and put herself to bed. She must have returned while I was over at Simon's.' concluded Joe.

John became aware of a quiet figure standing in the doorway that separated the kitchen from the bed/sitting room. The sound of Joe's bellowing voice had obviously woken her.

'Any chance of a cup of tea dear?' she enquired, apparently oblivious to the conversation between to two men.

'We've got a visitor.' remarked Joe, stating the obvious.

'Oh, hello there. It's John, isn't it?' Jane responded. 'You'll have to excuse me in my nightdress. I've only just got up.'

Jane entered the kitchen and sat down opposite John. Meanwhile Joe busied himself at the stove getting the tea ready. The sun shining through the glass on her face brought a spark of life to her previously blank expression. She ran her thin pale fingers through her thin greying hair like a bird preening itself.

'And how is your wife, John? Um Sal, isn't she?' Jane enquired.

'Yes Sal, Jane. You know Sal.' answered John. 'She said she saw you walking along our track last night. Didn't you see her?'

'I'm not sure John. Joe, did I see Sal last night?' enquired Jane.

'Apparently you did.' said Joe, placing the mugs and the teapot on the table next to the sugar bowl. But you're not to go wandering off again so late in the day. We were worried about you. And I don't want you over visiting your cousins Peta and Simon either.'

'Oh, he's such a fuss pot John.' exclaimed Jane. 'He knows I like to explore all the tracks and the properties when I get down here. It's not as if I don't know my way around the place.'

John sensed an improvement in Jane's cognitive state, and the more the conversation went along, the more engaged Jane appeared to become with the conversation.

'She seems to benefit from having people here to talk to John.' said Joe referring to Jane in the third person. 'She really picks up when there's someone different for her to talk to. I'd appreciate it if you and Sal called in to see her from time to time while you are here.'

John nodded as if in agreeance and deciding it was time to return home, got up from the table to rinse his mug out at the sink.

'Leave it there.' barked Joe. 'I'll deal with it later.'

Having said goodbye to Jane, John let himself out. The early morning freshness had thawed considerably by now, and what had started out as a cool breeze was now warm and soft. Stepping into the fresh air John felt somewhat relieved to be out in the open again. There was something about the dark interior of the Tucker cottage that had a depressing effect on him this visit. Perhaps it was the confronting nature of Joe's dilemma. Perhaps it was the effort to converse with Jane. Maybe it was simply the lingering smoke that hung in the kitchen from the wood stove.

Moving along the shore John took in the sights and sounds of the now busy waterway. The joyful squeal of children's voices that one might describe as 'beach music' rang out above the steady background buzz of numerous boats passing by. A sightseeing plane droned lazily somewhere overhead. In the distance, bright coloured beach towels and sunshades were strewn haphazardly over the sand either side of the government jetty. At the entrance to his track John stopped to pick up the breakfast things and reluctantly surrendered his spot to a group of day trippers who'd come across from Minamurra for a picnic. In a rare moment, he took note of Alan Bagshaw reclining on a banana lounge in the sun, relaxing while reading a book. Then, moving along he soon left behind all the colour and activity on the lake for the comparative quiet of the coastal scrubland. The warm redolence of the bush put John further at ease and the gentle rattling of tea-tree branches in the breeze played like 'bush music' in his ears. Striding briskly, the flip flapping of his thongs, made an evocative sound of summer. Unfortunately though, John's peaceful state of mind was short-lived.

Like a hawk descending on its prey, Simon Scully suddenly appeared to land on the track before him.

'We simply can't abide it, John. That's all there is to it. And now you know for yourself too, don't you.'

Simon's whole face was enlivened, from his bright beady bespectacled eyes to his spittle speckled mouth.

'Ah…sorry Simon, I'm not with you. What is it you mean?' said John, reeling back as if hit by a shockwave.

'I saw you there this morning with that man. Yes I did, so you can't deny it. You were in the Tucker place. Yes you were. He would have told you about last night. So you know, don't you?' asserted the fired-up Scully.

'Oh, you mean the visit you had from Joe last night?' answered John carefully, trying to slow the conversation down and think about how he was going to respond. He did mention something about going over to see you.' added John cautiously.

John was at pains to select his words carefully. He was acutely aware that anything he said Simon's ears would capture like a data entry being made into a police brief.

'The man assaulted me last night. Assaulted me! And for no good reason. And he's a blasphemer! Yes, a blasphemer! Can you imagine my cousin living with a blasphemer?' expounded Simon.

'But didn't he just go over to see if Jane was with you Simon?'

'Exactly! And now you've just proved my point, John. Haven't you!' pounced Simon.

John could feel his heart sink. It was fast becoming obvious, that anything he said to Simon, Simon would use to further trap him within the argument.

'You see Tucker was over at my place because he didn't know where Jane was. Lost her he had! She could have been anywhere…. even up at "All Smiles", God forbid. And she's only been under his care here for one day. One day! Luckily for me Andrew and Aiden showed up to show him some reason, otherwise who knows what would have happened. He's a violent man John. A violent man! And now, God forbid John, you are an accessory in the eyes of the law John.'

'Hey, it's nothing to do with me Simon. This is a family affair.' protested John. 'And remember, I'm at pains to remind you, I'm nothing to do with your family Simon.'

'Ah yes, but you are a witness, John. A prime witness!' replied Simon, with an expression on his face like a chess player who'd just put his opponent in 'check'.

'Simon, I haven't witnessed anything.' declared John.

'I'm sure you've seen more than you're admitting to John. I know you, you're an observant man. And aside from that, you've witnessed Joe's temper and heard his blaspheming firsthand so you would know I'd consider he's unsuitable to care for my cousin responsibly.' asserted Simon.

John was tempted to challenge Simon's claims with Joe's side of the story, but he knew he'd be drawn even further into the argument simply by mentioning Joe's account of what had transpired. Just admitting he had knowledge of Joe's side of the story would be incriminating enough, particularly the explosive accusations about being bailed up with the gun by the boys, threats to shoot a hole in his beloved boat and whether 'pushing' Simon to get past him amounted to Simon being 'assaulted'. Somehow, in a way John didn't fully understand, Simon had managed to back him into a corner and had dug him into a hole. John needed time out to think through the situation clearly, without the withering bombardment of Simon's verbal artillery.

'Simon, I can't talk any longer right now.' pleaded John. 'Sal is waiting for me up at the cottage to help turn the mattress over. We're re-organising the bedroom.' Any excuse to get away thought John.

'Well, this isn't the end of it John.' warned Simon. 'My goodness no, not the end of it! You'll be hearing more about it in the coming days. Do you know that? Yes, you will.' finished Simon......and with that, he strode off with his typically purposeful forward-leaning walk (hopefully John lamented), to a place a long way away.

John stepped into the kitchen where Sal was preparing some late morning tea. The cottage was still cool inside which seemed to help subdue his inflamed nerves. He decided not to mention his meeting with Simon to Sal, as he knew it would only embroil him in a further heated conversation.

'You look a bit pale John.' observed Sal looking up from a tray of fresh scones. 'Maybe you need to go back to the doctor'.

'I'm fine Sal. Perhaps I was a little taken back with Joe and Jane's situation just now.'

'She's alright then John?' Sal asked.

'Yeah, she's fine. She apparently wandered off for a while last night without Joe realising, but she eventually returned and put herself to bed. I had quite a bit of a chat with her, which she seemed to enjoy. You should call in and see her sometime. Maybe this afternoon when Frankie and I go fishing later. Joe seems to think a visit from you would do her good, you know, get the neurons connecting again.'

'I'll have to see how I feel. I'm a busy woman. You've left this place in a hell of a state while you've been on your own down here.' growled Sal, gesturing to the various parts of the cottage in need of tidying and cleaning.

John joined Sal on the outside decking for their morning tea. He was particularly fond of her scones served with strawberry jam and cream and didn't hold back when it came to indulging in an extra one, or maybe two.

'Well, you won't be needing any lunch after eating all that. Will you?' stated Sal, whisking the remaining food away from under John's nose.

John took on the appearance of a petulant kid who'd just lost his 'pet rock'. But rather than try and enter a plea for leniency, in the hope of perhaps just one more scone, he sought solace in the thought of his impending surf-fishing session with Frankie later that day.

To occupy his time pending Frankie's arrival, John busied himself readying the fishing gear he'd brought down with him from back home in Melbourne, a job he found pleasantly therapeutic. He cleaned down the rods with a damp cloth soaked in soapy water, serviced the reels, inspecting each one in turn, pulling them apart and lubricating all their moving parts. Then came the task of selecting the appropriate hooks and sinkers from his tackle box. He carefully assembled the rigs, paying particular attention to tying and tightening the knots and trimming the loose ends. It gave him something relaxing to focus on and took his mind off other things best left for another day.

Around mid-afternoon John strolled down to the estuary to see if there was any sign of Frankie. It was hot by now and the landscape on the other side of the inlet shimmered above the water. John flicked his thongs off, and the sand over which he walked, burned his feet. He waded a short way into the water and enjoyed the relief that the sensation of cool wet sand provided him. He stood there for quite some time, entertained by the water-borne activity. He watched Joe in the distance as he undertook a repair to the damaged cleat that Emma sustained during the earlier altercation with Simon's boat. He observed Rick Head a little closer, lying on the sand, seemingly fast asleep in the full sun, his brown torso glistening through a heavy layer of tanning oil. Next to Rick an equally brown and shiny Gloria lay on her back reading one of those 'coastal living' fashion magazines through a pair of oversized prescription sunglasses. A group of children plied the shallows, buckets and nets in hand chasing the many schools of tiny fish that darted about. Another group of younger children armed with buckets and plastic spades were busy digging a hole near the water's edge to construct a moat around their sandcastle fort.

Eventually John spotted a little blue dot on the horizon which he reasoned must be Frankie's runabout. As the little blue dot grew in size John could make out Frankie's shock of red hair above his colour coordinated rosy face. About halfway in, the bow of the boat dropped suddenly as the spluttering engine appeared to lose power. Because of the distance between John and the boat there was a short delay between what he could see, and the familiar sound of Frankie's high-pitched voice.

'You BASTARD!' bellowed Frankie.

By the time the words reached John's ears, he could already see the man feverously pulling the starter cord on the dead outboard. Every three or four pulls, a puff of black smoke would rise above the motor, then a moment later the sound of a muted splutter accompanied by another expletive from Frankie's mouth. Frankie's ability to personify mechanical objects amused John, especially Frankie's reference to their parentage. He also noticed another figure in the boat, sitting quietly up the front as if ignoring the theatre occurring up the back.

'Oh, that's good.' thought John. 'It looks like he's brought Faye with him. Sal will be pleased.'

Eventually Frankie's motor roared into life and created a smoke screen obliterating the horizon behind it. Frankie drove the boat, motor screaming on full throttle in John's direction.

It was as if he was punishing it for its bad behaviour. Frankie managed to hit the shallow water close to full speed. The runabout came to such an abrupt stop that Faye almost rocketed over the windshield onto the dry beach.

'You know my boat hates coming over here.' snarled Frankie as he jumped out, managing to bark his shin on the gunnel as he went.

'I think the boat just hates you.' thought John to himself.

'Hi Faye.' greeted John, ignoring the angry little Welshman standing next to him. 'Sal's up at the cottage. She'll be so glad to see you. It's been ages since you two last caught up.'

Frankie lent over the edge of the boat and hauled out a large ice chest.

'Here, take this up to the shack will you, while I do my business with that Dickhead.'

He lent over the edge of the boat again and this time lugged out Rick Head's generator. Neither of the two men had noticed Rick until he cleared his throat by way of announcing his presence. John felt embarrassed that Rick may have overheard Frankie's derogatory reference to his name, but Frankie obviously couldn't give a stuff. Gloria seemed to have made herself scarce. It was her usual habit to avoid Frankie whenever possible.

'Where do you want your generator?' asked Frankie.

'Up on the veranda if you'd be so kind Frank.' replied Rick. 'How did you go with it?'

'The bastard's rooted.' snapped Frankie. 'I've managed to get it going, but the rear seal's stuffed and the brushes are nearly worn out. So, it's up to you if you want to use it as a boat-anchor or a doorstop when it breaks down next time. Only I don't want to see it ever again.'

'Now, about the fridge.' Rick began to enquire.

'Yeah, yeah. I'll have a look at it after I take the 'genny' up to your house. I might have to come back down for some tools but.' muttered Frankie.

'All the fishing supplies are in the ice chest John. I'll grab me rods and the fishing creel on the way through and I'll see you when I see you, at your place.' continued the Welshman.

John left the heavy chest behind some bushes, while he accompanied Faye up to the cottage and retrieved the trolley to make moving the heavy chest easier.

He announced Faye's arrival calling out. 'Sal! There's someone here to see you.'

Then, leaving the two women to meet and greet, John took the trolley back down to the estuary to recover the ice chest.

Manoeuvring the chest onto the trolley John was surprised to see Frankie, already back by the shore.

'Aren't you meant to be looking at Rick's fridge Frankie?' asked John.

'Yeah, I looked at it.' replied Frankie bluntly.

'Well?'

'Well...... let's go fishing.' continued Frankie without offering any further explanation.

Frankie had an annoying habit of only ever providing the minimal amount of information in reply to a question. He'd often say 'Is it something you need to know, or is it something you'd just like to know? If it's the latter, then it's probably none of your business.'

This custom of Frankie's was something John had learned to expect, and as such there would be no point in asking further. It would be a matter of waiting for Frankie to volunteer the information during the course of normal conversation, should he choose to do so.

John led Frankie along the path, beyond his cottage and further up through the coastal tea-trees towards the sand dunes overlooking the expansive surf beach at the front of the block. A sea breeze tempered the heat from the sun but offered nothing to dull the glare from the brilliant white sand.

'We'll leave the esky up here in the shade.' announced Frankie. 'We don't want the beer getting too warm eh.'

Frankie lifted the lid on the ice chest and took out half a dozen cans placing them in his fishing creel. They descended the sand dune towards the water that lay immediately ahead of them. Frankie squinted against the glare, surveying the beach contours in search of a suitable fishing spot.

'Here's as good a place as any 'Johnny boy'.' announced Frankie, pointing his surf rod at the water directly in front of them.

'We don't want you having to trudge back too far to top up the beer supplies, do we?' he added, with a cheeky grin.

The two men set about organising their gear. John returned to the trolley a short distance back up the dunes and procured two fold-up camp chairs. Only when everything else was done did John ask Frankie where he'd put the bait.

'The bait? What bait?' said Frankie.

'The bait.' explained John. 'You do own 'Banister's Boat Bait and Auto'. You said the other day you'd bring everything.'

'Yeah, well I said I'd probably come over to drop a line in…. didn't say anything about actually catching fish. Did I?' taunted Frankie. 'Nothing worse than having to pull in fish while you're trying to enjoy a beer I reckon.'

Frankie's idea of fishing was creating an opportunity to sit down by the water, enjoy some peace, have a yarn and down a few beers. He couldn't see the sense in actually trying to catch a fish. If it's fish you want, he reasoned, it was much easier to get as many as you needed from the fish co-op, already cleaned and filleted.

John resigned himself to the fact that there'd be no bait forth coming from Frankie, but at the same time knew that Dieter would give him no end of teasing should he find out John had come home empty handed from his fishing efforts.

'I think I might have some old stuff left over from the freezer back home in Melbourne that I brought down with me.... a couple of pilchards and a bit of white bait. Better than nothing I guess.' lamented John.

'Well, if you're going back, you may as well bring another half dozen beers down from the esky. I'm feeling pretty thirsty in this sun.' said Frankie.

John made his way back to the cottage. It was only a short walk, but it annoyed him that Frankie knew he'd be expecting to catch fish, and only after he had set himself up on the beach and got comfortable, that Frankie would announce there was no bait.

Sal and Faye were outside on the decking enjoying afternoon tea and catching up on all the gossip. John didn't talk to them. He went straight to the fridge and started rifling through the freezer.

'What are you after John? I've just finished sorting the fridge out. I don't want you messing it up again.' called Sal looking in through the open door.

'I'm after the bait I had in here.' answered John, his head ensconced in the fridge.

'I put your stinky bait in the bin John. It stank the whole fridge out. Didn't you realise?' Sal asserted.

'Didn't Frankie bring the bait over?' called out Faye. 'Oh, he's a bugger, that man.' she continued.

John started sorting through the rubbish, and before long gingerly lifted out the odorous offerings he intended for the fish.

'When are you coming back in John? Faye has decided they're going to stay for dinner with us, so I need to know when to expect you both. It would be good to have some nice fresh fish too John, if you can manage it.'

'No promises Sal. I don't know that the fish will be overly tempted by this offering.'

John returned to the fishing spot to find Frankie was already into his third can.

'You've got a bit of catching up to do.' remarked Frankie, emitting a loud belch that blew his rosy cheeks out like two red balloons.

'By the way.' He continued. 'While I think about it, that bloke I was telling you about, you know, the one I said I brought across here a little while back, the one in the suit. Well, I spotted him down at the estuary just now as I was going up to the Head's, only he wasn't in his suit this time. Looked like he'd come off one of the boats. Anyway, 'Dick Head' reckoned he'd just been up to his place and made him an offer on his property. Reckons he asked Head if he thought anyone else might be interested in selling their land.'

'Did he say who he was?' enquired a keenly interested John.

'Nup.' answered Frankie in a dismissive tone. 'You'll have to ask Head.'

John baited up his line. The stale pilchard was so soft he had to wrap it up with some cotton thread to keep it from falling off the hook. Wading into the shore-break, he carefully cast his enticement out into the deep gutter just beyond the rollers. He made a mental note to see Rick first thing in the morning in the hope of finding out what this 'bloke' was all about. But for now, there was nothing more to do but to sit back, take in the sea air and enjoy Frankie's cold beer.

To John's surprise it wasn't long before there was some interest in his smelly offering. He managed to hook up and to his delight, landed a slimy mackerel. While these oily fish weren't regarded as much for eating, when cut into small pieces they provided excellent bait for Australian salmon.

The afternoon drifted on while the sun tracked slowly across to the western sky and closer to the horizon. Frankie sat back, comfortably settled in his camp chair, beer in hand with his empty surf-rod standing motionless in its rod holder. John was much more active, baiting up, running down to the shore break, casting out and retrieving in a continual cycle. A steadily growing pile of crushed cans lay strewn beside the Welshman. By some strange coincidence it seemed, every time John managed to land a fish, Frankie would want John to go and fetch another beer. What John didn't realise was that every time he turned his back to fetch another beer, Frankie would dip into the fishing creel and return the freshly landed fish back to the sea.

By day's end, the now deep red sun appeared to dip into the grey blue ocean. A thin slither of crescent moon timidly appeared above the Eastern horizon.

'I wonder what the poor people are doing?' exclaimed Frankie.

'This is so beautiful.' lamented John. 'Where else would you want to be at the moment I ask you? I just wish I'd brought my camera down.'

'Why would you want to do that?' asked Frankie. 'I can't see the point in taking your own photographs when you can just as easily get them from a magazine if you want.'

'But don't you ever feel you want to capture your memories, so you can look back on them later and re-live the magic moment?' replied John.

'Nup, never.' retorted Frankie. 'Nothing wrong with my memory. I don't need pictures for that.'

As much as John liked Frankie, his apparent complete lack of any romantic sentiment was just another side to him that irritated John. Perhaps the strongest bond between the two was one of mutual dependence. John relied on Frankie to provide him with mechanical services, gas and a secure place to park, while Frankie benefited from John's business, particularly when John came down to Paradise in the winter months when business was otherwise slow or almost non-existent. Frankie also considered John to be 'not completely stupid', something which he thought that many of his other customers to be.

'God must love stupid people; He made so many of them.' he'd say.

For someone who ran a service-orientated business, it surprised John to hear Frankie expound; 'Why do I have to like anyone? Do I look like a fucking people person?' Faye and Sal's relationship on the other hand, stood on a foundation of common interest and empathy.

In the last moments of the fading light, while there was still enough to see by, the fishermen decided it was time to pack up and head back to John's place. With a final loud belch Frankie struggled out of his chair, which by now had sunk considerably into the soft sand. He scooped up his empty cans and dropped them noisily into the open fishing creel on top of the few fish that John had caught, which hadn't been tossed back into the sea.

'Do you need a hand with the creel.' asked John. 'It must be fairly heavy with all those fish I brought in.'

'Nah, it's as light as a feather.' answered Frankie, not letting on about his ill doings.

Back at the cottage Sal and Faye had moved indoors. Warm lamp light danced delicately across the walls. Several pots boiled busily on the stovetop and the aroma of roasting potatoes seeped from the oven. The very last rays of the sun reflected off the sink and illuminated a small orange patch on the exposed ceiling boards.

'So, you've finally decided to come home.' said Sal to the boys. 'Did you catch anything?'

'I caught a glimpse of that Head woman in her bikini earlier.' slurred the cheeky and obviously inebriated Welshman.

'Frankie didn't, but I managed to get quite a few.' interjected John. 'Mainly salmon'.

'Ew…. salmon taste a bit strong for my liking.' announced Faye.

'In that case John, we might have the fish tomorrow and cook the steak tonight instead.' suggested Sal. 'But I'll let you two cook the meat outside on the barbeque. I don't want the cottage smelling of cooked meat.'

Frankie put his hand up in front of his mouth in an attempt to stifle a tipsy giggle. He knew that with John now cooking steak, the discovery of all the missing fish probably wouldn't be realised till after he'd left.

'What's so funny Frank?' snapped Faye. 'I hope you're not too drunk. You still must get us back safely across the water tonight. Have you remembered that?'

'It's not a problem Faye. I could find my way back blindfolded if I had to.' assured Frankie.

John lit the hurricane lamp, placed it beside the barbeque then went to gather some wood. Frankie pulled up a seat next to the fireplace and opened other can of beer for himself.

It wasn't long before a fire blazed brightly below the heavy iron hotplate. A sweet smell of tea-tree smoke rose into the still evening air then drifted away through the bush. Once the hotplate was sufficiently heated John poured a jug of water over it to sterilise and clean it down. Frankie finished his can and threw the empty container into the fire.

'What did you do that for?' exclaimed John.

'Not many people know this my friend, but you can actually burn aluminium. You just need the fire hot enough.' explained Frankie.

John was far from convinced, but knew there was nothing he might say that would have the slightest influence on Frankie's actions. And so, as the cooking commenced so did the number of charred cans collecting in the fireplace grow. Inside, the women were readying the table under lamplight, setting out the plates and cutlery in readiness. Sal had earlier picked some banksia flowers and hyacinth orchids and placed the floral arrangement in a vase in the centre of the table as a final table decoration. Apparently, the subtle ambiance was lost on Frankie as, when he burst in through the door, tray of sizzling meat in hand, Frankie blurted out; 'You'll need to get that bastard off the middle of the table (referring to the vase) to make room for the meat Sal.'

'Frank! No wonder we never get invited out for dinner. You've got no idea, have you?' commented Faye.

'It's alright Faye." said Sal diplomatically. 'Frankie, I thought we might put the meat dish on the kitchen bench and then we could all just help ourselves to what we wanted.'

'You'll still need to move the bastard but. It'll block our view of each other.' grated Frankie.

John took a back seat and kept his mouth shut. There was no point trying to reason with the Welshman when he was in 'full flight'. The two women acquiesced also and moved the offending arrangement to a mutually agreed position on the sideboard at the end of the table. For the next little while, the dinner group, with the exclusion of Frankie who sat simmering in his own juices, moved round the dinner setting helping themselves to the various bowls of vegetables and meat. Faye filled a plate for Frankie with an extra portion of steak before serving herself with much smaller portions. John delved into the lower compartments of the sideboard and retrieved a couple of bottles of wine for the table, one white and one red. Frankie was the only 'red-drinker' amongst them, so after pouring three glasses of white for himself and the girls, John left the bottle of claret in front of Frankie where he could help himself.

The passage of dinner was negotiated largely with small talk …. local town gossip in the main. The subject was changed as required when Frankie had some derogatory remark to say about a thing or an individual at the centre of the conversation.

The evening moved on quickly and soon after the plates had been emptied and stacked in the kitchen Faye remarked; 'Oh dear is that the time? Frank you've got work in the morning. It's time we got going back to Minamurra, if you think you can manage it.'

Frankie, having consumed nearly the entire contents of the bottle of red, in addition the earlier beers, looked ready to settle in for the night.

'You can both stay over if you think that's safer Faye. We've got the guest room made up. It wouldn't be any bother.' Sal offered.

'That might be a good idea, Frank.' suggested Faye.

'No.' interjected Frankie. 'It'll only take us fifteen minutes to get back. Too easy.'

John shuffled around in the kitchen and returned with a torch. 'Here Frankie, in that case you'll probably need this then.'

Frankie declined the offer of the torch on his earlier premise that he could find his way back to Minamurra blindfolded. He also declined John's offer to at least shine them down the track to the boat.

Faye and Frankie stepped out into the night, and it wasn't long before they left the illumination provided by the hurricane-lamp hanging on the porch. A thin crescent moon, still low in the sky, offered little to shine their way. Frankie, leading a less confident Faye into the darkness, may as well have been blindfolded.

Back in the cottage, John and Sally were immersed in the still silence of the night. Thinking the Bannisters must be well on their way, John ventured outside to check that the fire was extinguished and to tidy up the barbeque area. He noticed Frankie had taken off and left the ice chest, his fishing creel and all his rubbish behind. Remembering the fish were still in the creel, John grabbed a bucket to claim his catch, only to discover under the empty cans, most of the fish had gone. He was about to vent out his disapproval of Frankie's behaviour, when suddenly two dark shapes appeared from the bushes on the edge of the property.

'Is that you two Frankie and Faye?'

'Frankie's got us lost!' called out Faye.

'No I haven't.' blurted out a defiant Frankie. 'We just took a wrong turn, but we're fine now.'

'You sure? What about your Esky and your fishing gear? And by the way, where did all my fish go?' asked John.

'Yeah, we're all good......I'll get it tomorrow sometime.' said the voice in the dark, ignoring the last question about the missing fish.

The stillness and silence returned to the bush for a little while. Then shortly after, carried up from the inlet on the night air, John could the hear the familiar sounds of Frankie's repertoire of expletives, then the stuttering sound of an outboard motor. John returned indoors to help Sal with what was left of the tidying up, and while they chatted, they became increasing aware of the outboard motor sound which continued to burble away in the background.

'I think I'd better check on what's happening.' said John after a while.

John grabbed the torch and made his way to the estuary. The lights of Minamurra twinkled in the distance through the pitch-black night. He could hear a conversation out on the water. He was sure it was Faye he heard asking Frankie how much longer before they arrived back in town.

'We're nearly there.' barked a male voice.

'But we don't seem to be getting any closer Frank. Are you sure this is the right way?'

John directed the torch beam out over the black water. The light picked up the back of the Banister's boat. Frankie had the motor roaring away, unaware the leg of the outboard had not fully depressed into the water. The torch beam off the white foam as the propeller churned ineffectively just under the surface. John yelled out to the boat, hoping his voice might be heard above the din of the noisy engine.

'Frank, turn the engine off. I can hear someone calling us.' shouted Faye.

The engine dropped down to an idle. John yelled out again and alerted Frankie to the fact that the prop wasn't submerged sufficiently in the water.

'You bastard!' shouted Frankie, referring to the tilt lever which had jammed.

Several loud metallic bangs rang out, then the clunk of gears engaging once more. Eventually the boat took off, roughly in the direction of the Minamurra lights. John waited by the shore until the noise had subsided sufficiently to indicate the Banisters were finally making headway. He turned away from the estuary and headed back, unaware all the fuss had woken most of the boat people on the government jetty.

The following morning John awoke with the sun shining on his face. He squinted through the window scratching his thick head. Although he'd consumed far less than his fishing companion the evening before, it was still enough to leave him with a decent hangover. He dragged on a pair of shorts and made his way to the inlet. He had a nagging thought in the back of his mind that Frankie's boat may have reappeared. But he had nothing to fear, there was no sight of the wayward Banisters or their little boat.

Back home Sal had arisen and was busy making coffee and toast. John decided he'd make an early trip to Minamurra for supplies and to return Frankie's bits and pieces while he was there. He also remembered what Frankie had mentioned about the mystery man, and how he was supposedly interested in the Paradise properties. He was also keen to call in at the Head's on the premise of asking if they wanted anything from town, while at the same time enquiring what business the man may have had with Rick.

John loaded up the trolley with Frankie's stuff along with some rubbish bags to be dropped in the dumpster at the fisherman's wharf. He wheeled the trolley out onto the private jetty and parked it next to his boat. Dieter had also come down to the jetty, his large presence taking John by surprise.

'I saw you and dat Banister bloke fishing on the der beach yesterday. So, show me der big fishes you caught.' taunted Dieter.

'We threw most of them back. Frankie took the rest home last night.' answered John defensively.

'Sure.' replied Dieter in an unconvinced tone.

John, not wishing to take the conversation any further on the subject of fish, attempted to divert Dieter's attention by asking if he need anything brought back from Minamurra.

'Sure, der truth John.' answered Dieter with a cheeky smile.

John left it at that and took off for Rick's place. As per usual, the early warning system activated while he was still some distance from the house, and he was forced to run the gauntlet of ear piecing yaps and snapping teeth. Gloria appeared at the door, still in her night dress.

'Good morning John, you're out visiting early.' greeted Gloria, seemingly unperturbed about being seen in her scanty nightwear.

'Rick's still eating his breakfast but do come in.' she continued. Did that Banister man go up and see you yesterday afternoon John? You know he called in here to look at our fridge. All it needed was the pilot light adjusting and he charged Rick fifty dollars for two minutes work. The man's got no scruples.'

After hearing what Gloria had just said, John was reticent to admit seeing Frankie, but suspecting she may have observed the two of them together when Frankie arrived, thought it safe enough to say Frankie had dropped in with some beer and bait for him. Anyway, in light of the rumours about Paradise land being acquired, he was keen to learn what information Rick had on the mystery man.

'Rick, I just called in on my way over to town to see if you needed anything, but I was also wondering if you had a visitor yesterday. Frankie mentioned seeing a chap he'd brought across some time ago, who he said had called in here and made you an offer on your property. Is that right?'

'We did have a chap call in yesterday as a matter of fact, didn't we Gloria.' replied Rick.

'Did he say he was off one of the boats?'

'That's what he claimed.' said Gloria. 'I didn't like him at all. He was a pushy little man. Asked if we would be interested in selling, then when Rick suggested a price, he made a sort of 'scoffing' sound and told us we were dreaming. Said all the properties would be worth a lot less than we thought. Something about it being remote from the township…fire risk, or something. Anyway, we told him we weren't interested, so that was that as far as we were concerned.'

'Did he say who he was though?' asked John.

'He had something to do with Real Estate or property development I think.' piped up Rick. He didn't exactly say that, but it was inferred on his business card. Unfortunately, I think we may have burnt it. Sorry John.'

'You may still get to see him John. added Gloria. 'He said something about 'Did we know of any other property owners here who might consider selling?' But really, he didn't exactly look like the type of person who'd fit in here.'

Far from providing John with some reliable information and assurance, the visit to the Heads only served to niggle at him more. Something didn't seem right.

As John went to let himself out, he managed to step on one of the dogs again, sending the three howling and snarling while they took cover behind Gloria's bare scaly legs. Arriving at his boat, he threw in the fishing stuff and the garbage and motored out on the water as quickly as he could. Rounding the government jetty, the boat lizards were already out catching the early sunrays. As he cruised past, he could hear snippets of deck-chatter, which was largely about what the commotion on the lake was last night. The theories that were expounded varied from it being a dispute between two commercial fishermen, to a domestic between two drunken boaties. Someone even suggested it might have been murder being done.

Somehow John felt relieved to be clear of Paradise for a bit. The property acquisition thing, Simon Scully's badgering and Dieter's teasing all seemed to weigh on his mind while he was there. But the body of water that now stretched between his boat and the land, afforded him a sense of separation.

John's first stop was to drop off the rubbish in the council dumpster near the end of the jetty. Then there was Frankie's stuff to hand back, pick up another gas bottle, and retrieve his car from the compound.

Arriving at the servo, John found Frankie busy out the front arguing with a customer. Faye was in the shop going over the books.

'How did you go coming over last night Faye.' asked John.

'It was a bloody nightmare.' replied Faye, who rarely swore, if indeed saying 'bloody' were to be considered swearing. 'We ran aground three times. Then we ran out of petrol in the middle of the channel, and Frankie had trouble swapping the fuel line over to the fresh tank. Finally, if that wasn't the worst thing, Frankie somehow managed to get the mooring line wrapped around the prop just as we were in reach of the first landing at the beginning of the road. He had to jump out of the boat into chest deep water and pull the boat into shore, then we had to walk the rest of the way to the shop, him drenching wet and shivering with cold. He's only just returned from bringing the boat back up now.'

John passed Frankie as he drove out from the servo.

'So how did you go last night?'

'Sweet! No dramas John. A couple of small issues, nothing too serious. As I told you; Could have found my way back blindfolded.'

'Glad to hear Frankie. We were a bit concerned when you left, but obviously all good in the end, eh.'

John continued on his way. First up was the general store where he found Jeff Evans busily stacking shelves, signature lolly in mouth. As usual, John's shopping trolley ended up with much more than was on the original list.

Meeting at the till, Jeff rolled his lolly to one side of his fat cheek and greeting John, asked with the usual; 'And how are we today?'

John noticed a trickle of sweat roll down the store owner's temple, such was the effort of unpacking boxes and filling shelves. Jeff pulled out a bright handkerchief and lightly patted his face dry, before doing his dancing finger act over the buttons on the cash register.

'Can I interest you in the chocolates today? They're on special, two for four dollars fifty.'

'No thanks.' replied John politely.

'The crisps then?'

'No thanks.'

'Boiled lollies?'

'No.'

'Well then, that will be sixty-two dollars and twenty cents. Let's call it sixty-two shall we?' uttered Jeff while skilfully changing cheeks with his lolly.

Next on the list was the butchers, to replace the meat they had been eaten the night before, then finally the pub for wine and beer, where John took extra care not to make eye-contact with any of the fishermen who were in for an early drink.

John returned to his boat and began loading the shopping. Paradise was very much at times about loading stuff into boats, carrying loads up the track and back to the cottage, and lugging all manner of things back on the return trip to Minamurra, when it was finally time to head homeward at the end of their stay. Frankie was there at the jetty too, giving an outboard a test run.

'By the way John, that bloke I was telling you about. You know, the one I took over your way earlier this year. The one I said I saw there yesterday. Well, he was over here this morning out the front of the shop talking to some other blokes. Looked like they were some kind of businessmen.'

'Could you hear what they were talking about?' enquired John.

'Nar, I wasn't that interested. Told them they could have their little meeting elsewhere 'cause they were blocking the driveway, so they pissed off.'

'Well, let me know if you hear anymore won't you. With all that talk about land acquisition and him having an interest in buying over at Paradise, there seems to be something shifty going on, but no one seems to know what.'

Heading back to Paradise John mulled over in his mind if there could be any connection between this mysterious 'person of interest' and the wider Scully family. He doubted the local real estate agents would have any knowledge, for surely, they would have indicated some interest from any 'would be' buyers. Likewise, if one of the government agencies were looking to move people off the land, surely by now they would have shown their hand. He was also aware certain members of the original Scully family still held strong beliefs in the Adonai-Shomo philosophy, and in their rights to the original Paradise selection. But he was obviously reluctant to approach Simon with his concerns, and as for the other Scully members, well they were even more difficult to deal with than Simon. Reclusive and fanatical in their belief in the so called 'Truth', many of Simon's siblings, nephews and nieces had made no effort in the past to integrate with the rest of the Paradise community, and in fact seemed to discourage any contact.

The last week hadn't exactly gone how John would have liked it to have been, but his foot was so much better, and the weather was good; 'So why let this issue, which is probably nothing, spoil my time here?' he reasoned.

Chapter Six

The Night Stalker

*Rev. 21:27 "The abominable, and murderers,
and whore mongers, and sorcerers, and idolators,
and all liars, shall have their part in the lake
which burneth with fire and brimstone:
which is the second death."*

It was close to lunchtime when John got back to the cottage, laden with the shopping.

'How did you go over at town?' greeted Sal. 'And don't go inside with your shoes on.' she continued. 'I've just washed the floors trying to get rid of that terrible smell you left in here when I arrived. So, did Faye and your alcoholic friend make it back alive?'

'Yes, they're both fine, although it sounded like they had a few issues on their way home. The boat people down the jetty were still talking about all the fuss on the lake last night when I came past just now.'

'I don't know why you encourage that man to come over here. He's a bad influence on you. A bit fuzzy in the head today are we then?' taunted Sal.

John could sense Sal's mood wasn't conducive to sympathetic conversation, and whether it was the remnants of his hangover, or the bad feeling he harboured in relation to the 'mystery man', he wasn't feeling particularly hungry anyway, so rather than enquiring timidly about lunch he decided a good long walk along the ocean beach might be a better option, considering the current circumstances.

'Then don't expect anything to eat when you get back. The kitchen will be closed.' added Sal with a parting remark.

As he set out along the open beach, the fine white sand squeaked under each laboured step. Parallel to his own tracks, other footprints, further apart and deeper, suggested Alan Bagshore had paced along earlier on his morning run. The Ninety Mile beach stretched ahead of him, seemingly forever. He wondered how far Bagshore's tracks would go before they turned back or in toward the coastal scrub. A brisk sea breeze tempered the heat of the sun and the constant washing in and washing out of the waves completed this pleasant and uncomplicated picture. The salty air helped to clear John's head, and his thoughts drifted with greater ease as he found a comfortable walking rhythm.

The ceaseless breaking of the waves along the shore and the simplistic vista of sand, sea and sky combined to lull John into an almost hypnotic trance, and it was probably over an hour before he realised how far along the beach he'd wandered. Now at least five kilometres from Paradise, he felt as if he could be the only living sole on earth. Soothed by the sense of total isolation and freedom John shed his cloths and continued to walk on, naked to the world. He wandered into the shallows and indulged in the pleasure of feeling the surging tide washing over his bare feet. This was truly what being in Paradise was all about.

Despite drifting into this euphoric state, a nagging feeling soon began to overtake John's sense of wellbeing, a feeling that he was being watched. He glanced back to see how far back along the beach he'd left his cloths, but the object that caught his attention was not of clothing but that of a dark sinister looking figure crouched in the sand dunes just above him.

'Oh shit!' yelled a startled John involuntarily.

'You nearly scared the crap out of me!' he continued, addressing a wild looking aboriginal man, who seemed to have appeared from nowhere.

The wiry black man, wild hair and dressed in a khaki shirt and frayed denim shorts stood up and laughed at John balefully.

'What you frightened of eh, 'rudie' man?' the black fella taunted, his pearly white teeth braking through a board open smile.

John instinctively closed his legs in a pigeon-toed manner and bowed over, holding his hands in a protective cup in front of his shrinking genitals.

'You look so funny man!' said the beaming black. 'What you doing way up here?'

John, trying to compose himself, and with as much authority as he could muster replied, with a wavering voice; 'Looking for some peace and privacy. And I may well ask. 'What are you doing here?'

'I live up these parts. My mob belong to the Guniakurnia people. This is my place for peace and privacy! You come up from Scully's place eh.'

'Paradise.' corrected John, stepping forward and straightening up to his full height defiantly.

With that the black man's demeanour changed suddenly. The broad smile evaporated, and the previously smiling eyes focused on John with a fiery glare.

'You call it what you like then fella. It's a bad place now, and about to get worse for all you Scully mob.'

'I'm sorry, I didn't catch your name, but I'm not a Scully. I bought my place from one of Scully's relatives some time ago.' the still naked John replied.

'They don't know the difference. They don't care ...... my ancestors. Scully people did terrible things to them a long time ago. Now they want revenge. Even I don't go down there no more.'

With that the black man, began to tell his story; 'Down there was my people's place, and when the Scully mob arrived, my people were even happy to share because there was plenty of game, plenty of fish and Scullys didn't get on with the town people just like my people didn't. Everything was OK in the start, but part of that land Scullys occupied was sacred. Many of my ancestors, old men and women, and even kids who died there over the years before Scullys, were buried in them sand-hills overlooking the sea. The Scully people cleared the land, including the scrub that grew on the dunes. They pushed my people off that land, further out into the bush past that 'All Smiles' place they made. They dug up many of the remains at rest in the burial site and souvenired the skulls. Soon, without the scrub to hold the sand, the storms came and washed the sand hills into the sea. What remained of my people's burial grounds were washed away, their bones and spirits lost to the sea. It is said that every so often, when king tides come in at night and the wind blows from the south, the spirits of the young and old come in with the flood to search for their proper resting place. They want their land back. The spirits are very angry with the Scully mob and bad things happen to those who are there at that time. It's a bad place to be till the spirits drift out with the tide again.

It's been about sixty years since my ancestors came back in on a king tide while white fellas were there. Bad things happened to Scullys then, and this time they may not be happy to return to the sea. You lot should get off the land now, for good.' warned the animated black fella.

John simply stood there blinking. He wasn't sure what to say. Then, briefly turning away from the stranger, staring out to sea for a moment in an attempt to try and unpack what had just transpired, John spun back with finger pointed to deliver his rebuttal. But the stranger had gone. He thought momentarily about trying to follow the man back into dunes, but remembering he was still embarrassingly naked, instead turned on his heels and began what was to be a long trudge home. The tide had come in somewhat during the course of his walk and his discarded clothes, initially thought to have been left safe above the high-water mark were spread over several hundred meters of shore break drifting languidly back and forth in the wash. John pulled on in his wet sandy rags, the chill and eventual chafing adding to his irritation as he stomped his way doggedly home along the beach.

It was after three when John appeared at his front door.

'Look what the cat dragged in.' remarked Sal to Susan Weeks, who had called in for a visit. 'Don't think you're coming inside looking like that.'

'You look like you've been for one hell of a walk.' added Susan. 'Did you fall in the water?'

'Did I ever tell you; never turn your back on the sea.' replied John, trying to deflect the question.

It was a relief to have Susan there. Without company, Sal would have surely served up a real grilling, and John was reticent to disclose his encounter with the dark stranger up the beach. He needed time to try and make sense in his own mind of the un-nerving experience. It was well known that the activities of young Albert and William Scully in the late 1800's, apart from collecting aboriginal artefacts from exposed gravesites, also included collecting skulls and selling them to a local dentist for pocket-money. But the idea of vengeful lost spirits drifting in from the sea was something surely no-one would take too seriously, so it was something perhaps better not shared with anybody else, at least for the time being. John could just imagine Dieter's reaction for instance, on being told the story. He could just imagine Dieter saying; 'Sounds like dat bloke took you for a 'Patsy' Johnny boy. If you believe any of dat, you probably believe in der fairies at der bottom of der garden.'

Yes, better not shared for now, but disturbing never-the-less. One thing for sure, thought John: 'Stuff long walks up the beach for some time.'

Still, he wondered what Simon Scully might make of it.

'You'd better let him in.' a consolatory Susan said. 'He looks totally spent. Look at his pallor, poor chap.'

'Well, if he's overdone it, I can't help that. He can be his own worst enemy you know. Better come in then, but for God's sake clean yourself up, we do have a visitor, in case you hadn't noticed.'

While the women chatted idly on, John did his best to keep out of the way. He busied himself cleaning and refuelling the kero-lamps, splitting some kindling and lighting the old copper outside to heat water for a much-needed hot shower, together with any other small jobs he could think to do in preparation for the evening. Susan left before dinner time, and after an early evening meal of what remained of the catch of salmon John, feeling decidedly done in, opted for an early night, while Sal quietly read a book under lamplight.

Whether, because of the day's events, or the fact he was over-tired, or more probably the combination of both, he drifted into a restless sleep. That night he tossed and turned through countless shadowy dreams. A confusion of thoughts and actions crowded his mind, and he woke often in fits and starts. In one dream he found himself wandering embarrassingly naked around Paradise, going door to door asking if anyone wanted supplies in Minamurra, while at the same time searching for his wet clothes, which he could never find. In another dream which repeated over and over, he was desperately digging holes trying to re-bury skeletal remains in the sand dunes, but as fast as he could dig, the sandy soil kept caving in. In common to all the dreams, he found himself under the shadow of the black man, those fiery eyes and glistening white teeth hauntingly vivid in their apparent reality.

In his final awakening soon after dawn, he clambered out of bed from beneath the overheating doona that stifled his sweaty body. He struggled to emerge out of the mental fog that had set in during the long night. Only after moving outside into the crisp morning air could he regain some sense of engaging back with reality.

'I think you need to take it easy today, John.' said Sal, as she prepared a light breakfast.

'I think you tried to do too much yesterday. Heavens knows why you went on such a long walk up the beach after shopping in town. Then you came home in a state, hardly talked to our guest and later kept me awake all night with your tossing and turning. It's not fair John!'

Intending to try and explain his behaviour the day before, together with his concerns over the security of their land holdings, and of course his encounter with the black man, John decided on reflection that it would be all too hard. And anyway, perhaps he was blowing everything out of proportion. Maybe he was reading far too much into what he had seen and heard over the past couple of weeks and overthinking it. There was certainly no direct connection, or hard evidence to suggest anything was awry with the future of Paradise, just that gnawing feeling that something was changing under the covers.

But, in the bright sunlight and with a hot coffee consumed, he managed to put aside the dark thoughts and get on with enjoying the amenity Paradise provided him.

Following a perfect lazy day, a peaceful evening descended quietly over the land. The Williams dined outside on the decking. The warm lamplight created a cosy glow in an otherwise cool moonlit night. They shared a bottle of wine over a more relaxed conversation. Soft, comfortable chatter drifted well into the evening, and by bedtime John was feeling, for once in a while, relaxed and at peace with the world again.

Around midnight however a strange noise roused him from a deep slumber. At first he didn't know what it was, only that it had woken him. Noises and things that go 'bump' in the night were not unusual in Paradise. Possums, hog-deer, kangaroos and other nocturnal creatures proliferated long after the day-dwellers had settled in for the evening. A network of spidery tracks formed random lace patterns through the scrub, along which the night dwellers noisily scuttled or thumped in search of food, company or shelter. Waterfowl, nightjars and the occasional owl could often be heard calling out their soulful night cries, which would echo through the stillness. At this time of year also, noises from the boat people were not uncommon, a raised voice or a late-night party tune might be heard drifting up from the water. One of John's early morning pastimes was scouting through the scrub looking for tell-tale tracks in the sand, little clues by which he might identify what creature had passed through and woken him the previous night.

John raised his head from the pillow and strained to hear. Nothing....... silence, save the distant background roar of the surf on the ocean beach. But then, there it was again briefly. A child's voice perhaps? Someone giggling? John slid out of bed quietly so not to wake the rhythmically breathing Sal beside him. He felt round for the torch, pulled on a pair of shorts, and slipped quietly outside. The darkness enveloped him like a dank heavy blanket. The dull torch-beam struggled to penetrate the sea mist which shrouded the bush in a ghostly veil. The usually friendly environs took on a cold unwelcoming appearance that night. Silence once more, save the sound of his own laboured breathing. John held his breath, straining to pick up the source of the noise in the darkness. He clicked off the half flat dolphin torch. Adjusting his eyes to the darkness he scanned the ghostly silhouettes of the tea trees which stood out against the faint diffused moonlight. Then, there it was again, a high-pitched childlike giggle coming from somewhere down the track. Yes, a child or perhaps even a woman giggling for sure! As John moved cautiously in the direction of the sound and toward the inlet, he felt the dewy sand beneath his bare feet and wondered who would be out wandering around in the damp of a misty night. He shivered briefly, perhaps from the cold or perhaps from his nervousness.

'Hello?' he called out, feebly at first.

'Hello there?'

No answer.

'Hello?' he repeated cautiously, but a little louder, venturing slowly towards the inlet.

John reached the water's edge. The inlet lay out in front of him, black in emptiness and silence. The mist-shrouded boats spread along the shoreline to the government jetty all sat still and silent and in darkness. Nothing stirred, save the brief rustle of a night breeze which sent a chill up John's bare back and caused him to shiver again. Then the noise could be heard once more. This time it came from back towards the cottage. He retraced his steps, slowly shining the torch along and to either side of the path. He was not calling out now but listening intently. Ahead of him the shadowy shape of the cottage stood there in the dark, still and silent like the foreshore. But then, there it was again, from somewhere up the ocean track this time. John ventured forward with a little more sense of purpose, for what if it was some poor soul wandering around lost in the bush? They'd need to be found and brought to safety.

'Hello? Over here!' John called, time and time again.

He followed the track all the way onto the beach. It was a full tide and the dark sea appeared restless and gloomy.

But like before, as he moved toward the sound, nothing. Then suddenly it came to mind; What if it's Jane wandering around?

John continued to pursue the sound for some time, but with every attempt to track it down, as he moved in, it allusively seemed to be coming from yet another place again. Only when he started to feel decidedly chilled and the beam from the trusty Dolphin torch had almost reduced to a dull glow, that John finally decided to check on Joe Tucker's house for any sign that Jane may be missing. It was well after midnight and by now the promise of some stronger light from the late rising moon had vanished as brooding clouds gathered in the eastern sky to mantle the land with a feeling of iniquity. He made his way awkwardly through the bushes in the darkness, at times forced to re-trace his steps when he unwittingly stumbled down an opening in the bushes that led to a dead end. Eventually, perhaps with some good luck, he found himself once again on the main path that would lead him to Joe Tucker's place. Along the way he was sure he could still hear children's voices far behind as if mocking him for his pathetic attempt to find them.

Well aware of Joe's short fuse, John was reluctant to disturb him unnecessarily, particularly at this ungodly hour. However, it would be equally unforgiving not to alert him should Jane indeed be out alone in the middle of the night. John crept around the outside of Joe's place as quietly as he could. He peered gingerly into each window to see if there were any signs of movement or life inside. Finally, he made his way onto the front porch. There was no way he could prevent the old boards from creaking, but moving as quietly and as slowly as one could, he hoped his presence would not be detected. He leaned forward and carefully pressed the latch on the front door to see if it had been left unlocked, perhaps indicating that someone had left the house without thinking to close it properly.

Contrary to what John had anticipated, instead of the door resisting his pressure, or acquiescing with a subtle inward movement, it was almost wrenched out of his hand.

'What the bloody Christ in hell are you up to you bugger?' barked an animated Tucker, the door flying open, his anger accentuated by the dull radiance of John's torch in his face.

'You're lucky I didn't blow your fucking head off John! This is the sort of lowdown antic Scully would try to play on me, you bastard......I never expected this from you. Fuck off or I'll do you some serious harm.'

Stunned by the sudden and unexpected threat from Tucker, John just stood there agog with his mouth dropped open for a time. Then, remembering he was half naked, saved only by the hurriedly thrown on shorts to which the fly had been left undone, this wasn't a good look. He felt seriously vulnerable.

'I...aaah, I.' muttered John, in an attempt to try and explain himself.

'You heard me, Williams! Fuck off!' interjected the infuriated old man.

As much as John desperately wanted to clarify the reason for his presence, in the face of Joe's overwhelming tirade, the best he could manage was to stumble backwards apologising profusely and suggesting that it might be better if he tried to explain everything in the morning. So eager was he to get out of Joe Tucker's face that he spun round and turned smack into a veranda post, further accentuating his sense of vulnerability.

'I was worried about Jane.' he blurted as a parting gesture.

'Whatever...keep moving!' came the final angry response from within the shadows.

The now injured John, bloodied nose and bruised eye arrived back at the cottage to cop a second barrage.

'Where the hell have you been?' demanded Sal. 'I wake up.... no John. Crawling around in the dark looking for the torch...no torch. What's going on John? You've been acting weird for the past couple of days.'

'I want to go home Sal' he declared. 'I've had enough of down here for a while.'

'You can't go home; I've only been here for a short time and you're not going to leave me on my own. Anyway, you've always loved being here.'

John rattled around for some matches, lit a lamp and put the kettle on. There was no point in going straight back to bed now, and in the reassuring light he figured it was time to share what had plagued his mind, if Sal was prepared to listen. The pair sat in opposite chairs either side of the light while John worked his way through all the sharp edges that prodded his thoughts.

He told of the chit chat in Minamurra the week before Sal's arrival, the mystery man Frankie had spoken of and who had shown an interest in Rick's property. He worked his way through all these separate things, till finally he spoke of his encounter with the black fella.

'That doesn't explain were you've been just now. And how did you managed to get a bloody nose?'

'I heard some noises outside a bit earlier. It sounded like someone might have been wandering around in the bush. I went over to Joe Tucker's house to see if Jane had perhaps wandered off without Joe knowing and got lost. Joe caught me at his front door. I think he thinks I might have been spying on him. He was furious. I didn't even get the chance to explain what I was doing before he sent me packing.'

'I can totally understand that; You, half naked sneaking around in the middle of the night. Really John!'

'I guess I'll have to see him in the morning and explain everything. Perhaps I'll wait until I catch him on the jetty though. I don't think going to his front door again would end well. Hopefully he will have simmered down a bit by then. I've never encountered a man so angry!'

'I think you've got it all a bit out of whack.' said Sal, in a conciliatory tone. 'Let's talk about it more in the morning. I'm sure ever thing will be OK.'

Sal returned to bed, happy to leave John by the lamp with his thoughts. John felt a huge sense of relief having got it off his chest, and after reflecting on the night's events, was content with leaving things there for now and return to bed also. He lay back, took in a deep breath, to chance he might drift off into sleep. But what was that? A teasing little giggle came in through the window once more, from somewhere outside.

'Did you hear that, Sal?'

But Sal was already asleep.

Despite his interrupted sleep that night, John was keen to get out at first light and search for clues that might reveal the source of the 'voices' that had taunted him.

Once outside in the daylight he was relieved to observe that the bushland appeared friendly and inviting once more. He retraced his steps from the night before, carefully studying the sandy ground for imprints or markings that might disclose who or what had been there during the hours of darkness. He followed the tracks all the way to the beach and back down to the inlet, searched the clearings where he'd detoured into the tea trees, but the only evidence of someone having been there was his own footprints.

Later, after breakfast John returned to the inlet. He was hoping to catch Joe Tucker away from his house, who as part of his usual morning routine, would often wander out to the landing to check on his beloved 'Emma'. John hovered nervously under a grove of casuarinas just back from the water and waited for Joe to appear so that he might make his entrance, arriving as if just by coincidence to be at the lake. He shuffled awkwardly back and forth in the sand for what seemed an eternity before Joe finally made his appearance.

'I can see you Williams, skulking over there under those trees.' growled Tucker.

'Oh, hi there Joe!' called John, trying to act nonchalantly.

Joe ignored John's greeting and busied himself adjusting the mooring lines on his boat.

'Joe, about last night.'

'Williams, did I say I wanted a conversation with you?'

Joe turned his back on John and started moving toward his cottage, but John, desperate to pursue what might be his only opportunity to explain his nocturnal visit, hurried after him.

'Joe, can you wait a minute? Be fair; at least allow me to state my case.'

Joe hesitated. 'Well, I've never been accused of being un-fare, but make it quick. I've got better things to occupy myself with than pander to you, you sneaky bugger. And no need to come any closer to the house you prick. You already crossed the line last night John Williams.'

Trying his best to compose himself, John told Joe of the strange noises and of his concern that it may have been Jane out wandering alone and reminded Joe that it was he who had asked him to keep an eye out for her, as she was prone to wandering. John tried hard to assert his story, but found great difficulty with making eye contact, such was Joe Tucker's intimidating, glowering stare. He imagined Joe's laser beam eyes piercing his forehead probing the depths of his mind in search of the truth.

'The funny thing though Joe.' persisted John, aware he was taking liberties with Joe's time by now. 'I searched around this morning for any signs of tracks in the sand and nothing, save some wombat scratchings and a few wallaby tracks!'

'Did it ever occur to you it may have been a possum calling after a mate, or some bird chortling .... and you, out on a wild goose chase, so to speak?'

Then it suddenly came to mind about his encounter with the black fella way up the beach, the talk of the spirits coming in with the high tide and all of that, which he now foolishly chose to share with Joe at this point of time.

'Would it surprise you to know John that the Scully's are still on the nose with the local Aborigines these days? Sounds like you came across old Jonny Starling. I wouldn't be letting anybody else in on your story if I were you. When they find out that you'd been entertaining him by listening to his wild stories, you'll be laughed out of Paradise!'

As much as John felt belittled by Joe's rubbishing of his account, he was at the same time grateful that he hadn't mentioned it to anyone else.... especially the Dutchman!

'Did I ever tell you John, that everybody seems normal, until you get to know them? And in the future.' he continued. 'In the unlikely event you feel the need for us to talk again, do me the courtesy of either knocking, or calling out first .... Good day!'

Joe turned once more, and meandered off, hunch-shouldered and in a manner that in John's imagination resembled a grumpy old wombat.

John reeled away, and feeling somewhat vilified by Joe's brusque dismissal, decided to have one last search through the bush for any feasible explanation to explain his concerns. Crawling through a thicket closer to the ocean beach he startled a feeding Wompoo pigeon. The bird took flight and clattered noisily up into the high branches of a tree and, staring down indignantly let out its characteristic low gurgling call. John raised his eyes from the ground for the first time to follow its ascent and spotted what he had missed in his earlier searches. Hanging from a branch, just out of reach, was a tiny stick figure crudely bound together with blades of sword grass. Faceless, it seemed to stare at John menacingly none the less. He moved on further, his gaze fixed in the trees this time. Squinting into the shafts of sunlight that penetrated the canopy, it wasn't long before he spied another, then several more, each a little different but similarly constructed. It reminded him of that creepy movie that once scared the hell out of him 'The Blaire Witch Project'. One looked like it had long shaggy hair. Another appeared to be carrying a long stick or a spear. It was impossible to know how long they had been there, or who might have been responsible for them. As all of them were just out of reach anyway, John thought it was probably better to leave them in situ till the time when he decided who best to show them to. But oddly he still couldn't find any footprints anywhere.

After lunch John decided to look further afield to see what else he might uncover. He headed west from the immediate Paradise precinct into the more heavily wooded bushland that was dotted with mahogany gums, nearer the Scully properties. What he wasn't expecting to come across was Simon.

Scully rose out of a dense patch of brush like some Godly apparition and startled John.

'Damn you John Williams, damn you!'

'You frightened me, Simon! What are you doing out here?'

'And you frightened the birds off, that's precisely what you did, didn't you. So, I need to ask you; What are you doing out here? …. Don't I?'

This unexpected meeting gave John the opportunity to see whether Simon knew any about the goings on during the previous night. But he wanted to be careful not to allude to the fact that he thought Jane may have been the source of the mystery calls. In fact, he wanted to be careful not to allude to anything that might be construed as anything out of the ordinary. He had a healthy respect for Simon's ability to twist what is said around and take charge of the conversation.

'Just stretching my legs Simon, I haven't explored up this way for a while.'

'No, well you'd have no need to. Would you? No need to at all.'

'Sorry Simon, but you haven't answered my question about what you are doing here.'

'Before you interrupted, I was counting bird species, wasn't I. I've recorded fifty different species this time down at Paradise. Fifty, would you believe!'

'And does that include nocturnal birds too Simon?' ventured John carefully.

'Nocturnal birds John, nocturnal birds! Why would you specifically ask about nocturnal birds? Is there something about nocturnal birds that particularly interests you John? You've never mentioned you were interested in birds before.'

'Oh, nothing specific Simon. I just wondered if you'd come across a bird that calls out at night and sounds a bit like a giggle. I think I may have heard such a bird like that the other night and just wondered what it might be.'

'A giggle, a giggle John? Are you trying me on John? Well, are you? Did you ever think you might have heard someone off one of those boats instead? They're drinkers you know, and blasphemers too! Always up to some hanky panky. Did you bother to go out and investigate? Well, did you?'

John could feel the conversation going down the same old slippery side that Simon always managed to get him on. Still, John knew that Simon would only delve deeper if he didn't answer.

'I did go and investigate actually, but I couldn't find the source of the sound. But I can tell you there were no footprints to suggest a person had been wandering around.'

John hoped that his answer might preclude what he thought would be Simon's next question; 'How could you be sure it wasn't Jane out there?'

'So, you initially thought it could have been Jane did you......Did you?'

'Well maybe.'

'Well, so that just goes to show you too have doubts about Tucker's ability to look after Jane, does it not. Well, does it?'

'Simon, I had no idea what it was making those strange noises out there in the middle of the night. I simply investigated all possible causes, and like you say, maybe it was coming from one of the boats....... anyway, got to be going.'

John turned on his tracks and smartly strode off before Simon could seize the opportunity to have the last word. John was aware Simon had a reputation around Paradise for pursuing divisive issues. Some matters he would persist with for years, holding on to them like a dog with a bone. John could remember one time Simon was in dispute with his own brother over the width of an easement that ran through his property.

John recalled the time he was busy loading up his boat, getting ready to leave Paradise for the winter period, when Simon trapped him on the jetty.

'My brother Gordon's cleared a wide track right through the middle my property. Right through it! Four metres wide would you believe! He's no right to do that, no right at all! Some rubbish about natural justice. Says he's entitled to access to his property from the private jetty through my place. Natural justice be damned!'

'But doesn't the land titles map show an easement through your place Simon.' John replied politely.

'Exactly, an easement.... an easement! Not a confounded highway. I'll be taking the matter to court. I don't mind a track, but he's not having a highway! Wouldn't you agree John? Well, wouldn't you?'

It would be the better part of the year before John ran into Simon again, and on encountering him, just as John pulled alongside the jetty, even before John could say 'Hello Simon, how are you going', Simon in an animated manner declared 'We won! We won!' talking as if he'd been having the earlier conversation that year only a day or so ago.

'That's natural justice John!'

'Oh, sorry, do you mean the easement matter you were having earlier this year Simon? Is that what you're referring to?'

'Of course I do. Of course! What else would I be referring to, what else!'

Simon then went on to explain all the details of the court decision, how the easement had to be re-surveyed and re-aligned in accordance with the original deed. How the easement had to conform within the limits of the allowable width. The requirement for a remediation plan to re-vegetate the cleared sections of the track etc etc........ all at Gorden's cost. It left John in such a befuddled state, he was lost for words with which to form any coherent reply.

And the matter didn't end there. Sometime after, Simon's boys, Aiden and Andrew, strung a volleyball net across the path in defiance of Gordon's 'natural justice', probably just to 'stick it up' him even further, and it seemed to have the desired effect. Gordon, finding his way blocked by the boys, took matters into his own hands and, when push came to shove Gorden lashed out. Throwing a perfectly timed right jab, he managed to dislodge several of young Aiden's teeth. So back to Court they went, this time with a restraining order taken out on Gordon. However, it didn't all go Simon's way. The Judge, tiring of Simon's persistent applications against other members of the Scully clan, warned that his next appearance would see Simon at risk of being declared a vexatious litigant.

There was always some issue or another and John could never understand why the Scullys appeared to be eternally feuding. For a family who displayed such generational religious fervour, and who all enjoyed successful careers and seemingly had everything they could want in life; Why put so much time and energy into fighting one another?

Chapter Seven

Love Thy Neighbour

*Psalms 1: Blessed is the man that walketh
not in the counsel of the ungodly,
nor standeth in the way of sinners,
nor sitteth in the seat of the scornful.*

Arriving back at the cottage John found Sal settled in with a favourite book and a frosted glass of chilled white wine. The afternoon was still young, and with nothing else demanding more of John's attention, he decided he might try his luck fishing in the lake. The background hum of activity from the government jetty deterred John from collecting mussels from the weedy piles and instead, for bait, he thought he'd try netting some shrimp, which at this time of year proliferated in the sea grass beds covering much of the shallows around the estuary. He wandered up to old Wheatcroft's shed where he kept his collection of tools, more fishing gear and other oddments, which Sal refused to have kept in the house. Finding the key in a jar hidden behind the old shed, he levered the corroded padlock apart. The shed door opened with a loud rusty creak. He was met with a heady waft of rat droppings as he entered the darkened, fetid interior. A scuttling noise rose from the direction of a pile of cardboard boxes in the far corner, and out of the corner of his eye a dark fleeting shadow scurried under a roll of old lino. Little pins of light penetrated the gloomy room around the blackened walls. As John's eyes adjusted to the darkness, across the room he could see the stand of fishing rods leaning up against the corner. There also stood a long-handled fine meshed landing net, with which he planned to catch the shrimp.

John grabbed the rods and backed out into the glare of the afternoon sun, cracking the back of his head on the low doorway on his way.

'Bugger you Wheatcroft!'

He squinted at the bundle of rods. It was obvious the environs of the shed did no favours to his fishing gear. The varnish on the poles had started pealing and the ferrules were sullied with corrosion. Worse still, he discovered the rodents had chewed into several of the foam and caulk handgrips.

'I can't take all my fishing stuff back to Melbourne each time I leave here, Sal will just have to put up with these in the cottage from now on. No arguments!'

The rods felt sticky in his hand, and he took a whiff of his fingers …. they too stank of rats now. He made his way back to the cottage and filled a bucket with hot sudsy water from the copper. With a sponge borrowed from the kitchen, he exorcized the evil odour from his equipment, and himself. Using a wad of steel wool John rubbed away any sign of corrosion from the reels, then sprayed them with an ample layer of penetrating lubricant. The hand net needed some attention too. There were several holes in the mesh where the rats had had their way, which John repaired as best he could with a length of nylon thread he found at the bottom of his fishing-kreel.

Finally, after an hour of repairs and preparation, bucket, rods and net in hand, John sauntered down the trail to the lake. He selected an area where the seagrasses covered the shallows, and wading out, scoured the grass patches with the long-handled net. Every so often he would return to the shore and empty the contents of the net onto the dry sand, then sorting through the weeds, pick out the darting shrimp and drop them into his bucket.

Occasionally he would call out 'Oh there's a big one', or 'Arrr, he got away!' as if conversing with some imaginary fishing mate.

Half an hour of foraging harvested enough bait for a good session out on the estuary. John took his catch and fishing gear to the private jetty, loaded it all into his boat, cast off and headed out west into the quieter reaches of the lake away from the other craft and beach goers. The little motor spluttered away quietly as John surveyed the water looking for a likely spot to cast a line. The best places were those where the sandy patches opened up between the weed beds, and along the edges of the sand banks between the shallows and the deeper gutters where the currents ran. After some deliberation John finally settled on a spot to drop the anchor. There was still a little time before the slack water gave way to the runout tide when the fish would be biting, time enough to get his rods organised and time enough to absorb the surrounding environs; the scrub-lined shores of bullrushes, melaleucas and boobialla, behind which spread distant blue hills, flocks of black swans, some with their cygnets in tow, the cormorants and looking skyward, the scudding fluffy white clouds.

John stretched out, his back leaning against the warm shiny black cowling of the outboard motor. He focused his sight on the rod-tips through the glare of the sun. The air was still and silent, save the gentle lapping of wavelets against the aluminium hull.

Reflecting on his shrimping session, his mind drifted back to when he was a young boy. He remembered the times when he would go yabbying in a dam that was part of a small farmlet across the paddocks from his house next door. All that was required to catch the yabbies was a small piece of meat (typically pilfered from the lamb chops in the fridge) attached to a short length of string, a kitchen colander and a bucket to keep them in. After flicking the meat out and letting it sink down into the muddy water it took a little patience, but once the yabbies started pulling on the string it was simply a matter of retrieving the bait.... ever so slowly, until the yabbies, unwilling to let go of their meal, could be scooped out and dropped in the bucket. The owner of the local newsagent who liked to go fishing in Lake Eildon from time to time, would pay John a cent for every yabby he could get. Small yabbies were the preferred bait for redfin which proliferated in the lake, so the newsagent would only accept the ones which were under a certain size. The larger yabbies John would take home and cook them in a boiling saucepan of water, much to his mother's aversion. He remembered being so thrilled to receive his 'yabby money', it was all his and something he didn't have to ask for from his mother and, something he could spend on whatever he liked, which was usually lollies.

Life back then had a simple innocence. Catching yabbies in a muddy dam was an adventure, and receiving payment for the catch, however meagre, was as good as a king's ransom. And during the lead up to Guy Fawkes' night John could purchase fireworks that he would stash in his bedroom ahead of the annual 'cracker night' celebrations, although many a cracker was detonated earlier to blow up ants' nests, or the occasional letterbox. The big '*threepenny bungers*' were his favourite ordnance.

Life back then was uncomplicated. Little things held so much value. Relationships were uncomplicated and had a pure simplicity about them, unlike that requiring careful navigation as those at Paradise. And at days end being tucked away securely into a cosy bed guaranteed a night of comfortable, uninterruptable and restorative slumber.

Tap-tap ... bang! One of the rods contorted suddenly, rousing John from his daydream. He lurched forward, barking his shin on the centre bench seat, and before he had a chance to loosen off the drag, the full weight of the fish overcame the breaking strain of the line and broke loose.

'Wow, bugger! It's always about the one that got away.'

While John set about re-tying another rig he reflected on his past, when even in his wildest childhood dreams, he could never imagine having the opportunity of fishing from a boat. And now here he was, captain of his own vessel, be it only a four-and-a-half-meter run-about. His was a childhood with very few amenities that other kids seem to have as staples. Neither parent drove, nor ever owned a car. Getting around meant catching a bus or a train, or walking miles. In the home, only when John entered into his teens did his father relent and purchase a second hand black and white television set, and even then, it was on condition it was not to be kept in the house, instead it occupied a small space in an old bungalow out the back. It was fitted with a homemade aerial that restricted reception to half the commercial channels. Yet his childhood memories, as spartan as they seemed, were full of wonderment and dreams. Being starved of modern niceties in no way diminished his sense of freedom and fulfilment.

After the initial excitement, the remainder of the fishing session was slow, but John somehow didn't mind. The open water and vast expanse of sky helped unclutter his mind. It provided him with the space to think about his past and reflect on where he'd come to in life. He reasoned that compared to the life his mother and father had, he could consider himself a rich man.

It was late in the afternoon, although the sun shone brightly, still well above the horizon, when John's thoughts drifted back to the present. He'd gone out without a hat or sunscreen, and he could feel the sun's bite on his arms and the back of his neck. The last of the shrimp he'd caught were now floating in the bucket of tepid water, lifeless and milky white. Having neglected lunch, early pangs of hunger signalled it was time to think about heading back in.

John retrieved the keep-net hanging off the side of the boat. Two small whiting were all that occupied the net. Not much to show for the afternoon's efforts, but at least enough for a feed he reasoned. He wound in his lines from the water with the bait still intact, then reaching round pulled several times on the recoil starter till the little motor coughed and spluttered into life. While the motor warmed up, he dragged the anchor in and briskly dunked it up and down like a teabag to release the clumps of dense black sediment and weed sticking to the tynes. He motored off, noting the dark muddy cloud left floating behind.

Approaching the private jetty, but still a little way off, John scanned the landing and surrounds to see if there was any sign of Dieter or his boys. He could still hear the voices echoing in his head, when during the last time he came in with only two small fish, the Urquharts took delight in belittling him on the net worth of his catch.

'My Got, look what der cradle schnatcher's pulled in!'

'When are you going to become a real fisherman and go out into der ocean and catch some proper fish?'

John was well aware of the dangers of 'going out' across the bar and into the unprotected waters of Bass Strait. The timing of the right state of the tide and the rolling swells dictated a narrow line between safe passage and disaster. The ocean was unforgiving, and in a small tinny, only the very brave or foolish would think to venture out. But that didn't stop the Urquharts from goading him at any opportunity. He would have jumped at the opportunity, if invited, to venture into the ocean to fish with the Urquharts, but the invitation was never on offer. When it came to fishing the Urquhart boys kept much to themselves and were always guarded in disclosing such details as the best bait, or their favourite spots.

Occasionally Dieter would go fishing out back in the surf, much like John and Frankie had a few days earlier. From the hummocks at the top of John's block, Dieter could be seen, his generous frame overflowing fatly in a faded green plastic chair on the sand, surf rod in hand, esky on one side and folding table on the other, staring out over the waves looking more like King Farouk attempting to hold back the tide. John joked with him once, asking if he would like a pillow and a blanket to make himself more comfortable. Dieter, eyes not moving from the horizon simply retorted 'fuck off'. John thought it was funny though.

By now the sunlight had begun to turn golden. Long shadows stretched along the foreshore. A salmon-pink haze faded into a purply-blue hue above the horizon. Tomorrow would be another warm and clear day. John opened a now warm can of beer he'd saved in the boat. It fizzed vigorously and frothed up, overflowing in his hand. He finished cleaning his fish, then cleaned out his boat and wiped clean the rods and bait-board. The warm beer caused him to belch loudly which made his eyes water.

As he traipsed up the track, bucket and rods in hand, he could smell the sweet tea-tree smoke coming from someone's BBQ. Alan Bagshaw jogged past, all dressed up in his 'active wear'.

'Evening John. Fish for dinner?'

'Just a couple of whiting.' was the reply, but Bagshaw had run on, out of view.

John gathered some kindling for the BBQ fire while Sal prepared a simple salad. When the fish were done they served themselves outside on the decking. Little brown wrens busied themselves round about, catching evening insects as they darted between their legs. With the sun now settling below the treeline, they sat in the shadows sipping the last of Sal's chilled wine until the bite of cool air, drifting in from the ocean, signalled it was time to move inside and light the lamps before the daylight began to fade completely.

Around 10.00 PM Sal finished reading her book, clapping it shut before blowing out the last of the kero lamps and joining John, who was already dozing off in the bed. The warm radiance of the lamp light was transformed into the thin cold luminance of the moon shining in from the window.

Sal dropped into a deep sleep in what seemed like only minutes; however, John, having been roused by Sal's shuffling into bed, lay awake staring into the dark ceiling, ears straining above the noise of his own breathing for any strange sounds like the ones which had him creeping around the bush, nights before. At some stage John must have drifted off, because he suddenly woke to a noise from somewhere outside. Noises at night were not unusual around Paradise during the night. The shuffling and bumping of wombats, the flapping of some water bird on the water, scurrying possums or the soft thud-thud of a wallaby or kangaroo passing by were all common nocturnal sounds. John pressed the light on his watch...... 2 AM! He'd been asleep for a while, long enough for the adrenalin rush to set his heart beating with an audible thump.

'Well, I'm wide awake now' he thought. 'I may as well have a look around outside.'

Sliding carefully out of bed, so as not to disturb the slumbering Sal, John reached for his shorts in the dark, grabbed a torch, and crept out the door. A high moon shone brightly in a cloudless sky, it's light muted only by a thin layer of low-lying sea fog. John left the torch off allowing his night vision to adjust to the subdued light. He moved carefully away from the cottage, his bare feet crunching quietly on the twigs and leaf litter. Nothing, not a sound other than the distant waves crashing on the ocean beach. A cold breath of air made the hairs on his neck stand on end and set the trees of the night whispering. John retreated to the track and shone his torch briefly at the ground to see if there were any signs of fresh footprints or tracks. There was nothing.

Reflecting on Simon's earlier comment about the demeaner of the 'boat people' he decided that while he was up anyway, it might be worthwhile wandering down to the government jetty to see if there was any activity down there. From his vantage point on the foreshore, in the moonlight he could see the ghostly outlines of the cruisers and the sailboats moored on the landing. The dark water glistened with silvery threads and the boats, all bar one, were dark and silent rocking ever so gently at their moorings. Approaching closer, John could make out a faint glow coming from one little trailer-sailor moored near to the shore, and on further inspection he could make out a solitary figure quietly reading a book by torchlight. John turned to wander back home, and thoughts of Jane's wellbeing entered his mind once more.

'Maybe I should check on Joe's place? No…..bugger that, not doing that again!'

So, John traced his steps back a way, then diverted into the Bergen once more. He remembered the little grass figures he'd seen in the trees after the last disturbing night. His torch beam threw a yellow arc of light up into the branches of the tea-trees where he'd spotted the effigies before. There was no sign of them. They were all gone. He returned his attention to the ground, but the only tracks he could see were his own.

For what remained of the night John tossed and turned uncomfortably, until in the early morning he succumbed to a deep slumber. Sal had woken earlier and must have gone out somewhere to leave him in peace. It was mid-morning when he rose and dosed his foggy head with a strong cup of coffee. He decided he would ask around the neighbours to see if anybody else had been disturbed in the night.

Down the track Alan Bagshore was busy fussing around with a rake clearing up some dry leaves.

'Morning Alan. How's it going? By the way...... just wondering if you've noticed any strange noises over the past few nights.'

'Can't say I have. I'm training for the veteran's half marathon in Saint Kilda at the moment. I'm out to it just as soon as my head hits the pillow. You could fire a gun off, and it wouldn't wake me. Might have been Urquhart's dog, I hear it's been wandering around a bit at night.'

John continued further down to the Head's. It was already hot, and John found Gloria out the front on a sunbed baking her scantily clad brown leathery skin. The ever-protective guard dogs bared their teeth and snarled at him from under the safe cover of the bed.

'Oh, hi John.' called Gloria, casually swinging an oily hand across the dog's muzzles.

'Don't mind them. If you're looking for Rick, he's in the house fiddling with the fridge that Banister bloke was meant to fix the other day.'

'Actually, you'll do, I just wondered if you or Rick may have heard anybody sneaking around the place over the last couple of nights.'

'The only sneaking around I hear in the night is Rick when he gets up to have a pee, and that's the only time you could hear anything above his terrible snoring. I shouldn't say this, but we've had to sleep in separate rooms for a few years now, it's become so bad.'

John, not wanting to get into the Head's personal lives, acknowledged Gloria's remarks with a nod, then moved quickly on, while all the time keeping a wary eye out for any rear-guard attack from the dogs.

He wasn't game to asked anyone on the Scully side of the creek about the nocturnal events, and he wasn't in Joe's good books, so no need to go there for now either, and as for the remainder of those he asked, they all seemed quite dismissive, as if strange noises were just part of any Paradise night.

Scuttling furtively past Joe's place, John arrived at Susan's. The two women were sharing a pot of tea on Susan's balcony.

'Oh, the midnight cowboy has arisen, has he? Feeling fresh like a little buttercup, are we? You thought that I was asleep didn't you.' Sal continued. 'But I was aware you were out and about snooping around like the boogie man last night.

'It's not like that, Sal. Somethings don't seem right around here just now. I can feel a bad vibe in the air. It's not just the strange noises at night. There are other things that have bothered me which I mentioned to you the other night.'

'It's none of my business.' Susan butted in, 'But if it has anything to do with the Scullys, well there's always something they're up to that doesn't seem quite right.'

A familiar barrage of profanities from out on the water interrupted the conversation. John swung around to see Frankie's flushed face scowling from the helm of his boat. John went over to where Frankie beached his tinny, and before he could offer any greeting, Frankie blurted out; 'I told them it was rooted, now I'm back here trying to fix the bloody thing again!

It's too bloody hot in the workshop anyway, so I've left Faye in charge of the servo for the rest of the day.' he continued.

'Stuff it, I'm going fishing after this …… and I've got some bait this time. Your shout for the beer if you're joining me Johnny boy.'

'Yes well, I've got nothing else on, so I may take you up on that.'

While Frankie went off to deal with the Heads', John returned home, prepared an early simple lunch, and between mouthfuls of sandwich and tea, he rigged up a couple of surf rods and sorted out a camp chair and what cold beer he had in the fridge. All the while, John could hear the incessant sound of Alan Bagshore buzzing around somewhere with a hedge trimmer (God knows why?), and further off, Gloria's three poodles barking feverously, punctuated every now and then by the raised voice of Frankie shouting, 'You bastards!'

A little time later, after a short period of silence, Frankies nasally voice could be heard again, this time much closer.

'Well, are you coming or not Williams? The fish haven't got all day.'

John quickly scribbled down a note to Sal to let her know what he was doing, then shuffled out and followed Frankie's cursing utterances into the sand dunes and on down to the beach. There was a nice deep blue gutter that had formed out the front of John's property, and so here they set up their rod holders and other bits and pieces. The first thing Frankie did was to delve into John's esky in search of a beer.

'Shit, is this all you've brought yah bugger? I thought we were going fishing, not just paying the beach a quick visit', he grumbled counting the number of cans in the box.

'There's more back home, but they're warm…and that's all I could fit in my little fridge.'

'Well …. you need a bigger fridge then! Anyway, I don't mind a warm beer now and then, not that you'd ever want to call me a Pommy bastard.'

The hot afternoon drifted on. The brilliance of the white sand competed with the glare given off from the whitewash in the splash zone as it surged relentlessly about their sunburnt feet. A lone puffy cloud floated gently above the farthest horizon in an otherwise clear blue sky. John occasionally wiped the salt spray from his sunglasses, and Frankie, glasses-less, gazed seaward in a continuous painful squint. By mid-afternoon Frankie had coerced John to make a second, then a third trip back to the cottage to resupply the Esky with warm beer. Somehow Frankie managed to consume two beers for every one that John downed, and with every can consumed, his banter and storytelling became more animated.

'There's not much happening fish wise.' commented John after some time.

'Of course not.' barked Frankie. 'It's the wrong time of the day. To be honest I only came here fishing to avoid going back to the servo, if you need to know. Faye and I had a 'blue' this morning. Reckons if things don't change, she won't be putting up with me for much longer.'

John nodded in silent acknowledgement, maintaining his focus on the tip of his surf-rod …… then, something quite unexpected happened. Like a bolt out of the clear blue sky, Frankie spun round and slapped John squarely to the side of his face. The loud smack sent John reeling off his seat.

'Jesus! What the hell was that for? What's going on?' a clearly shocked John responded from the sand.

'You weren't listening to me!' shouted Frankie.

'Faye threatened to leave me this morning. We were arguing over the books, and then she started with 'she wanted to have a say in the way the business was being run, and to make some changes around the place'...... So, I told her; I was the one who wore the pants around the servo, and she was only there to support me. The thing is, she's the glue that holds our business together. She does all the books, the accounts, the orders, and she deals with all the difficult customers I'd otherwise be telling to bugger off. You probably hadn't noticed, but I'm not really much of a 'people person'. I'm the workshop guy, the petrol pumper.... you know, the back of office, the 'boots on the ground'. People irritate me ...... even you do sometimes. You know, without Faye behind me I don't think I'd cope. I think I'd rather 'top' myself.'

John nudged his sunglasses above his eyes and backed off for a moment to let Frankie's sudden outburst sink in. Mentally unpacking what Frankie had just said, he reflected on the way Faye always appeared to be the stable one of the pair, the one who always seemed to have the more sensible ideas and cautions, but who would invariably be overshadowed by Frankie's colourful raucousness and 'in your face' demeanour.

Additionally, John was vaguely aware the lease on the Banister's Boat Bait and Auto site was due for renewal sometime soon, and that the lessors, who were somewhere back in Melbourne, had new plans for the property, hoping to reap a better long-term investment by developing it into a medium density residential complex. Should Faye walk out of the business, John reasoned Frankie would most likely pack it in too, meaning the site would probably be re-developed. That would mean no more easily accessed fuel, no boat servicing and no more secure car parking in the backyard. It would be a great loss to many in Minamurra, but particularly those in Paradise.

'I'm sure you can patch things up Frankie. I'll tell you what, I have to come over to town tomorrow to get a few things for here. I'll bring Sal with me if you like, and maybe she can have a talk with Faye, if you think that might help.'

'S'pose it can't hurt ...... that's if Faye's still there...'

From that point on there was little reason to stay on the beach much longer. Frankie, having finally found a way to get things off his chest, be it at John's expense, downed his last can and slumped languidly on his seat. His rubicund face toned in with his reddened watery eyes and his shock of ruddy hair.

Frankie packed his things together, stood and stretched his sunburnt frame for a moment before striding off into the scrub, and out of sight.

'See you tomorrow then, eh Frankie.' John shouted out to him. But there was no response.

John tidied up the remainder of the gear and crushed down and stashed all the empty cans Frankie had managed to litter the beach with. He gathered everything together and with his cheek still feeling the sting of Frankies open palm, stumbled home on tired and sunburnt legs, empty handed.

Fortunately, the night went by uneventfully. John and Sal woke refreshed, and after a hearty breakfast of bacon and eggs accompanied by a strong pot of coffee, they ventured out into the crisp morning air. They packed their little trolly with the empty esky, an empty kero tin, a few shopping bags and a big bag of rubbish which would be put into the dumpster over at the fisherman's wharf in Minamurra. John had briefed Sal on Frankies outburst, and it was decided that John would do the shopping while Sal took Faye out for a chat over some morning tea.

After tying up the tinny beneath the shadow of the huge overhanging bow of one of the fishing trawlers, John parted ways with Sal, she going in one direction to Frankie's, and he taking his bags and shopping list in hand down the main street to Geoff Evans' mini-mart. The familiar aroma of liquorice greeted John at the door as he scanned the 'specials list' on the front window, giving his eyes time to adjust to the dim light afforded by the old fluoro tubes in the store. With what he could find that was on his list, John rattled the wonky trolley to where the ever dapper but fat Evans manned the register.

'Can I interest you in one of these loaves of bread? It's day old, but perfectly alright and half price.'

'No thanks Geoff.'

'Maybe some mince beef? I over ordered it. I've marked it down for quick sale, perfect if you want to eat it tonight.'

'Ah ....no thanks. Just what's in the trolley today.'

'Crisps?'

'No.'

Geoff danced his stubby little fingers over the register while he made sucking noises with the usual boiled lolly held between his pursed lips. 'Well, that will be seventy-two dollars and twenty-five cents then. Let's make it seventy, shall we?'

John returned the groceries to the boat, placing the refrigerated items in the esky, but not before checking the pub as he passed to see that his bung-eyed adversary from the other day wasn't there to hassle him when he called in next to replenish his beer stocks.

The last item on the agenda was to call into Frankies for some ice and kerosene. When he arrived, Sal and Faye were still out somewhere having their 'heart to heart'. Frankie was out back in the workshop as usual, personifying some inanimate object in expletive terms above the rasping screech of an angle grinder. A gust of wind stirred up the orange dust in the dry yard, stinging John's eyes and coating the cars and shiny boats parked there with a gritty layer of dirt. The dogs growled menacingly from within the confines of a shed at the farthest end of the yard.

'Faye's still out with yer missus John.' yelled Frankie through the workshop door over the din.

'How were things when you got home yesterday?'

'I dunno, Faye's still not talking to me. I slept in the workshop last night, and I haven't been in the shop since she fronted this morning.'

John knew better than to probe any further with the still irritated little Welshman. Instead, he called in through the door that he was grabbing a bag of ice and four litres of kerosene, if Frankie could put it on his account.

'Tell Sal when you see her I'm waiting for her at the fisherman's wharf.'

Back at the boat John made himself comfortable perusing the local paper he'd grabbed from the mini-mart to put himself back in touch with the outside world. Every so often he would glance up to see fish boxes being trolleyed along the jetty. He could hear the voices of the fishermen talking about the sea conditions during last night's session. The men also discussed what fish were running, and who had registered what with the co-op.

An hour or more seemed to slip past effortlessly before an all too familiar voice called down. 'I'm here John, have you finished the shopping?'

'I'm ready to go ......you've been a long time.'

'I'll tell you about it later, when we get back home.'

They cast off and left the glassy shadowy waters of the harbour. Further out under the late morning sun a stiff easterly met them, pushing up a short chop against the bow. The spray splashed up and, caught by the breeze, drifted across the boat. They passed a flock of black cormorants feverishly feeding on a school of baitfish, and crossing nearer the entrance to the ocean, watched as a pod of exuberant dolphins played in the swell that rose up against the run-out tide.

Over at the government jetty the boaties were all out and about, some already busying themselves preparing an early BBQ lunch, others sprawled out on their decks soaking up the sun. Several children were jumping off the jetty into the clear blue water, their shrill squeals rising above the general bluster of the boats. A few people were sitting beneath colourful sunshades on the beach, either reading or simply chilling out. A little further on, reclining on a sunlounge under the shade of an old pine tree, Gloria's sun-dried figure could be seen near the edge of the scrub, her three poodles sitting defensively from under the safety of the bed. Dieter and his boys were tied up on the private jetty cleaning their catch from an early morning session out on the ocean.

'I seen you and dat Banister bloke over on der beach yesterday.' blurted the dutchman.

'Looked like you two were playing funny buggers. Banister looked pretty angry mit you. What did you do to upset him?'

'He just got a bit carried away Dieter...... all good now.'

John transferred the shopping from his boat into the trolly, and back at the cottage, when all the unpacking was done, he and Sal settled down to lunch.

'I wish that Dieter would keep his nose out my business ...... always looking at having a go at me, can't take a joke himself though. Anyway, how did you go with Faye?' John enquired.

'I don't know exactly what to say John. Poor thing, she really has nobody much to talk to for advice, and it's not my place what to tell her. She seems to have grown out of Frankie, but he's such a dominant partner, there's not much room for anything else in her life. She's been repressed for so long and she really needs the chance to get out a bit and spread her wings.'

John was aware how bigoted and cavalier Frankie could be. With Frankie, there were no shades of grey, only black and white. He had few, if any social graces. He had a short fuse, a personality that could grate and a politically incorrect approach to most issues raised in conversation. Faye, on the other hand was thoughtful, reflective and empathetic. She was smart too. It was only the bond of love that allowed her to tolerate him most of the time.

'Do you think she would ever leave him Sal?'

'Well, she's finally put him on notice. It wouldn't surprise me.'

'Sounds like they need some marriage counselling, but I couldn't imagine Frankie ever agreeing to that!'

'I recon if she did leave him, that would be the end of the business. Frankies's hardly your astute businessman. If that happened that would be a real blow for us here in Paradise. It's not just the convenience, but the security of our cars and trailers.'

Sal had a less circumspect view; 'The place is a bit of a knockdown anyway, rusty old sheds and all. If it closed it would provide an opportunity to see some redevelopment, which no doubt would improve the site no end. And I'm sure Frankie would find some type of work elsewhere. I'm sure we could find somewhere else to park our car and trailer securely without the local vandals getting at them.'

John left the conversation there. He'd brought with him a novel he'd been wanting to get into for quite some time, and with no further pressing matters to distract him, he put all thoughts of Frankie aside, pulled up a deckchair under the shade of and old banksia tree, and immersed himself in the book for the remainder of the day.

At day's end John treated himself to a warm hipbath. Wanting a decent uninterrupted night's rest, he took a sleeping pill he'd found in the bottom of Sal's shower bag. He enjoyed a warm cup of milk in bed, and in no time at all drifted off into a deep night-long slumber.

Chapter Eight

On Stranger Tides

*Psalms 54:7 For he hath delivered me out of all trouble:
and mine eye hath seen his desire upon mine enemies.*

John woke to the chorus of the kookaburras. Feeling a little
hungover from the effects of the sleeping pill, but at least well
rested and refreshed, he ventured out for his morning sojourn
to the lake. Bagshore was already up and on the edge of the
water in his *Speedos* and bathing cap, polishing the bottom of
his surf-ski. Susan was also there doing an early bird count of
the pelicans for the Minamurra Birdwatchers club. There was no
sign of life on the boats floating motionlessly by the government
jetty, save a couple of silent silhouettes out, casting a line into
the water against the first rays of sun.

'It's going to be a hot one today, Susan.'

'Yes, I thought I'd get out early and get my chores done
before the heat sets in. I've been watching the pelicans.' she
continued. 'But you know what, see how fast they are drifting
past with the current! I know how fast the current flows past
here sometimes on the flood, but if a south easterly springs up
later, we're really going to see some high water later tonight.'

It was John's habit to get an ocean beach walk in most days.
He was once told that if one spent an hour by the sea daily
watching the waves, most times it was almost impossible to ever
suffer from depression. With Sal likely to be still sleeping, and

considering the forecast of a hot day, he decided rather than returning to the cottage now, he would stride out through the tea-tree scrub across the back of the properties and along the ocean foreshore. The rising sun was at his back and the sand felt damp and cool to his feet. Footprints that were trodden in the sand the day before, which lay ahead of him, were being gradually eradicated by the wash of the incoming tide. After about half an hour, the footprints ceased. John became aware he had walked beyond those who had walked the beach before him. Then suddenly the memory of his encounter with Jonny Starling the other day came to front of mind. He glanced up furtively into the hummocks and was reassured by the emptiness around the tussocks and pigface. But then, in the next heart sinking moment, a now familiar voice called out; 'You back up here rudie boy? Haven't forgot to put ya pants on this time eh!'

John strained his eyes into the sand hills, and like a shadowy apparition, a dark face with fiery eyes rose up into view.

'Are you spying on me? Jonny Starling's your name, isn't it?'

Ignoring the question, the black man replied 'I've been keeping an eye on you for a while this morning, Scully person ...... or whoever you said you are. I told you you're not welcome up here you know.'

'Well, it's not your beach to start with, and by the way; Have you been sneaking around my place the past few nights making weird noises and sticking little effigies up in the trees?'

'So, it's started then! I warned you this would happen ...... bad things, very bad things! I told you the other day, even I don't go down that Scully place no more. You should tell that Simon Scully something's going on round your place. It may surprise you what he has to say.'

Simon was the last person John wanted to talk to, but from what this man was saying, he was keen to get to the bottom of things once and for all and put it all behind him.

A sea eagle swooped low over John's shoulder, distracting him momentarily.

'Why should I talk to Simon about it?' demanded John. But the apparition had disappeared.

During the long walk home John pondered how best to broach the subject with Simon about his meetings with Jonny Starling and his dire warnings. Obviously, Starling thinks Scully must know something about the strange goings on, he reasoned.

It was late morning by the time he approached the little clearing which signalled the way into his property. A brisk south-easterly had sprung up, and a thick sea-fog began to roll in causing the tea-trees to rattle. It was an unexpected change from what had earlier promised to be a still, sultry day.

Sal had been up long enough to tidy the cottage, pay Susan a visit and have lunch prepared.

'Where have you been for so long? Susan said she'd seen you down by the lake earlier this morning. I was beginning to wonder what had happened to you.'

'Just been on my usual beach walk. John replied. 'Took a bit longer than usual. It was quite hot to start with, but now the wind has swung round, and it's cooled off considerably.'

John avoided mentioning his encounter with Jonny but explained to Sal he wanted to go over and talk to Simon about certain matters.

'You be careful what you say to Simon then, you know how he always manages to twist things around to his advantage. And I don't wish to hear he wants you to appear in court as a witness to attest to some family issue. Oh, and before you go, I had a call from Faye this morning. She's very worried about Frankie.

She went for a part time job interview yesterday and when Frankie found out about it, they had an almighty 'blue', so she decided to stay over with a friend last night. Anyway, when she turned up at the servo early this morning there was no sign of Frankie. She went home to the farm to see if he might have slept in and found the gun case empty and no sign of Frankie. So, she called the police. They apparently found him at the bottom of their property with the gun. He told them everything was good, and he was just out to shoot some bunnies. He returned to the house with them, and they left.'

'So, what's Faye's worry then?'

'Apart from the fact they're not speaking now, Faye said; Firstly, he always likes to get to the servo early in the morning, and secondly, the only time he takes the gun out is when he goes off deer hunting in the hills with his mates .... maybe only once a year.'

'I'll check in on him next time I go over if you think, but you know what he's like, he'll probably tell me things couldn't be better.'

With that, and after finishing lunch, John headed over to Simon's place via the lake front. He passed Alan Bagshaw on the way, in a pair of waders, his boat up on the sand, busily polishing the hull (for some reason that was beyond John).

Crossing the creek, John paused to look down. He noticed the salty water was running upstream. There must be a big run-in tide today he reasoned. He took in a deep breath as he crossed the rickety foot bridge that led to the Scullys. He felt like an advanced scout heading into enemy territory. What added to the confrontational atmosphere were the sharp cracks of Aiden and Andrew shooting targets somewhere out the back. John hadn't even got near the front door before Simon burst out to intercept him before he reached the front steps.

'Well John this is unexpected, very unexpected. Wouldn't you agree.?'

'Sorry, I didn't want to surprise you Simon, it's nothing important really, just something that was on my mind recently.'

'Well, you wouldn't be over here for no reason. Nobody comes over here for no reason, do they? …. No, they don't. That's a fact …. a fact! Is it something to do with our Jane is it? …. Well, is it?'

John had to do some quick thinking, and he was worried the eagle-eyed Scully would see through his guise.

'No, no, nothing to do about Jane, Simon. I've always been interested in the history of this place, ever since I bought here. And I thought the best thing to do, other than ask other people what they knew, was to go straight to the source. I didn't like to approach your brother Gordon as I've never had much to do with him.'

'History of the place? You've never said you had an interest in the history of the place before this …. No you haven't, have you? Why this sudden interest now, I ask you.' enquired Simon, standing his ground.

John was feeling quite uncomfortable at this point, and there was no indication Scully was about to invite him in for a friendly chat over a cuppa, not that the Scullys partook of tea or coffee anyway. Peeking over Simon's shoulder he could see in the background Peta peeking surreptitiously between the slats of a venetian blind lowered over the front window.

'I've heard a bit about your grandparents here.' continued John nervously. 'But apart from them, I know very little of your mother and father, and you had some uncles I believe who used to spend a lot of time down here, and well, you also mentioned years ago when I first purchased my place about a caveat on the sale of my property.'

'Yes, a caveat indeed. That was part of my late aunty Katherine's last Will and Testament when she divided up the settlement, but as I said to you at the time, I doubted whether it would still have stood up in court. And if it was the case, you wouldn't be here now, would you? ...... No you wouldn't!'

As was Simon Scully's way, John could feel he no longer had control of the conversation, and perhaps it was time to 'man up' and come to the point of why he was really paying Scully the visit.

'Actually Simon, to be honest, apart from your knowledge of the history here, there was one other thing on my mind.'

John then began to explain how he had had two encounters with who he thought to be a certain 'Jonny Starling' way up the ocean beach during the past week. He brought up the matter of strange nocturnal occurrences, which he had earlier mentioned to Simon, and the connection between those and the prophecies of the Starling man. To John's surprise Simon focused in intently on what he was saying, like a hawk hovering above its prey.

'This Starling chap, if that's who he is, said some bad things had happened down here, about the time I imagine you would have been coming here as a youngster with your family. And he reckons bad things were about to start happening again. Probably all a load of rubbish, but he did mention your name and said to mention it to you, and I'm truly sorry if I'm wasting your time with this.'

Simon stood unusually quiet for a moment, staring at the ground.

'Starling! That heathen! Is he around again? ...... Is he? Witchcraft, curses and spells! That's what those Gunnakurni mob are about you know ...... curses and spells! You could be in danger John. Do you know that? Well, do you?'

'He seemed to have a bent on the Scully family actually, well your great grandparents in particular, but also the current descendants.'

'It's the people on this land John, not just Scully related occupiers.' Simon replied. 'They put a curse on this place, something about angry spirits wanting to reclaim the land, or some such thing. So, anybody coming over here can be affected. The last time this occurred so many years ago I was just a youngster and didn't properly understand what was happening. My father, who was not strong of '*The Faith*' got very sick, and my younger brother Nathan started having seizures. Nathan never fully recovered and died before he reached his teens. I remember a fierce wind springing up and a big king tide that washed much of the beach away. A couple of the cottages nearer the beach were taken into the sea. There was a terrible fire too, and some of Paradise got burnt out. Only those of the family who still held strong to '*The Faith*' were immune to this heathen witchcraft. Those who held fast to the belief of the '*Wonderous vision of the purpose of the Lord*' and who strongly believed in the proof of the existence of divine Providence, which had delivered our people here in the first place, were untouched. Are you of '*The Faith*' as taught by my grandfather Thomas, John? Well, are you? ...... No, you are not .... you are not! This is why I know you and the others to be at risk. It might be a good time to think about leaving Paradise before people get wind of the curse on the land. You'll get nothing for your property if people think it's cursed ...no you won't, nothing!'

For what seemed like ages, John stood there speechless, transfixed as if by some strange force. His mind struggled to put all the events of the week together in the context of what Simon had just said ...... his injury, the doctor's rumours, Jane Tucker's declining condition, the mystery man enquiring about land for sale, the prophecies of the black-man, the strange happenings of the night, Frankie's problems, the unusually high tide and Simon's extraordinary statement just now. It was all too much to digest and try to make rational sense of in the moment. There was a good chance, he reasoned, that much of all these things were purely coincidental and he knew damn well how Simon had a reputation of turning any conversation, regardless of what subject, to his advantage. He needed time to unpack it and think it over in a calm and logical manner, and he knew he couldn't do that while Simon was in his face.

'That's an amazing story Simon. I never knew.' said John finally, trying to steady his demeanour.

'It's not just some story John. No John, not just some story. It's a warning John, do you understand? A warning!'

With that John excused himself and left Simon standing there, like some sort of religious sentinel in the front yard. The sounds of intermittent gunfire fell silent out the back. When John got to the creek he stared down at the water, hoping somehow not to see the water flowing in anymore, but unfortunately, noting the surging current, that was not the case.

Further along the foreshore Alan was still hard at it scrubbing his boat. As John walked past, Alan caught his eye.

'A pity about this sea-mist rolling in. It was meant to be a nice hot sunny day.' Then returning his attention to the job at hand continued. 'You've got to keep on top of these jobs John. If you let them get on top of you, you'll never keep up with them. There's always something that needs doing.'

'So, no problems with your lot recently? I mean, nothing untoward?'

'All good with us, but there you go, I hear the Beechams have had all sorts of issues with their place recently, which is why it's so important to keep everything ship shape eh!'

'What sort of issues Alan?'

'Oh, well ...... Their concrete stumps have started cracking, you know, the salt getting into the reinforcing steel. Concrete cancer they call it. Apparently, their water tank has begun leaking from somewhere under the stand and will need replacing, and a sudden gust of wind the other night caught the open back window, and it slammed shut and smashed. It's all started happening in the last few weeks they said. Anyway, they were saying they're getting too old, and with all these issues occurring recently, they just can't keep up with the maintenance anymore. They say their children aren't particularly interested in coming down here and using the property these days ...... so the next thing I hear, some bloke who was over here the other day, had a talk to them and put in a low offer to buy the place. As far as I can tell they've decided to accept the offer.'

This extra bit of news further troubled John. He never really knew the Beechams that well .... save only to say hello on passing, however he knew them well enough to think this was out of character.

Arriving back home, John found Sal on the front deck immersed once more in her favourite book.

'Oh John, I got a call from Faye while you were over at Simon's. She's staying in town tonight at the motel. Frankie's told her he's got some sort of business back in Melbourne and she didn't want to be out at the farm on her own. She's asked if I could go over and stay the night with her. If I do, would you be alright here on your own?'

'I don't mind you going over, but I'm a bit concerned with the change in the weather and getting you over there though. There's a south easterly building, and the water in the lake is rising quite fast. I reckon it could even get up to the track by tonight.'

'That's OK, I enquired at the government jetty while you were out and there's a charter boat operator going back to

Minamurra later today who can take me across. You'll just need to collect me tomorrow morning, or a taxi boat might bring me back if it's still too rough for you. I've already packed an overnight bag.'

The afternoon passed with the sea fog continuing to blanket Paradise, shadowing from the warm summer sun. Around five PM Sal took her overnight bag down to the government jetty and waited for the charter boat operator to round up the passengers he'd earlier brought across for a day trip.

John polished and refuelled the lamps in readiness for the night. It was getting too windy to risk lighting the BBQ, so instead he put aside some sausages and onions and got out an old tin of 'tiny taters' from the pantry to accompany them. He was quite happy to be without Sal's company for the night for it prodided him some space to clear his head and to try and make sense out of everything.

As darkness fell the wind continued to build. The tea-trees rattled incessantly below a menacing sky, and their trunks buckled and swayed under the strengthening gale. He threw a jacket and cap on before venturing outside under torch-light to check the water-level in the lake. Halfway down the sandy track he was surprised to see the water had already backed up and had started to cover the lower reaches of the path. Little wavelets blown along by the gusts trickled up the lower reaches of the track to meet him. Then, casting his torch beam across the tall sedges that bordered the creek, he watched the stems flowing in waves away from the torch light into the blackness as the wind blew over them. Once he turned for home, he was comforted by the sight of the soft glow of lamplight radiating out through the windows, the warmth and safety beckoned him in. He sat alone in his chair, his mind wandering through a thousand thoughts. The little cottage shuddered ever so slightly as the tempest buffeted the walls and beat down on the roof. He pictured Sal and Faye over in Minamurra, sitting in some cosy dimly lit restaurant, chatting equally about the issues at hand and other small talk over a bottle of wine, oblivious to the weather.

It wasn't too long before sleep enticed John and he succumbed to the idea of an early night. As the last lamp got snuffed out, the blackness of the stormy night outside enveloped the room. John laid on the bed under a comforting dooner. Eventually he drifted off to sleep, despite the noise of the tempest that clamoured outside his retreat.

Sometime in the middle of the night a loud crashing sound roused him from his slumber. For the second time this stormy night John ventured out into the gloom. He shone his torch around the cottage and discovered the source of the noise had come from a moonar branch which, ripped off a tree was sent crashing onto the roof. The other trees were dancing wildly, and his thoughts were directed to how his boat was faring down on the lake. Braving the blackness, he shone his way along to the lake front. Over the last hundred meters he was forced to wade knee deep through the flooding water. The estuary was a tempest of rolling white caps that stood out against his torch beam. He could just make out the boats moored bow-first along the private jetty. They were rising and straining against their mooring lines like a line of bucking stallions. He noted one boat closest in had been tied up stern-first into the wind with the waves crashing in over the transom. He figured it was probably Dieter's vessel and that it would most likely be on the bottom before daybreak. Looking east to the government jetty he could make out a number of lights burning from within the many cruisers and yachts, their skippers, no doubt, out on the decks adjusting fenders and lines in the storm.

Suddenly, behind him there was a crack of splintering wood and a tea-tree crashed down over the flooded track splashing water up and soaking him.

'I really shouldn't be out here in all this.' John mumbled to himself.

Stepping over the fallen trunk he decided to make a hasty retreat back up from the lake. He was almost back to the cabin when an alien sound pierced the din of the tempest. It sounded like a woman crying out, or maybe a small boy, he couldn't quite tell. He moved into the scrub toward the sound but couldn't seeing anything. Then, there it was again, only this time more like the strange giggling noises he'd heard the time before. He moved on further, but it was hard to separate the strange sounds from the roar of the wind and the clatter of the branches around him. He made his way up into the sandy hummocks overlooking the sea and was hit by the full force of the south easterly. The ocean let out a deep rumble. It appeared like a boiling cauldron and the spindrift pushed his hair back and stung his face. The beach was without light or visible horizon as if the boiling ocean and the angry sky were as one.

Another crack of splintering wood and a second tree blew down near him.

'That's it, I'm done out here.' John shouted

But, as if mocking his cowardice, a horrible wailing sound came through the noise of the storm once more. As John beat a hasty retreat, he shone his light up into the branches for fear of getting clobbered by another wayward limb. To his horror, he saw that the little straw effigies were back hanging in the trees, dancing frantically in the storm.

As he entered the sanctuary of the little cottage, John took care to lock the door behind him, something he normally wouldn't bother to do. He lit all the lamps, pulled the curtains closed and turned the transistor radio on in an attempt to normalise this seemingly hostile and lonely environment in which he found himself. The radio reception was terrible. Two different all-night broadcasts came in through a heavy band of static, one on top of the other, so neither channel made any sense. Despite the poor reception he turned the volume up as high as it would go hoping to drown out the din continuing outside. There was still four or five hours till daybreak, too long to try and stay up. He rifled through the cupboard and found half a bottle of cooking sherry left over from his last stay in Paradise. He took a deep slug from the bottle, which he struggled to keep down, then took another and another, till his head started to spin. He collapsed back into bed, pulled the dooner up over his face and drifted off into an alcohol induced stupor.

Morning came and John was woken to the incessant ringing of his cell phone. One of the four lamps he'd lit in the middle of the night was still burning, the remainder had burnt dry, and the radio batteries were dead. He felt hungover and ghastly. The storm had blown itself out, the wind had abated, and the sea fog had burnt off giving way to a clear sunny morning.

'So, how did you go during the blow last night John?' A bright chirpy voice enquired over the phone.

'It got pretty wild over here Sal. I haven't been outside yet, but I know we've lost a few trees. We copped a branch on the roof and I'm not sure how much beach is left. I won't keep talking just now, I'm keen to see how the boat is and to check out any damage to the house. Assuming the lake has calmed down a bit I'll come over about mid-morning to bring you back over if that suits you.'

Clearing the cobwebs from his mind, John trod tenderly barefoot over the debris. Halfway down the track Alan Bagshaw, dressed in a smart pair of crisp clean overalls, had already started the task of clearing things up.

'Bit of a blow last night, eh John. It'll take days to tidy everything up. I've already been down to our jetty. Your boat is OK, but you've got a fair bit of water to bail out before you go anywhere in it. I couldn't see Dieter's boat, not sure if he's out on the water, although I hardly think so.'

By the time John got to the jetty himself, Joe Tucker, with smoking pipe in hand, had nearly finished surveying his beloved Emma. Dieter Urquhart and sons were in the middle of playing the blame game, peering down over the side of the jetty to where their runabout sat firmly on the bottom. Joe acknowledged John's presence with a momentary glare, then turning his back on him and retreated to his cabin.

John got to work with his bailing bucket. There was at least a foot of water in his tinnie. It seemed like it took forever to get all the water out, during which time young Daniel and Mark had cut the strained mooring lines to Dieter's submerged boat and had duck dived down and fixed a line to the bow.

'Come on boys, it's not going to bloody pull itself up onto der bloody beach. Pull harder!' yelled Dieter trying to motivate the boys.

'One of you moored der bloody thing arse-about-face last night. I don't care which one it was, but it's up to you two to retrieve it and get it going again, or I'll be getting rid of der bloody thing, and you can bloody well swim across here next time!'

John finished up and returned to the cottage. By the time he'd fixed some breakfast and cleaned himself up it was time to motor over to Minamurra to collect Sal.

There was still a bit of chop on the estuary which made the crossing slow going. Passing by the government jetty John could make out a number of conversations relating to last night's gale. It was obvious that not much sleep was had between all the boats, and some of the owners were talking about moving on to look for more sheltered moorings, lest another blow should happen. But out on the water with a fair breeze on his back, it was almost as if last night was just a bad dream.

Arriving at Frankie's, John found Faye at the bowser mixing some two-stroke fuel for a customer. She appeared to be wearing a dress that John imagined she would have worn the night before when she dined out with Sal. He thought it looked somewhat incongruous, and why wasn't Frankie helping with that? In the shop Sal was taking money from another customer who had just purchased some bait.

'Where's Frankie?' enquired John.

'He hasn't returned from Melbourne.' answered Sal. 'Faye had to leave the motel early this morning and open up. Just as well I decided to call in and wait for you here, she would have been run off her feet otherwise. She's quite concerned about him. I think she's going to ring his brother, when she gets a chance, to see if he knows anything.'

'Well, if you think she can manage by herself now, we'd better be heading back. There's a bit of cleaning up to do about the place after last night's storm.'

John and Sal left Faye to cope with the daily business on her own, but assured her they would stay in touch in case she needed help with anything. Hopefully Frankie would return later in the day, or at worst, if he was still tied up with whatever it was that required him to be in Melbourne, his brother would come down to help her out.

After a somewhat bouncy return crossing, they tied up at their mooring, but before they could get to their track Gloria confronted them in an animated state.

'Oh John, Sal, we had the most terrible night last night. All that wind and noise! We've got a sheet of roofing iron that has come loose at the back and pulled out the cable to our solar panels. Rick is up there trying to fix it now, and he should never be allowed to be up a ladder at his age. I've tried to ring that Banister fellow, such a difficult man! He won't answer his phone. John, can you help us?'

'Frankie's away in Melbourne right now Gloria.' John informed her. 'I've got a bit to do at my own place first, but perhaps if it can wait till later this afternoon, I could have a look at it for you then.'

'Well, I don't have much choice then, do I? Thankyou John.'

Leaving Gloria, John noticed the Urquhart boys had stripped their outboard motor down. Surrounded by spare gaskets and various engine parts, and partly obscured in clouds of dense smoke emitting from the spluttering motor, they had somehow managed to get the thing going ...... well sort of.

On their way up the track John broached the subject once more about the strange noises and sights in the night. He implored Sal to follow him into the bushes so he could show her the little figures hanging in the tree branches, however the tumult that had preceded him in the wee hours appeared to have erased any evidence of anything unusual, and try as he may, he could not find a single effigy in the tree canopy. There was simply nothing to show.

The remainder of the day went uneventfully. Paradise buzzed with the sound of chainsaws and leaf blowers cleaning up the branches and leaf litter brought down in the storm. John cleared his track to the ocean beach and carted the wood back to be used to burn under the copper at some later date once it had dried. He managed to fit in Gloria and Rick's job later on, after which both he and Sal were invited to share some late afternoon snacks, where Rick broke out a bottle of aged whiskey as an accompanying aperitif.

Sal took a call from Faye that evening. Frankie had returned during the day, but they had argued again over Faye's role in the running of the business. Faye had decided to take on the part time position she applied for with a local solicitor, which she said she was really looking forward to, however Frankie on hearing her decision had stormed off back to the farm in a rage. She told Sal that a girlfriend in town had offered her the use of a bungalow in her backyard, and that for the time being, until she could sort things out with Frankie, she had decided to stay there. John pondered the possibility of a visit from the angry little Welshman at any time, and what he might possibly offer him as advice, but to his relief the visit didn't eventuate.

The coming days were hot and dry, signalling the arrival of a late summer heatwave. Several times each day John and Sal went down to the lake to cool off, their footsteps crunching over the dry leaf litter. A sporadic puff of wind over the dry landscape caused the Mahogany gums to shed some leaves, which when falling upon the corrugated iron roof, oddly mimicked the sound of raindrops.

'So much for the recently cleaned gutters.' John thought.

The occasional community of Paradise soon unwound back into the summer rhythm of eating, swimming and relaxing. Strolling along the water's edge towards the government jetty the evocative sights and smells of summers past filled the senses. Brightly coloured beach umbrellas, bikini clad women and fat bellied men in their trunks, the shrill melody of children playing in the shallows, the smell of sunscreen and insect repellent, and the countless tanned or sunburnt bodies recumbent in the sun. Many enjoyed evening drinks together by the lakeside watching the warm dusky light give way to the cool pastels of the evening. The flooding tides had abated, and the sparkling water of the estuary was crystal clear and cool. Over on the ocean, white crested waves rising from a deep blue sea, washed gently over fine yellow sand. The sounds of bright conversation and merriment drifted through the tee trees into the night on the scent of enticing smells from any number of campfires. To John's relief, there were no more strange night sounds nor bad events that happened in the coming days. Even Joe Tucker's brusque manner toward him appeared to have softened somewhat. Perhaps all was good and right in the world after all.

But sadly, it seemed it was just too good to last.

'John, I've got some bad news, so brace yourself.' declared Sal, interrupting John's afternoon nap in the shade on the decking.

'Something awful …I mean really awful, has happened!'

'Well, come on then. Don't leave me wondering.' replied a bleary-eyed John.

'I've just had a call from Faye. Frankies been found dead! It looks like he's hanged himself in the back shed on the farm.'

John sat bolt upright, staring into the bush momentarily, stunned by Sal's blunt delivery of the bad news.

Lost for words, he returned his gaze to Sal. 'What! …. Just like that? I mean, when did this happen? Who found him? Where's Faye now?'

'Faye's out at the farm right now being interviewed by the police. They've cordoned the farm off and set up a crime scene until they can check out the circumstances and prepare a brief for the coroner.'

Sal sat down and began to apprise John on what Faye had told her. 'Apparently the reason Frankie had travelled to Melbourne was to see a solicitor and have his Will changed. He stayed with his brother while he was there, and after leaving to return to the farm, his brother phoned Faye to say he was very concerned by Frankie's demeanour. As you know, Faye had been staying with a friend in Minamurra, so his brother decided to call Frankie at the farm just to make sure he was alright. When Frankie didn't pick up, or return his brother's calls, his brother made the decision to travel down early the following morning. Faye says he took a thirty-minute break at a truck stop halfway to get some breakfast and let her know he was on his way. When he got to the farm he found the house was empty and the back door wide open. He went outside and down to the shed, and that's where he found Frankie. The awful part about it was that had he arrived just half an hour earlier, he thinks, Frankie may still have been alive in the house.'

'That day on beach when he slapped me, Sal. It was so out of character; I should have seen it coming.'

'The police have told Faye that he probably had this planned for some time. They found an extensive note he had left on the bench, where he basically blamed Faye for everything, and how he couldn't come to terms with the possibility of losing her. He must have known Faye was growing out of their relationship some time ago. He'd even gone as far as to detail how he wanted his funeral to be conducted ...... and this is where you come into the picture John, he wrote that he wanted you to deliver the eulogy!'

'Oh hell, I wonder when the funeral will be. I'll have to apply for more leave from work I suppose.'

John rose from his chair and paced around the decking for a time. He then went about collecting his fishing gear, a bucket and a landing net. If there was one useful thing he'd learnt from Frankie, it was that being in a quiet spot with a fishing line provided the perfect excuse for allowing one's mind to wander and think about things while appearing to be occupied doing something that was purposeful. He made his way down to the private jetty, his racing thoughts all but blocking out the sights and sounds around him. At the end of the jetty, he sat down, his legs dangling over the edge. He cast his line out. His gaze followed the cast out, then further over the water and beyond into the distance hills.

The fluid nature of the reflections on the water had a meditative effect on John, and he let his thoughts drift freely in and out of his troubled mind. After a while, sitting there quietly, he began to feel a sense of peacefulness descend over him. Unfortunately, his peaceful state wasn't long lasting. A cogent voice from behind penetrated his meditative state.

'So, a little bird tells me that Banister man has come to a sticky end. Indeed, a very sad situation, wouldn't you agree John. Well, wouldn't you? I never really liked the man, but you did, didn't you? And don't say you didn't, because I've seen you both fishing on the beach together. He was a blasphemer and not as one with our Lord. Nevertheless, it's a bad thing that has happened, and I warned you bad things could happen to people who frequent this place and who are not of The Faith. I warned you didn't I. Yes, I did!'

"Well, so bad news travels fast Simon. How did you get to hear about it? ..... I only found out myself a couple of hours ago. And anyway, please, it's not the time to be bandying your crazy ideas around.' remarked John defiantly.

'Half the town knows about it already John. Half the town! Crazy ideas are they now? You know, our blessed Saviour will succour those of The Faith during times of danger but will not hesitate to smite those who mock his 'Wonderous vision of the purpose of the Lord'. For those of you who choose to walk along the street where only rats can run, and who shun the 'house of the Lord', can certainly be accommodated in his 'house of pain'.'

At this point John started to wonder whether Simon's increasing religious fervour was a sign he may be becoming a little unhinged. He decided the best course of action here was to cut the conversation short.

'Well thank you for your advice Simon, but I'll have to leave it there for now. I have a few things requiring my attention back at the cottage.'

And with that he collected his things together and beat a tactical retreat from the barrage of Simon's verbal artillery.

Chapter Nine

It's an Ill Wind That Blows No Good

Psalms 1:4 The ungodly are not so:
but are like the chaff which the wind driveth away.

A warm north wind sprang up late in the afternoon, and even after the sun had set, a balmy breeze persisted into the evening. In the warmth, many of the Paradise residents, and those on the boats, stayed up late, shunning the idea of withdrawing inside for the night.

Before retiring to bed, John made a mental list of the things he wanted to do the following day. Amongst other things, he intended to try and find out more about this mystery man who'd been running the traps enquiring about those who might be wanting to sell their properties. From what he could determine, no one had been approached yet from the Scully side of the creek. Surely somebody would have kept his business card, or some other ID. The other thing he needed to sort out was over in Minamurra. He needed to find out what was happening with the Banisters .... what arrangements were being made about the funeral, and what was happening with the servo in the interim period.

It was quite warm inside the cottage, and John and Sal lay on top of the bed next to an open window. The sounds of distant conversations and laughter from different quarters were carried along and in on the wind. John drifted in and out of sleep throughout the night, woken from time to time by the freshening northerly as it pushed its way through the tree canopies which surrounded the house. Peering out the window, an otherwise black sky appeared clear and blazing with stars.

The Williams didn't rise until around 9 AM that morning, and already the sun was high, and it was hot. John ventured out, dressed only in a pair of shorts. A scorching blast burned against his face. They sat inside preferring a light breakfast and coffee in the comparative coolness of the cottage. These hot windy days of midsummer made John edgy, so he decided, rather than visiting Minamurra he'd stay close to home ....at least until there was a break in the weather. After breakfast he thought it would be a good idea to start raking up some of the dry leaves about the house and trim back many of the tree branches which had begun to impinge on the building following the good winter rains.

It wasn't long before his face dripped with sweat. Soon his t-shirt stuck to his back in an uncomfortable manner. After about an hour, red faced and with a dry throat, working in this heat soon became very unappealing. John stopped raking, lent the rake against the tank-stand, put the handsaw down and cupped his hands under the running tap. He took a long sip of the cool fresh water and splashed the remainder over his face and over the back of his neck. He stretched up peering skywards and noted what he at first thought were thin puffs of blueish cloud drifting overhead. He moved out from under the shade to get a better view of the skyline. It wasn't cloud, it was smoke. He walked down to the creek to get a better idea of where the smoke might be coming from. It appeared to emanate from somewhere out to the west, but he couldn't be sure how far off. A couple of wisps floated low over John's head. It didn't have the usual 'sweet' smell of a BBQ or a campfire, it was acrid, and it stung his sinuses.

John raced back to the house. He burst in through the door, nearly falling over Sal who was busy sorting out a bottom cupboard.

'Sal, I think there's a fire somewhere!' he exclaimed.

'It's probably just someone burning off someplace John. You do get over overwrought on these hot windy days. And look at you, you're as red as a beetroot. You'll probably have a heart attack if you keep going on like this. Why don't you go down and cool off in the lake for a while? It's far too hot to be running around with a rake and saw like you are.'

'Who'd be silly enough to burn off on a day like today? Really Sal!'

Still, the suggestion of a swim did sound good, but rather than the lake, John opted to go across to the ocean beach side instead. That way he could drag the branch tailings he'd earlier trimmed and dump them in the eroded places in the sand hills.

He peered over the sand dunes at the top of his land. The ocean out front sparkled invitingly under the clear sky. The offshore north wind had blown the waves flat, and all that remained of the swell was a gentle little shore break. The water was clear save the occasional dark patches of weed stirred up during the storm from the other night. John slipped off his sandals and tip toed in a strange dancing manner over the scolding hot sand down to the water's edge. The dry sand squeaked with every tentative step. In contrast to the estuary, which was dotted with numerous boats and people, the ocean was quiet and empty, and John found he had the whole place to himself. He stripped off and plunged into the crisp tingling seawater.

During certain weather conditions the ocean could be a dangerous place to swim. The gutters and rips were often hard to make out, and an unsuspecting swimmer could soon find themselves in great difficulties with nobody in sight to render assistance. But on days like these when the conditions were benign, cooling of in the shallows of the surf beach was simply magic, and John could never figure out why more people didn't take advantage of this.

Rocked softly by the passing tidal surges, he floated on his back for some time. His heart rate settled in the comfort of the water. The brilliant sunlight, combined with the saltwater, caused him to squint and almost close out his surroundings, leaving him in an almost trance-like state. He stayed in the water until he could feel his feet starting to cramp up, then clambering out onto the beach his gaze was drawn westward once more. The smoke he witnessed earlier was not only still visible, but if anything, had become darker and thicker.

As John returned through the scrubby bush, he became aware that something was different. Save the rustle of the wind, the bush was eerily quiet. The usual crack of the whip-bird and the banter of the wattle-birds were absent. A black snake crossed his path, like a trickling rivulet of molten metal. Already in a heightened state of alertness, it startled him to the point where he lurched backwards and tripped over a fallen log. He struggled for a moment to catch his breath, and when he eventually entered the cottage, he was still pale from fright.

'What's wrong with you John? You look like you've just seen a ghost.'

'No, a snake Sal. I nearly trod on the damn thing. Scared the shit out of me! I'm lucky I didn't get bitten.'

'Well, I'm always at you to wear long pants and proper footwear when you walk through the bush.'

'Anyway, have you had a look outside? John asked. 'That fire, wherever it is, appears to be getting bigger. If this wind keeps up from the same direction, we could all find ourselves in trouble at some stage.'

Despite the heat of the day, the prospect of a bushfire impacting Paradise worried John sufficiently to resume his cleaning up around the cottage, he even got out his ladder and inspected the gutters for dry leaves again. From across the creek, he could hear that Dieter was also out busily clearing around his house. He ran over to Dieter's place to confirm that Dieter was aware of the fire and to see what he knew. Dieter told him that he'd heard the National Parks people had reported that a fire had started in the park just to the west of the Paradise boundary track. They thought they had it contained, but it had managed to spot ahead of the main front into private land.

'I'm about to get der boys back up here to give me a hand ...... fixing der boat can wait. If it gets into Paradise, we'll all be buggered. All der tea-trees and der dry grasses, dis place will go up like der tinderbox!'

Dieter's comments further raised John's concerns and he thought it prudent to return to the cottage to re-assess whether further clearing around the place was needed. In his haste he failed to recognise Joe Tucker's lumbering gait as Joe trudged doggedly along the track in front of him. John would have preferred to have avoided him, but the need to get past took precedence from the risk of further conflict with Joe.

'Sorry Joe, just need to get past .... How's Jane?'

'Jane is fine, thank you for asking.' grumbled Joe, without lifting his eyes from the track.'

'By the way, have you noticed all that smoke Joe?' John added.

'You may think I'm stupid John, but I'm not blind. Of course I'm aware there's a fire somewhere west of here. Probably one of those Scully's trying to burn us all out.......mad thoughtless buggers, the lot of them! I just hope if it comes this way it gets rid of what's left of that 'All Smiles' abomination once and for all, and even better, Simon's place.'

John, not wanting to 'rattle the dog's chain' any further, stepped past Joe and continued on without attempting to make any further small talk.

As the day wore on John paced down to the estuary every half hour or so to get a better view of the origins of the fire and to see if it was getting any larger, or any closer. At one point he noticed Simon out on the private jetty, also presumably checking on the fire. Oddly, John thought, despite all that blustering the day before about the '*Wonderous vision*' and the '*blessed saviour*' providing succour to those of the *Faith*, Simon appeared to be particularly flustered and concerned. He also noticed many of the other residents appearing at the lake from time to time presumably equally aware and concerned by the impending threat. In contrast, the day trippers, the yachties and those on the cabin-cruisers seemed to be either unaware, or unconcerned by the looming danger, they continued to enjoy their drinking and dining, their swimming and sunbaking on the lakeside.

By mid-afternoon the sun had taken on a deep orange hue. It cast an eerie yellowish light over the landscape. Wafts of hot smoky air permeated the land. The place was devoid of wildlife, even the shore birds had moved elsewhere.

In contrast to the transient boat people, the Paradise community had begun tuning into their radios and watching their cell phones for any information that might provide them with advice or warnings relative to their current situation. As the afternoon progressed, the north-westerly wind continued to freshen.

John hunted round the house in search of any buckets or empty bins he could fill with water. He made sure the old copper was full and went inside and filled the bath and the kitchen sink as well. He returned outside and tapped the side of the water tank to determine how much water it held, and to his dismay he discovered it was half empty, not that that would make much difference anyway, for without an axillary pump to pressurise the pipes it was impossible to get any sort of firefighting stream out of it. Sal, who by now shared John's angst, brought out half a dozen towels which John placed in the copper to soak. With a length of twine and a couple of tee-tree poles, he fashioned two crude beaters and left them in strategic positions near to the filled buckets he'd placed about the cottage.

Still dressed in his t-shirt, shorts and thongs, John thought it prudent to go and check on Alan Bagshore. He found Alan busy outside his house, line trimmer and chainsaw in hand, dressed in a pair of bright yellow overalls, accessorised with a red bandana, white construction helmet, goggles, heavy leather gloves and leather boots. It truly amazed John how Alan seemed to have the perfect outfit to suit every possible occasion!

'They say it could impact this area anytime from late afternoon to sometime tonight. There's a cool change on the way, but it all depends on when that arrives.' Alan advised.

'Where did you hear this?' John asked.

'I heard it reported over the marine radio. It seems the Coast Guard are tracking its progress and getting half hourly updates from the weather bureau. The bureau has issued a weather warning for boating in this area. They're predicting gale force north- westerlies swinging round to the southwest later today, and then turning southerly sometime later in the evening.'

John moved on to check on the Heads. He found Gloria and Rick loading their boat with their personal belongings, and of course the three dogs.

'Oh John, this fire situation is an awful thing, don't you agree? Do you think it will get to Paradise? I've told Rick he's much too old to be fighting fires, so we've decided to pack our things and move across to Minamurra for the night.'

'I'm quite fit enough to look after the place if we had to John. What Gloria can't see is that if we leave the property and lose the house, I am too old to re-build over here.' argued Rick.

'Well, all I can say to you both is I hope it doesn't get to that.' John replied.

But by late afternoon the sky had darkened to a deep red. The landscape went dark as if nightfall had arrived prematurely. The usual cacophony on the lakefront in midsummer had disappeared and was replaced by a strange silence. A great smoke column all but completely blotted out the sun, and the fire activity to the west, forebodingly underlit the dense clouds of smoke generated by the fire front. Yet it still appeared to be some distance away. A few of the cruisers on the government jetty, and more of the beach moored boats, decided to leave the area for safer places of refuge. The remainder of those on the visiting boats who had remained, stood guard along the shore keeping watch to the west as the fiery monster advanced easterly towards them. At some stage a loud hailer from a police launch echoed across the community, advising residents they should leave the area, or evacuate to the water without delay. A coastguard launch pulled up at the government jetty and off-loaded a team of volunteer firefighters armed with a portable pump and some rudimentary firefighting equipment to protect the government assets, and to check on the welfare of the residents. Contrary to the general movement of evacuees, a couple of large boats arrived from Minamurra, carrying no doubt, well-meaning friends of some of the Paradise people to see how they could help out.

Within the next half hour, fragments of blackened leaf matter and burnt bark started to fall out of the smoke layer and settle on the water and the land. The ocean beach was delineated by a black tidal mark separating the tidal wash from the white sand. Everything glowed a dark red, as if at any moment the vegetation all about them could spontaneously burst into flames in the stifling heat. Any thought of the Banister's situation, or the so-called mystery man couldn't have been further from John's mind at this time. Both he and Sal stood out on the decking, their gaze fixed westward trying to ascertain how far away the inferno might be.

As evening drew closer, so too did the continuing threat of fire. The hot northerly wind continued to freshen, and there was no sign yet of the promised southerly change. The dark horizon started to take on an ominous bright glow. By the late afternoon, their energy sapped by the heat and the relentless stress, the little community was starting to feel a growing sense of fatigue. People had been on high alert for most of what now had begun to seem like the longest of days, going over and over their plans and preparations for what might, or might not eventuate and obliterate them. The boats moored along the private jetty were filled with personal belongings and valuables in case a last-minute evacuation be required.

Nightfall eventually arrived, appearing more like an Armageddon dawn. The bright glow of flames, still not visible from Paradise, filled the sky and the burnt fragments of vegetation began to rain down in glowing brands like a thousand fireflies sweeping across the land by the devil-wind.

John set out into the scrub with his makeshift beater and headlamp checking for any evidence that the glowing brands may have ignited the dry brush around his property. Sal stayed with the cottage checking the gutters, under the house and the decking areas for any embers which might have lodged and started a spot fire.

Finally, the flames appeared on the horizon, rising into the night air as if in slow motion, terrifying yet strangely fascinating to watch. 'It's somewhere at the back of the Scully property' John thought. There was a commotion across the other side of the creek. Voices raised in urgent tones indicated a spot fire had ignited somewhere between the Urquhart's and the Scully's. John raced across, and by the time he got there, a half-dozen silhouettes had surrounded the blaze and were frantically beating out the conflagration with whatever they had at hand. Turning on his heels, he raced back home and, on the way, noticed the back of the Head's place all lit up. He could see torches darting around in the bushes and hear a pump-motor running flat out by the shore, and so assumed the volunteer firefighters had come up from the government jetty and run a hose line out to defend the place. Passing Alan's house, he saw Bagshaw up a ladder where flames were rising from a small section of guttering. He thought it looked so strange.

The dull roar of the main fire in the distance was drowned out by the clamour of the wind, the shouting voices, the screaming chainsaws and boat engines. Paradise was under ember attack. It was a scene of frantic activity and much confusion in the darkened smoke logged environment. It was hard to know what was going on, but it was evident the roaring flames of the main blaze were advancing ever closer. John continued to patrol his property for any spot fires. The air was hot and heavy, and painful to breathe. At one stage he thought he felt ants crawling over his head, only to discover his hair had been singed.

Finally, around midnight, the searing wind suddenly abated, however the glowing embers continued to rain down for some time. Then, during the very early hours of the morning, well before daybreak, a fresh southerly breeze advanced in from the sea, cleansing the smoky air, and bringing with it a sudden drop in temperature and a light drizzle of rain.

John, like most of the Paradise people, had remained up all night in the face of certain annihilation. As the cool change swept in, he felt the rush of fresh moist air caress his smoky body. Then, the sudden onset of exhaustion, swept over him like a heavy blanket. Sal, who had retired to bed several hours earlier when the wind had died down was sound asleep on the bed. John, still sweaty and smelling of smoke, collapsed into bed next to Sal. The two of them didn't stir till late in the morning.

The day was overcast, and in contrast to the previous day, a cool pleasant breeze dominated the weather. As they arose, the area continued to buzz with the sound of chainsaws and distant voices. Neighbours were checking their properties for any smouldering remnants, particularly concentrating on any dead trees that harboured signs of live embers. The acrid smell of bushfire smoke pervaded the landscape, and apart from the man-made noises, the bush remained eerily quiet and still.

After doing a final inspection of his own property, John set out to see how the others had faired. To his relief, the majority of Paradise had remained free from fire damage. Alan Bagshaw was up on his roof pulling off a section of roofing-iron to check for any fire extension from the ignition in his guttering. The backwall and an adjoining shed at the Head's place was damaged, but the firefighters had done a good job to contain it from doing any further harm. All the other houses appeared to have come through unscathed. The fire, it seemed, had only come as far as Simon's place before the cool change had turned it back. Had the wind-change arrived an hour later it would have been a different story John reasoned. He noted Joe Tucker was on-board Emma with the red sails raised, assessing a number of burn holes where embers had penetrated. There was no sign of Jane and John wondered what she would have made of all the commotion the day before, or even if she would have been aware of the situation they were in. Around the Urquhart's there were several areas of burnt scrub where spot fires had taken hold. Dieter was directing the boys who were raking over the burnt areas checking for any remaining hot coals, their blackened faces testament to their desperate efforts during the night.

The government jetty was a hive of activity. Those boat owners who chose to remain were out with buckets and mops cleaning off the wind-driven ash from the windows and decks. A Coastal Parks barge was pulled up on the sand and a small delegation had alighted to check for damage to any of the government amenities. The estuary itself was otherwise devoid of boats.

For the remainder of the day John and Sal spent their time cleaning off the ash from the decking and windows. Despite the water tank being half empty, John disconnected the downpipes so that when the next rains came, the ash covering the roof didn't wash into the tank and foul their drinking water. Beyond that they did very little else. Around afternoon teatime, Sal ventured over to Susan's to compare notes from the fire event while John had a nap.

Chapter Ten

Farewell to Friends and Foes

*Psalms 1:1 Blessed is the man that walketh not in
the counsel of the ungodly, nor standeth in the way of sinners,
nor sitteth in the seat of the scornful.*

The following days passed quietly in Paradise. The motor-launches, cruisers and yachts began to return to the estuary shores, and the pleasant summer smells and sounds gradually eroded those of trauma, that which had been endured earlier in the week. It gave John time to reflect on recent events and the last conversation he'd had with Simon Scully. His mind also turned to the matter of Frankie's suicide and what actions on his part needed to be addressed in the coming days. It had all been one hell of a stay here in his normally benign place of rest and recreation.

'I was thinking I might go over to Minamurra later today, Sal. We could do with a few things from Evan's mini-mart, and I need to chase Faye up to see how she's travelling and what arrangements have been made regarding Frankie's funeral …. and not least of all, what's happening with the servo in the short term.'

'Yes, we need to know. Do you mind if I don't come with you? I just feel like I need some quiet time to myself after all that's happened recently. I'll make you up a list of things we need from the shops.'

John too was happy to have some time to himself. He felt the trip across to Minamurra would provide him with some space to put things in perspective, maybe even catch some scuttlebutt from the townsfolk about the happenings in Paradise. Beside the lake he ran into Dieter who was inspecting his beached boat and the waterlogged outboard motor, which by now was in many pieces.

'If you're going across to town John, would you mind giving one of der boys a lift across? We need to pick up a few spare parts for der motor, udderwise we can't get it going properly again.'

'Happy to help Dieter, but I don't know what's happening at the servo, you know with Frankie gone. I guess it's still open, so we can get to our cars in the compound, but other than that....'

'Der boys know what they need, so if someone is there, they ought to be able to find der parts they need themselves. I'll get Mark to come across mit you.'

The two men motored across the lake without conversation. Dieter's son was happy to sort out their needs, then wait at the boat while John attended to his. John was relieved to find the servo still open. He dropped his outboard fuel tank at the bowser ready for filling before going into the shop. What he saw standing behind the counter shocked him.

'Frankie? I ...... I thought......?'

At that moment Faye appeared from within the office.

'Oh John, sorry if you were startled. This is Frankie's brother Timmy. They're a couple of years apart, but people often mistake them for twins. Timmy looks so much like Frankie. Wouldn't you agree? How did you go with the fire? I hear it was a pretty close call for you all.' she continued.

Faye looked fragile and diminished. Frankie's death had obviously taken its toll on her, particularly the accusations contained in his suicide note, blaming her for his demise. She stood there, her shoulders hunched and her normally shiny blonde hair looked dull and bedraggled. Her eyes had a haunted look about them. John felt so sorry for her.

Following that first awkward encounter with Timmy, the two men introduced themselves, after which John could see that beyond the physical similarity, Timmy's personality, while not entirely different to Frankie's, reflected a far more moderate demeanour.

'Timmy's going to stay with me for a while John till we can sort out what to do with the servo and the farm. It may be some time before they release Frankie's body, so Timmy and I think it's best to have a memorial service for him. We're organising it for next week. If you're still around, Frankie had requested in his note that he would like you to deliver the eulogy.'

John thought it was odd that Frankie would want him to speak at the service, but Faye explained while most of the town knew him, they didn't really have many people they considered to be 'friends' as such. And as Frankie would say, he was not a 'people person' and his often sexist and racial remarks, plus his habit of swearing in front of customers, put many off. He also didn't suffer those who he considered to be fools, and he let that be known to those unfortunates enough, who apparently fell into that category.

'Faye, I'll have to see if I can extend my leave from work first. They still owe me a few weeks, so it shouldn't be a problem. I have no idea what I'm going to say about Frankie though, but he was quite a character.'

The three of them became aware of the young man patiently standing at the shop front door.

'Sorry, I should have introduced you to Mark.' said John, gathering his senses. 'Mark is Dieter Urquhart's son. Dieter owns the white Hilux you've got parked in the compound. Mark has come across from Paradise with me. Their boat sank in that storm last week and Mark was hoping to pick up some parts to get the motor going again.'

Timmy directed Mark out the back to the workshop and explained he knew nothing much about boat engines, but that Mark was welcome to search through the stock himself to see if he could find what he needed. Meanwhile, John took himself off down the street to get what was on Sal's shopping list, while Mark sorted through the many racks of bits and pieces in Frankie's shed.

With his mind distracted by the Banister's dilemma, John forewent his usual avoidance of the Central Hotel while on his way to Geoff Evan's mini-mart. Unfortunately for John, midway passing the front of the pub, a drunken figure staggered out onto the pavement blocking his path.

'Well, if it isn't that dumb arrogant prick who chose to ignore me the other day.' blurted the drunkard.

It was Bill the fisherman, replete with a fresh black eye, who John had the misfortune of encountering at the doctor's surgery several weeks ago. John had earlier been comforted in the belief that this objectionable character had never recognised him. However, here he was, assuming a wide gait in John's path, rocking precariously on a pair of worn-out thongs, glass in hand, his bung eye struggling to focus on the image in front of him.

John's earlier thoughts were instantly snapped back into focus by this pathetic yet menacing image of what stood in the way of him and his shopping duties.

'I seem to recall seeing you at Dr. Stephen's surgery a little while ago...... Am I correct?' John asked diplomatically.

'Arrr .... that bloody Stephens bloke, I'd rather see a bloody vet...only we ain't got one of them here. Are youse a mate of his then? ..... Yes? .... Well, that would figure, yar big pansy!'

The drunk lurched forward and nearly shirt fronted John, his breath, John recalled smelling something like what he imagined to be like the wind from Satan's bottom.

'No, my friend,' John continued, with his diplomatic approach. 'I've got a property over at Paradise, and I injured my foot one night. I had no choice but to come over here and consult him to have it attended to. I see your previous injury has healed up well.'

'Ha! Paradise you say?' the bung-eyed drunk replied. 'Those Scully buggers live over there, don't they? Can I tell you something about what's happening over there!'

'You mean the fire Bill...... Is that your name?' John politely asked.

'Yeh Bill ...... Nah, stuff the fire ...... That Scully prick's got a lot more goin' on over there, so me mates on the trawlers recon. One of the deckies on the Miriam 2 .... Jonny someone.... lives up the west end of the estuary somewhere. Well, he's been mouthing off about how that Scully bastard's been payin' him to scare the shit out of the other residents over there, you know, voices in the night and all that crap...... reckons it's a real bloody hoot.'

'You don't say Bill! Well, that answers a few questions for me then.' replied an astounded John Williams.

'Anyway'. continued Bill. 'I never told you nothin. It's not worth losing me job for mouthin' off, so piss off and don't ask me anythin' more about nothin' or I'll be happy to give you more than just a bloody nose yar prick.'

John hastened away, his mind racing into overdrive trying to make sense of why Simon would pay someone to do that sort of thing, and what he could possibly stand to gain from it. He decided it was best not to share this news with anybody else until he could first, verify what the inebriated blaggard Bill had said was in fact true, and second, form some sort of opinion about what possible motive Simon might have. He knew it was pointless simply fronting Simon with the allegations. He would no doubt deny it, and then have the ability to turn the story around and back onto his accuser. Anyway, it was enough for the moment to get his head around the Banister's situation and work out after talking to Faye, what the family might want him to say in his eulogy.

By the time he returned to his tinny, Mark was patiently waiting for him in the boat. There was a bag full of bits and pieces at his feet which he'd picked out from Frankie's shed. Faye had attended to his fuel-tank and Mark had re-installed it into the boat.

The trip back was devoid of conversation despite there being so much talk to share between the two. Finally, pulling up to the private jetty John broke his silence.

'Do you recon you'll be able to get your motor going now?'

'I recon we will. I couldn't find all the parts we need; the place was in a bit of a mess, but I should be able to modify some of the bits to fit.'

'Well, that's a relief for you then. Let me know if you're still stuck tomorrow and need to go over again. I'll have to talk to Faye and Timmy again before Frankies memorial service anyway.'

The two parted company, Mark chasing up his brother to help with the outboard, John carting the shopping up to Sal.

John found Sal and Susan out the front of his place imbibing in a late afternoon wine.

'Please join us and tell us all the juicy news from across the lake.' a relaxed looking Susan beckoned, waving a glass of Sauv Blanc at him.

John resisted the urge to share the sensational gossip he'd encountered outside the Central Hotel. Instead, concentrating on maintaining his best poker-face, he reported on what might be happening with the servo in the short-term following Frankies death, but also Frankie's wishes for his own funeral, as he had detailed in his suicide note.

Following that conversation, John, aware of Susan's interest in the local flora and fauna, (apart from her marine studies), then asked if she might have a trail camera he could borrow for a few nights.

'Why do you want to borrow a trail camera for heaven's sake John?' Sal interjected.

John hated the fact that Sal seemed to be working against him in Susan's presence, but he didn't want to elaborate about his request by divulging what Bill the fisherman had told him. He needed another reason for asking for a night-vision camera.

'You know about the possum with the hob nailed boots who lands on our roof each night, and the wombat that's been undermining the footings of our cottage for the last two years? Susan, the one thing that struck me prior to the bushfire impacting on Paradise the other day, was the silence of the bush. Apart from us, the birds and the other wildlife who usually reside here must have had a sense of the impending threat of fire. I've noticed since the fire, much of the wildlife we are accustomed to seeing here seem not to have returned. I was really keen to set up a motion-sensitive night camera on our property somewhere to see if any of our more elusive nocturnal friends had come back.' said John, fibbing about its intended purpose.

'I don't have one, but I know the Jenzens down near the government jetty used to have one. Earlier this year, while the place was still quiet, they were looking for evidence to prove the bandicoot could still be around this area. I hear some bloke made them an offer on their land the other day, so they may be selling up now, and not in need of it any longer. I can ask them if you like.'

'Thanks Susan, that would be great.'

In due course Susan brought the camera over to John. She told him the Jenzens were happy for him to borrow it for as long as he liked. According to Susan, the Jenzens had felt a bad vibe about the place recently and were considering purchasing another property further down the coast. Susan then added, that after the trauma with the close call from the bushfire the other day, they got back to the man who made the offer and told him that under the current circumstances they would accept it, albeit a lot less than they would have otherwise considered.

This further reference to the mystery man going about Paradise making offers to purchase, rang more alarm bells in John's already over-busy mind. The rumours in the doctor's surgery about a Coastal Parks acquisition of the properties, the apparent generational dislike of the Scully family over in Minamurra, and the recent strange happenings, plus the alleged shenanigans of this Jonny Starling person were troublesome enough. Then there were the fervent religious warnings from Simon about bad happenings for those not of the 'Faith' ......
Something untoward was going on, but he still just couldn't connect the dots. Worse still, no one else around Paradise seemed to share his concerns.

John fitted the camera with fresh batteries the following day. He took it out to the general area where the 'voices' and the little effigies had taunted him. Even considering the little camera was already inconspicuous with its 'camo' finish, John took pains to secrete it at the edge of a clearing overlooking a likely spot. If what that crusty old drunk 'Bill' had said was true, then just maybe the night camera might provide him with the hard evidence he needed to confirm Jonny Starling's nocturnal indiscretions.

With the trail camera set up in the bush, like he might set a baited nightline in the water to catch an elusive fish, John turned his mind to Frankie's memorial service that was due to happen in the coming days.

Faye and Timmy had desided to hire the local Mechanics Hall for the service in favour of the church, such was Frankie's wish in his letter. Additionally, they'd organised airfares to allow Frankie and Faye's adolescent sons to return from Western Australia, where the boys were working as jackeroos, so they could farewell their father.

John pondered on what he might say in the memorial proceedings, after all, apart from Frankies staunch agnostic views, not to mention his bigoted opinions on race, sexuality and all other socially sensitive topics, he really hadn't known Frankie that well. Another consideration was getting over there in time. If the weather was good, it would take him no time to make the crossing, dressed in his 'Sunday best'. But experience taught him that the fickle microclimate, where Paradise was, could make his journey anything but dry and easy.

John eagerly checked the trail camera first thing each morning in the days that followed, but frustratingly, like the local fauna, any evidence of the spectre of the night had disappeared since the fire event.

The day of Frankie's service finally arrived, and John, while a little apprehensive, was also relieved in the knowledge that by day's end the whole thing would be done and dusted, and he could then put it all behind him. In contrast to the sombre occasion, the day of the service was bright and sunny. Sal had asked John to leave a little early so she could find some flowers somewhere in town to take to the ceremony. While they didn't have any formal attire to wear, they nevertheless dressed in their best apparel which they kept in the holiday cottage. Their 'Sunday best' was formal enough though to make them feel oddly out of place amongst the other folk in Paradise. No one else in Paradise seemed too interested in attending Frankies send off, causing John to wonder how many, if any, of the Minamurra folk would be attending.

After making an uneventful crossing, they arrived at the servo to find the premises all shut up. There was a prominent note taped to the shopfront door stating the business was closed for the day due to tragic circumstances and, perhaps for the sake of those over at Paradise John thought, read 'Anyone needing to remove their car from the compound should ring Geoff Evans at the mini-mart for access.'

It was a bit of a walk from where they moored their boat to the Mechanics Hall, but easier than trying to organise getting their car out of the compound. Passing Geoff Evan's mini mart, Sal spied some flowers on a stand by the front window. On closer inspection they looked to be a little more than just passed their best, but in the absence of anything else available, she decided they would have to do. Geoff, always the consummate salesperson, stepped out from behind the register and engaged them at the shopfront.

'The flowers you see here, lovely people, are on special today, only $7.00 a bunch. I got them in especially on the sad occasion of Mr Banister's memorial service. They've been in great demand today, so if you are intending to go to the service and want any, I wouldn't hold back, or they may be all gone soon.'

'OK Geoff, can I have a bunch of the red ones, and a bunch of those blue ones at the back.' answered Sal.

'Not a problem Mrs Williams, and can I also interest you in some tinned spaghetti, they're also on special today, still perfectly good, just need to be eaten this week.'

'Thanks, but no thanks Geoff.'

'How about some smoked salmon, quite good too, if eaten this evening.'

'No thanks!'

'Very well then, enjoy the service.' finished Geoff, obviously miffed that he'd failed to upsell his 'special' offers.

John and Sal continued down the main street with Sal's now drooping blooms in hand. They passed the long line of cypress pines overhanging the trawlers by the harbour board walk, past the line of various retail strip-shops which formed a gawdy façade along the main drag, past the minigolf place and the dated slot-machine parlour.

Near where the main street morphed into the regional highway, close to the Mechanics Hall, much to John's amazement, there was barely a car space left in which to park. A large crowd was milling at the entrance to the hall. John wondered, considering Frankie's reputation around the town, whether given the tragic circumstances surrounding Frankie's demise, that many of the town people were here for no other good reason than to satisfy their sense of morbid curiosity, hoping to glean any juicy details that surrounded Frankie's untimely passing.

Not long after John and Sal arrived to mingle with the crowd a dark limousine turned off the road and nudged quietly into the throng. The Banister clan alighted slowly with heads bowed. They clung close to each other, seemingly oblivious to their surroundings. Dressed mainly in black, their appearance further set the small group apart from the rest of the mourners who were attired variously in a mixture of workwear and Sunday-bests.

The Banisters were led inside and down to the front of the hall first, then shortly afterwards the congregation filed in slowly past a fold-out market table where they were offered a program with Frankies image on the front and invited to sign a condolence book. John and Sal entered too and found their seats, John aware that during the proceedings he would be called out by the celebrant to deliver his eulogy. The small huddle of Banisters at the front of the crowd looked so diminished and fragile compared to the robust gathering behind them.

The service started with the usual 'tap-tap' on the microphone and a welcoming introduction from the celebrant, who struggled to be heard above the residual chatter and scraping of folding chairs on the dusty wooden boards within the audience.

'Can we all be quiet please!' called a voice from the rear of the hall. 'We can't hear back here!'

'Can you hear me up the back now?' asked the celebrant, adjusting the microphone to better suit her slight statue. This was followed by an ear-piercing scream of feedback from the PA system, causing some near the front to wince and stick their fingers in their ears. Then, after some technical adjustments to the PA, the service progressed more smoothly.

The celebrant, who had obviously never known the deceased, rattled on about what she had learned of the life of Francis Emanuel Banister, his upbringing, his life achievements and as many good points about his character that she had bothered to note down as conveyed to her during her interview with the family just a couple of days before.

John could sense the audience was becoming restless. Some were glancing at their watches; one or two others were escorting restless children outside where they could no longer be seen or heard. Then there were some, quietly mumbling between inquisitive ears. Finally, John was called to address the gathering. Negotiating his passage awkwardly out from his back-seat row, he took a deep breath, straightened up to full height, and strode confidently to the front of the gathering. He got a full view of the congregation for the first time. He estimated there must have been at least three hundred people packed into the hall. Sensing the growing boredom in the crowd from the over processed and benign nature of the service, John decided to ditch his pre-prepared speech. Instead, he began to describe Frankies quirkier side, and tell of some of the funnier encounters he had had with him, that others would probably relate to. After a few minutes, the atmosphere within the hall seemed to lift. There was a spark of energy in the gathering and people nodded in agreement and laughed at some of John's accounts. Even the Banister family, while still so bereft, appeared to show some relief on hearing of Frankie's lighter side.

One story that John was keen to share recounted the time he needed to get a replacement water-tank over to Paradise. The tank was too awkward to fit in his boat, so Frankie generously suggested to John he load it into a small runabout parked on the sand across the road from the servo and tow it over in that. John took up Frankie's kind offer, but on launching the little craft was concerned that there was practically no freeboard remaining, and should he encounter any chop on the journey across, the little vessel might take on water and sink.

'Don't worry about that, it's not a problem.' John recalled Frankie saying.

'But what will you do if I lose the boat?'

'Nothin'…… it ain't my boat.'

At that part of the story John noticed a large man near the front-row seats, who just happened to live next to the servo. The man looked him dead in the eye then gave him a 'knowing' nod. This chap had for years wondered who the bugger was that stole his little boat, and then mysteriously returned it a few days later, perhaps with an overwhelming sense of guilt. John sensed it was probably best to finish the story telling at that point before it got him into any more trouble. He concluded his address by reciting Rudyard Kipling's poem 'IF'.

'If you can keep your head when all about you Are losing theirs and blaming it on you, If you can trust yourself when all men doubt you, But make allowance for their doubting too; If you can wait and not be tired by waiting, Or being lied about, don't deal in lies, Or being hated, don't give way to hating, And yet don't look too good, nor talk too wise: If you can dream—and not make dreams your master; If you can think—and not make thoughts your aim; If you can meet with Triumph and Disaster And treat those two impostors just the same; If you can bear to hear the truth you've spoken Twisted by knaves to make a trap for fools, Or watch the things you gave your life to, broken, And stoop and build 'em up with worn-out tools: If you can make one heap of all your winnings And risk it on one turn of pitch-and-toss, And lose, and start again at your beginnings And never breathe a word about your loss; If you can force your heart and nerve and sinew To serve your turn long after they are gone, And so hold on when there is nothing in you Except the Will which says to them: 'Hold on!' If you can talk with crowds and keep your virtue, Or walk with Kings—nor lose the common touch, If neither foes nor loving friends can hurt you,

If all men count with you, but none too much; If you can fill the unforgiving minute With sixty seconds' worth of distance run, Yours is the Earth and everything that's in it, And—which is more—you'll be a Man, my son!'

John wasn't sure how much of Kipling's poem the crowd would have taken in, but they seemed suitably impressed with his flamboyant recitation and offered him a round of applause at the conclusion of his speech.

Directly following the eulogy, and before John could resume his seat, Frankie's last wish, as requested in his suicide note, was granted, in the form of a song he wanted played, as part of his send off. It was the pop star Anastasia's song 'Sick and Tired'. John thought it was a strange choice, but none the less a catchy tune he'd not heard before. However, looking down on the family, he could see it was causing them much distress and he couldn't figure it out, until he listened carefully to some of the lyrics;

*'A little late for all the things you didn't say
I'm not sad for you
But I'm sad for all the time I had to waste
'Cause I learned the truth*

*Your heart is in a place I no longer want to be
I knew there'd come a day
I'd set you free
'Cause I'm sick and tired
Of always being sick and tired*

*Your love isn't fair
You live in a world where you didn't listen
And you didn't care
So I'm floating*

Floating on air
Oh, yeah

No warning of such a sad song
Of broken hearts
My dreams of fairy tales and fantasy, oh
Were torn apart' . . . .

I lost my peace of mind
Somewhere along the way
I knew there'd come a time
You'd hear me say

I'm sick and tired
Of always being sick and tired

Your love isn't fair
You live in a world where you didn't listen
And you didn't care
So I'm floating
Floating on air . . . .*'*

It was Frankie's way of delivering a final cruel message from the grave, blaming everything on Faye for his demise, and in a way that made it brutally public via all those attending the service here. Faye broke down unconsolably and had to be physically assisted from the hall by Timmy past the assembled throng of voyeuristic eyes and the covert whispers. The two sons followed, embarrassed for their mum, but not fully understanding the gravity of the situation. If having to mourn such a tragic loss publicly wasn't difficult enough, now the tide of sympathy potentially turning to Frankie and against her, would make life living in this small community untenable. The gossiping, the sideways glances and the awkward interruption to normal conversation would mean that Faye would probably have to face the prospect of moving away from Minamurra somewhere, to try and start a new life for herself.

Another wish of Frankie's was that there was to be no wake to follow his service. He didn't like the idea of any freeloaders being entertained on the fruits of his earnings and hard work following his death. John and Sal caught up with the family briefly outside the hall. Amongst all the hangers on and for that matter, the potential rumour-mongers, there were a small group of mourners who were obviously keen to show their respect and support for Faye and the family. Faye had little to say, obviously still distraught by the finish to the service, but Timmy came forward to thank John for his contribution to the proceedings, and the boys followed close behind to shake John's hand in acknowledgement of his support.

The trip back over to Paradise following the memorial service provided both John and Sal with time for reflection. It wasn't as if their lives had been completely upturned by the recent traumatic events, as with the Banisters, however they still felt a sense that they'd both been put through an emotional wringer.

Returning to the cottage, John felt the need to take himself off and do a quiet spot of fishing. He thought that in some way, escaping out on the water with a fishing rod, as Frankie was often want to do, might help him make better sense of things and put his mind more at ease. Sal, on the other hand was keen to get across to Susan's to fill her in on the day's events and all the gossip.

However, when John arrived at the lake, he was greeted by the rather bizarre scene of Dieter's boys, Daniel and Mark, having an altercation with another man on the private jetty. The man was obviously not one of the Paradise lot; a small stoutish man, attired in a dark business suit and carrying what appeared to be a leather satchel. He looked quite out of place.

'Ah, at last, the mystery man!' John thought.

As John approached closer, hoping to hear the verbal clashes better, the meeting suddenly became quite physical. The older boy Mark grabbed the man under his arms from behind, while Daniel at the same time, restrained his kicking legs and raised them off the ground, rendering the wildly protesting victim quite helpless. To John's astonishment and shock, they bound the man hand and foot and bundled him into their boat. He was further restrained by a strip of gaffer-tape plastered across his animated mouth. They held him down, out of sight in a foetal position on the bottom of the runabout. Mark fired up the outboard, which despite all the work done on it since it's drowning, coughed and spluttered erratically and blew copious amounts of blue smoke. The two boys, together with their unfortunate captive, motored out well clear of the cruisers on the government jetty on a heading which would have taken them toward the entrance to the sea.

John, fearing something terrible was unfolding, hastened towards Dieter's place. There he found Dieter relaxing in a camp chair, beer in hand beside the BBQ.

'Dieter, your boys! ...... They've just absconded with some poor fellow in your boat! They're headed towards the entrance I think.'

'Well, it's his own doing. He picked a fight wid the wrong people dis time. That sleezy little dirt flogger's been doing the rounds for a while now, trying to capitalise on all the bad things occurring here of late, including more recently the fire, and other stuff he says has been going down during the past few months that we didn't know about. He reckons our property values are plummeting as a result, and putting der pressure on us to sell while our places are still worth something. I hear he has convinced some of der older folk to sell up, but be buggered if he thinks he can try it on us. Der boys are just trying to give him a lesson on my behalf. You shouldn't worry, in fact I think you should thank me, John.'

John returned to the lake front hoping to catch a glimpse of the Urquart's boat, but it had already motored out of sight. He walked out onto the jetty to where the unfortunate man had been press ganged by the boys and spotted the brown leather satchel the man had been carrying, floating in the water below. John managed to grab the satchel with a boat-hook. He hauled the sodden item onto the jetty and opened the latch to let the water drain out. The contents of the satchel consisted of a bundle of documents. They were all stuck together, equally sodden and at risk of becoming one solid mass of paper mâché. As much as John resisted the temptation to snoop, he decided to take the satchel and its contents home to dry them out, and hopefully preserve what was left of the paperwork.

He left his find in a safe place out in the sun, then returned once again to the shore-front, keen to learn the fate of this 'mystery man' at the hands of Dieter's boys, and to return the man's satchel to him. It would be nearly an hour before Daniel and Mark returned. John strained his eyes towards the still spluttering and smoky boat as it approached, hoping to see if their victim was still with them so he could return the man's bag. He could just make out what appeared to be a limp body strapped across the bow of the boat and the two assailants smiling smugly behind him. As they pulled into the jetty John looked on in horror at the sight of the visibly pallid 'mystery man', still trussed up and tied across the bow. The boys dragged him back into the centre of the tinny, his head and clothing dripping wet to the extent there were puddles of water forming in the bottom of the boat. They undid his restraints, tore the gaffer tape from his face and dumped him unceremoniously onto the deck of the jetty. John stepped forward to approach him, but to his surprise this pathetic figure suddenly came to life and without a word leapt to his feet and bolted off into the bush, nearly knocking John off the jetty in his flight.

'My God you pair, what on earth did you do to him?' John asked in shock.

'We just had a bit of good clean fun with him.' answered Mark smirking.

'It looked like you bloody well nearly drowned him!'

'We nearly did at one point.' added Daniel with a suppressed giggle.

The boys went on to describe what they had subjected the man to, obviously quite pleased in the manner in which they had managed to terrorise him. When they had initially confronted him about hustling them into selling their house and land, he had responded with vailed threats inferring that if they didn't agree to a sale, they would almost certainly incur a substantial financial loss if he was to return at a later date with a significantly smaller offer. When they reacted to his hard-line sales approach with threats to his wellbeing, he remained quite smarmy and condescending towards them. That's when they had had enough and decided to take matters into their own hands. They hog-tied him and muted him with tape before throwing him into the bottom of their boat out of sight of others. They told him they were going to take him out through the entrance and into the ocean to a spot far offshore, where they would toss him over with an anchor, never to be seen again, unless he could give them his solemn word he would never return to Paradise to cheat other people out of their land.

The boys went on to say that once near the ocean entrance, with no other boats in sight, they hauled him up onto the front of the tinny where he was most exposed to the rising swell that crashed relentlessly into the bow and threatened to wash him off into the turbulent waters over the bar crossing. From there they headed out to sea as far as they were game to go in their little craft with the dodgy engine. The water out in the ocean was a deep indigo blue and for all, could have been bottomless. The ocean swell slapped gently, yet somehow menacingly against the sides of the little boat. The boys cut the spluttering motor, then turned their attention to their wretched passenger. They wrapped the anchor chain around the man's legs before repeating their threats and demands, then hauled him overboard and lowered him into the deep, so only his terrified face was all that remained above the surface.

'That's when we nearly lost him.' chimed in Mark in a moment of admission.

'The bugger shouldn't have struggled so much! He was a strong slippery little sucker and managed to break loose of our grasp. He must have sunk down at least ten feet before we could haul him back up to the surface. Being totally saturated he was so heavy we struggled to drag him back into the boat. We nearly capsized! That's when we decided to bring him back in. We were going to drop him off at Minamurra on the way back, but thought better of it......you know, too many witnesses. Anyway, here we are then.'

The knowledge of what Dieter's boys had just done made John feel nauseous. He also wondered where the terrorised man might have run away to, given the fact that Paradise was across the water from where the mainland might have offered him sanctuary.

That evening John shared the happenings of the day with Sal following their return to Paradise, while she in turn reflected on what she had been sharing with Susan about the earlier events of Frankie's memorial service. Such an emotional and event filled day beckoned an early repose for the Williams. A soft, mild breeze that blew from the northeast, gently rattled the Moonar branches as the mild night moved in, complimenting John and Sal's desire for a peaceful slumber. Meanwhile outside under the eaves on the decking, the mystery man's satchel and documents remained untouched.

John woke next morning to the early sunlight streaming in through the bedroom window. For the first time since the fire, a chorus of bird songs filled the bush again. The air outside felt warm and fresh as too did John. Dressed only in thongs and shorts he left Sal in bed and wandered off to check out the ocean beach. He was greeted by the sight of the glassy flat blue sea. White gulls circled over the water searching for an early feed. The sand was cool and white, save a thin black tide line, a lingering reminder of the recent fire emergency. Gazing seaward, John began to think about what Dieter's boys did to the mystery man yesterday, and he recalled how the traumatised victim set off into the scrub toward the ocean beach.

'Why would he want to run to toward the ocean where he'd just earlier nearly drowned in it?' John wondered.

Shifting his gaze up towards the sand dunes John spotted a line of footprints that were yet to be erased by the elements. On closer inspection they appeared still crisp and well defined in the early light, so fresh that John's curiosity took hold, and he began to follow them. They led him down near the tidal zone, then headed west away from the Paradise properties. While

John was no detective, he could see by the forward force of the imprints that whoever left them was moving in a hurry.

'I'll bet these were made by the 'mystery man' yesterday.' John surmised.

He could feel his pulse quicken at the thought of tracking the man down. At various intervals along the beach the footprints had been erased by the hightide wash, but it was easy to pick them up again where the person had travelled over higher ground. Further along John spotted a discarded necktie on the sand, confirming his suspicion that the trail he was following belonged to the same man who had run off into the bush the day before. Unless the man was simply running off in a blind panic, John couldn't understand why he was heading out towards the uninhabited parts of the peninsular. Then it dawned on him that this was the part of the beach he had encountered that Jonny Starling bloke on the two earlier occasions. And sure enough, about where he last remembered seeing the black man, the footprints veered away from the water's edge and into the scrub. John wracked his brain trying to work out what possible connection there could be between these two dissimilar, but equally unsavoury characters.

Leaving the beach for the scrubby sand hummocks, the footprints became harder to distinguish amongst the leaf litter and dry grassy tussocks and John became guided more by an overgrown track which appeared to lead inland. A little way along, when he was just about to give up the hunt, he came across a small, corrugated iron humpy. He approached it cautiously, straining to hear if there was any activity inside, then, ever so carefully he pulled open a roughly hung shutter to reveal the gloomy interior. What he saw inside at first puzzled him. Apart from a thin, soiled mattress on the dirt floor, against the back wall, John could just make out what looked like two cushions, each one fitted with a leather strap sitting beside an old cassette recorder. Leaning on the adjacent wall was a small lightweight aluminium step ladder.

John cautiously entered the dark rank interior, which by now was feeling the effects of the hot morning sun on the rusty iron roof. Moving to the back wall, out of curiosity, he pushed down the play button on the cassette player to see if the thing still functioned ...... and there it was! Out from the machine came the same haunting noises he'd heard in the dead of night through the mists on his property. Echoey sounds of children laughing, intonations of suffering and wailing, they were all there just as he'd heard them during the night. Then, shifting his attention to the cushions he noted foot marks on the fabric under the straps. He slipped off his thongs and slid his feet under the straps, then pacing around out in the open found he could get about silently on the cushions, and without leaving any sign of footprints. The final piece of evidence consisted of about a dozen little grass effigies scattered over the mattress, and the small step ladder John reasoned would have allowed them to be hung in the trees, just out of reach of any passers-by.

'So, Bill the fisherman was right about Jonny sneaking down to Paradise trying to scare the hell out of us. But what would be Simon's motive for engaging him to do it?' pondered John.

The place was beginning to give John the heebie-jeebies, and he feared he might be under surveillance, so he moved on further into the bush in search of the man in the suit. A few hundred meters along he glanced a thin wisp of smoke rising out of the vegetation, at which point he began to crouch down and proceed cautiously in a crawling manner. He could hear his pulse racing through his veins, and his breathing quickened. The adrenalin rush caused a trickle of sweat to run down his temple. Concealing himself behind a thicket of Boobialla bush,

John observed two men in a camp clearing sitting around a fire on a pair of makeshift chairs. They were sharing a bottle of whiskey, taking alternate swigs from the bottle, which appeared to have been almost emptied. He recognised the two as being Jonny Starling and the 'mystery man', although the latter of the two, unlike yesterday when he looked as flash as a rat with a gold tooth in his business suit, now looked quite second hand, unshaven and obviously having a very bad hair day.

John settled into a prone position in a shallow depression on the ground and turned his ear to better eavesdrop on their conversation. Jonny, his tongue obviously loosened by the drink was lamenting how the cool change had come in and turned back the fire, which he had earlier lit, just before it tore through Simon Scully's place. He described how he had waited patiently for the right conditions to set fire to the land so that it would burn out the Scully properties as payback, after Simon had reneged on rewarding him for his 'nocturnal services'. Jonny was counting on Scully's payments to give him a break from working on the fishing trawlers, which he found hard and tiresome. While it seemed like a bit of fun at the time, Jonny felt Scully had set him up and cheated on him, just like Scully's forefathers had done to Jonny's mob in the early days. John knew it was no secret that there existed a deep generational distrust and dislike between the Gunakerni people and the Scully family. On the other hand, Tony Zaletta, as the mystery man would become to be known, was indebted to Simon. Tony, a dodgy onetime property developer had lost his real estate licence a while back after amassing a significant financial liability to develop a speculative estate on the outskirts of Melbourne. Without his licence Tony would be unable to see a return on his investment and would be bankrupted, unable to ever return to the only profession he had known .... flogging properties. Furthermore, Tony's shady debtors were not the type to take too kindly to those who owed them money. Simon, through his barrister connections, had promised to get Tony's licence reinstated through the courts if Tony agreed to work on his behalf to buy back such land in Paradise at a bargain basement rate, which had previously been sold out of the family in the later years. Apparently, from what Tony was saying, Simon had big plans for the Paradise area, and the combined efforts of these two accomplices were designed to drive down the property values below market value, but after his near-death experience at the hands of the Urquhart brothers, Tony now feared for his life more than his financial demise and was warning Jonny of a similar fate.

John's mind was ablaze with all this bombshell information, and how he might deal with it. Simon had proved to be such a tricky fellow in his past dealings with John, and John was reticent to show his hand before he could produce some concrete evidence to put to Simon. Hopefully, he thought, the long walk home along the empty beach might provide him with the space to think things out. Then he remembered ...... he still had in his possession Tony Zaletta's satchel! The anticipation of discovering its contents put a spring into John's step, although he still proceeded with caution, wading along the wash so that his retreating footsteps would not be discovered by Simon's two conscripted racketeers.

By the time he got to the cottage it was nearing lunch time. He was greeted by an empty house and the sight of two pieces of cold toast and an equally cold mug of tea waiting for him on the kitchen table. Only then did he realise how long he'd been away up the beach. His fear that Sal might be angry with him, was spectacularly justified when Sal appeared at the front door.

'Where the hell have you been John! I've been searching for you all over Paradise the last few hours. No one has seen or heard from you all morning. I've been worried sick. I've even been down to the government jetty asking around after you. Don't you ever do that to me again!'

John stood there like a scalded dog, not knowing which way to look, and not fully understanding why he was in so much trouble. Tired and hungry, and now starting to feel the discomfort of sunburn, it was also obvious Sal hadn't finished with him yet.

'I got up just after you went outside this morning and made you a beautiful breakfast, (which is now stone cold), thinking you'd be back in within a few minutes. You hadn't dressed to be going anywhere too far, so when you didn't return, I began to worry. Now look at you, sunburnt and dishevelled. God only knows what you've been up to.'

John did his best to explain how he initially intended to take just a quick look at the ocean beach, but thinking about yesterday's events and the fresh footprints in the sand, one thing led to another. He could see Sal still wasn't impressed, and the account of how he followed the tracks, discovered the shed and spied on the two men only brought further displeasure to Sal.

'You stupid man. You're not Dick Tracy! You could have been mugged or something way out there snooping on people in the bush, then we may not have seen you ever again. I can't believe you did that!'

John thought it was best not to argue and simply to cop it sweet, and besides he was hungry and keen to get into the contents of that satchel. He forced down his half-day-old breakfast before retrieving the case on the decking. Moving out into the sunlight he carefully removed the still sodden wad of paperwork from the pouch. The first few pages he successfully managed to peel off from the rest of the pile. They contained handwritten notes, which unfortunately had been written with a fountain pen, and the ink had run making the writing pretty much illegible. Beneath the handwritten notes were a number of folded sheets, which, when John tried to unfold them, started to disintegrate. Much of the remainder of the sheets were also inseparable. John spread out the bits and pieces on the decking to try and make sense of them. On one large fragment of sheet, he could make out part of a map of the Paradise properties showing the existing boundaries, over which proposed building footprints had been overlayed. He could just make out what looked like a chapel of some sorts in one place, and in another section, what could have been a dormitory hall. On another fragment there was a vague reference to re-establishing 'All Smiles' as part of a proposed major development. Although the severely damaged contents of the satchel were sketchy at best, and far from being definitive, they smacked of Simon Scully's intent all over them.

John wasn't sure what his next move should be. His extended leave from work was nearly over and in a few days he and Sal would be packing up and travelling back home to Melbourne ahead of the long cold Victorian winter, when few would remain in Paradise. As much as he wished to avoid any confrontation with Simon, nevertheless he felt compelled to challenge the man about what John suspected to be his sinister intentions.

John first gave thought to trying to get Joe Tucker on board in challenging Simon, but considering he wasn't exactly on top of Joe's Christmas card list now, plus the fact Joe already had his own battles with the Scullys regarding Jane's wellbeing, John thought better of it. The Bagshaws were already in the middle of packing up to return home, so John dismissed the idea of garnering support from them, and Dieter and his boys were probably wanting to keep a low profile after what they had done to that Tony Zaletta fellow yesterday.

After weighing up his few options, John reluctantly decided to make his way over to the Scully properties. He had a sense of Déjà vu as he crossed the creek over to the 'enemy territory' and once again heard the odd angry shot ringing out from somewhere out the back of Simon's place. Moving ahead nervously, John started to rehearse his opening remarks to Simon. John knew how skilled Simon was at turning the conversation in his favour, but at the same time, John's thoughts were giving consideration to what he wanted to achieve from their encounter. He wanted to make Simon aware that the people of Paradise were about to learn of Simon's nefarious intentions, and that his underhanded doings had been exposed. But once again, as in the past, Simon had the jump on him.

Before he even got to Simon's house, from a short distance behind, a voice called out from the scrub; 'Well, well, well! If it isn't the new invader coming to visit again. Yes, that's what you are John, 'Johny-come-lately', the new invader. In my family's time here, you are considered to be a relatively new 'invasion'. You're not one of our family, are you? No, you aren't!'

John trying to put himself on the front foot replied, 'You're sounding like Joe Tucker now Simon.'

'Well, you mention Joe Tucker and my dear cousin Jane, now that's an entirely different issue, and one that is none of your business, and I doubt one that brings you along my path here today anyway. And I should warn you, Aiden and Andrew are out hunting down some feral deer. It would be a terrible accident for them to mistake you for a legitimate target in all this scrub.

Then Simon continued. 'So then, what then is your business with me today, John?'

'Simon, there's been a lot of idle talk around town recently about people over here in Paradise being moved off their land to make way for some other purpose for the area. No one could pin down any specific details, and it was thought that perhaps the Coastal Parks authority might be wanting to take back the freehold properties to link up the coastal parkland precincts either side to the east and west of the area.'

Gaining a little more confidence, John continued. 'Simon, recalling our previous recent conversations about the unfortunate happenings around here recently, and your comments about your blessed saviour offering *'succour to those of the faith'*, I have become aware of the presence of a dubious character doing the rounds, mainly amongst the vulnerable landowners across the creek, trying to knock down their property values and pressuring them into selling out.'

'So, how has that got anything to do with me John? How then? I ask.'

'Well, firstly just yesterday, I witnessed Dieter Urquart's boys accost this man and take him out on the water to deter him from any further harassment to the landowners. During his struggles, he dropped his satchel in the lake, which I managed to retrieve. The contents of the bag appear to show plans for a big development here. They look awfully like some sort of religious complex.'

'So, let me get this straight John; yesterday you witnessed a kidnapping and assault, and apart from not intervening, took advantage of the situation and stole this man's property, then rifled through his personal effects. And don't deny it, because I saw you and those two assailants on the jetty at that time. Yes, I did John. Yes, I did! I could report you to the police right now you know. Do you realise that? Well, do you?'

'It was not my place to intervene, and anyhow I retrieved the bag to return it to the individual at a later time. Now, secondly, I managed to track the fellow down this morning where he had fled to, up at Jonny Starling's camp. I found a number of items Jonny had been employing to try and scare us at night, and I overheard their conversation which implicated you in their deceitful doings. What do you have to say about that then?'

Simon's hawkish eyes blinked erratically while he thought on his feet. 'You do realise John, that you have no credible evidence to associate me with these pair of crooks, only their word against mine, which I will deny vigorously of having any association with them. That Starling character is a disreputable heathen, and I have proof he tried to burn us out with that fire a few weeks back, so that makes him an arsonist and a criminal as well! He wouldn't dare speak out against me; I have too much on him that would see him land in gaol for a long time. As for the other one, he also is in my debt. One word out of place from him and I could send him into ruination for the rest of his life. And John, in the unlikely event that anyone should ask, I will also strongly deny this conversation ever took place.'

Simon then went on to reflect on his great grandfather Thomas's teachings and about the apostle Peter telling of how, just as the Earth was once destroyed by water, with the second coming it is to be destroyed by fire and renewed. Simon claimed that the events of the past weeks only strengthened the belief in the apostle's promise that we (the Scully family) would be able to look to new heavens and a new earth, wherein dwelleth righteousness, and that those without 'the knowledge' and 'Truth', such as the likes of John would have no place there.

It was clear to John that Simon's ambitious intentions were to re-establish the Adonai Shomo cult in Paradise and to return it to the exclusive realm of the Scully clan. John was never much of a chess player, but he could see that Simon had him in check.

Simon finished by issuing a veiled threat to John. 'May I give you some friendly advice John? Well, may I? Yes, I may! You'd do well to get rid of that satchel and its contents. Being discovered in possession of Tony Zeletta's property will implicate you in a way you could never imagine, should you think to hold onto it, or consider using it against me anytime in the future. I have some very influential friends in the legal profession. I do John, yes, I do.'

John would need quite some time to work through what had just been unloaded on him. He decided not to share the conversation with anyone else for the time being, not even Sal. Over the coming days he and Sal gradually packed up the little cottage in readiness for their return to the city for the winter period. Those of the remaining community were doing the same. One morning John observed the red sails of Joe Tucker's beloved 'Emma' diminishing into a tiny red dot in the distance as Joe with Jane onboard, sailed slowly toward Emma's winter mooring somewhere up the river. Most of the motor cruisers had left the government jetty, and the shoreline was devoid of the summer throngs. Simon was nowhere to be seen during the final days, and in fact, apart from where the scrub had been burnt during the fire event, it was as if nothing else had ever happened.

Motoring across to Minamurra for the final time, a chill wind hinted to an early end to summer. John pulled up near the wharf opposite 'Banister's Boat Bait and Auto'. The township seemed quiet, and the servo was shut up and closed. A 'Business for Sale' sign had been erected out front. He found the compound unlocked and open, so that those who needed to, could retrieve their cars. John's vehicle and trailer were the last ones remaining in the yard.

John and Sal were later to learn that Faye had decided to sell up and move over to the West Coast to be closer to her sons and hopefully start a new life, free of the local gossip which had persisted around town here following Frankie's memorial.

John felt a strange emptiness as he retrieved his boat from the water and he and Sal hit the road homeward bound. He was leaving behind Minamurra and Paradise, and all that had happened there during their stay this time.

Back across the water, Paradise was returning to the other creatures who called it home. A spiny echidna waddled slowly over the transient human footprints pressed into the sand in search of ants and beetles along the track that led to the estuary. An elusive bandicoot ventured cautiously between the secluded empty cottages in search of fresh ground to dig for food. A swamp wallaby surveyed the quiet landscape and scratched its chest. The swans and other water birds floated peacefully on the now quiet waterways. Once more the land was divested of the human stain and all the politicking and activity that went with hominal occupation. With the coming seasonal rains, the tea-trees and coastal Arcasia's which lined the cobweb of paths that crossed the land, would begin to grow over and heal the scars left by last summer's clearing.

Epilogue

Proverbs 28:6 Better the poor whose walk is
blameless than the rich whose ways are perverse.

Now safely back home, some months after returning from Paradise, the tyranny of distance helped separate John from the trials and tribulations which occurred during his extended summer stay. Immersed in his work and shrouded in the humdrum of urban living, last summer was not much more than just a past memory.

Occasionally he reflected on his moments with Frankie, and how Faye might be coping, and of course his last interaction with the Scullys, but it was all as if it had just been a crazy dream.

It wasn't until he randomly read a newspaper article reporting on crime that the gravity of what happened with his experience with Simon Scully and his unfortunate accomplices hit home. The article told the story of the mystery disappearance of two men in the East Gippsland area. Police were seeking public assistance in relation to the whereabouts of the two, who had no apparent previous connection to each other, but who had vanished under suspicious circumstances in the same area and at the same time. At this stage police had no credible leads and were appealing to anyone who may have known, or had contact with these men, or who may be able to provide any information in relation to where the two may have last been seen.

In this context, Simon's final advice to him suddenly flooded back into focus...... 'that it would be better for you to dispose of that satchel, which if found in your possession, may implicate you in a way you could never have imagined.'

A sudden sharp pain erupted in the heal of his left foot like a memory jolt.

'Hell! What did I end up doing with that bloody satchel during all our packing up?'

John searched his mind but couldn't recall what he did with it. Might the police conduct a search of the Paradise area? There was no indication that Paradise had been included in their investigations, but it left John with the uncomfortable uncertainty of where and with who the investigations might settle.

www.ingramcontent.com/pod-product-compliance
Lightning Source LLC
Chambersburg PA
CBHW031113030726
47496CB00002BA/528